Afterward . . .

There are many new islands. Wherever the land was low to the west of the Green Mountains the climbing waters intervened, carving them into new solitude.

Where the Lorenta and Hudson and Ontario Seas come together at the southeastern corner of the great Adirondack Island, outrageous tides tear about in a crazy Sabbat of the elements, and scour an unknown bottom. At a place called Ticonderoga small sailing vessels can often make fair passage to and from Adirondack Island, passing out of sight of land for hardly more than an hour if the wind is right.

As for crossing the Hudson Sea in the far south, that's for professional heroes. . . .

STILL
I PERSIST
IN WONDERING

EDGAR PANGBORN

A DELL BOOK

Published by
Dell Publishing Co., Inc.
1 Dag Hammarskjold Plaza
New York, New York 10017

These stories were first published as follows:

The Children's Crusade, The Legend of Hombas and *The Witches of Nupal* in the CONTINUUM series, edited by Roger Elwood, Berkley Publishing Corporation, 1974.

Harper Conan and Singer David in TOMORROW TODAY, edited by George Zebrowski, Unity Press, 1975.

Tiger Boy in UNIVERSE 2, edited by Terry Carr, Ace Books, 1972.

My Brother Leopold in AN EXALTATION OF STARS, edited by Terry Carr, Simon & Schuster, 1973.

The Night Wind in UNIVERSE 5, edited by Terry Carr, Random House, 1974.

Dell ® TM 681510, Dell Publishing Co., Inc.

ISBN: 0-440-18277-8

Printed in the United States of America
First printing—November 1978

Note: All characters in these stories are entirely fictional.
                                                          E.P.

And still I persist in wondering whether folly must always be our nemesis.

—JERMYN GRAZ

to
T. E.

CONTENTS

THE COUNTRY CALLED EDGAR

A Personal Memoir by Spider Robinson

Now do I repent me of my youthful extravagance.

A monthly book reviewer, required to wade through over a dozen science fiction books a month, is dismally depressed most of the time, by Sturgeon's Law. This has the paradoxical effect of inclining one to burst into ecstatic hosannas every time something marginally readable comes along. For a book that actually has something going for it, all the stops are pulled out, and a really *good* book has been known to generate incoherent babbling. And so I have squandered the superlatives of my youth, so thoughtlessly, and have nothing left fit to offer the genuine master who has come calling.

How's this?:

I resist with difficulty the temptation to worship Edgar Pangborn—he wouldn't have liked it. The most I will allow myself is to love him with all my heart.

No, that's no good. You probably think he was a dear friend of mine or something. I never set eyes on the man. I didn't know he existed until very shortly before he died—somehow or other I contrived to overlook his every published work for over twenty years.

All too many of us have made the same mistake. When Edgar died last year he was neither particularly rich nor particularly famous.

11

So perhaps I had best assume that you don't *know* Edgar Pangborn, that you're standing in some drafty bookstore leafing through this foreword in search of a good reason to spend beer money on this collection. It's a safe bet: if you do know Edgar Pangborn, the chances of your wasting time on words of mine in a book of his are negligible (although you just might be an Edgar-lover who has finished this book but isn't ready to leave the bathroom yet). How, then, in this age of easy hype and squandered superlatives, can I convince you that just this once you really are holding in your hand one of the Special Books, the finest collection available of a writer of the calibre of Mark Twain?

I'll begin formally, with track record: for when Edgar died, he was neither particularly poor nor particularly obscure.

He began writing in 1930; in that year he published a mystery novel, *A-100*, under the pseudonym "Bruce Harrison." He wrote many kinds of things, under an assortment of names, but according to Peter Beagle, Edgar himself always claimed that he truly became a writer with the publication of "Angel's Egg" in *Galaxy* in 1951. He set himself formidable standards, for the very least that can be said of that story is that it is one of the finest novelettes ever printed in a science fiction magazine. I defy you to read it without weeping. It was his first science fiction story.

He won the International Fantasy Award in 1955 for his novel *A Mirror for Observers*—the same award won in the previous year by Theodore Sturgeon's *More Than Human* and subsequently by Peter Beagle's *The Last Unicorn*. Those three books belonged together somehow.

His novel *Davy* was barely edged out for the 1965

Hugo Award (by Fritz Leiber's *The Wanderer*). Reading *Davy* has measurably and significantly changed my life, for the better, and I still have three-in-the-morning conversations with some of its characters. It spawned two other novels, *The Judgment of Eve* and *The Company of Glory*, both set in the same I-hope-hypothetical After The Holocaust future of *Davy;* both of them are exquisite. It also spawned the stories contained in this volume, and several others.

His story "Longtooth" was a Hugo finalist in 1970. A non-*Davy*-cycle story, it builds unbearable tension into warm sweet horror with incredible skill.

Davy and *A Mirror for Observers* both placed in the 1972 *Locus* Poll for Best All-Time Novel.

Science fiction is a specialized taste; as a genre it has produced any number of Great Works and Great Writers which could not possibly be appreciated or enjoyed by anyone but a science fiction fan. There's nothing wrong with that, and of course there are numerous exceptions. Edgar is perhaps the most outstanding; he transcended every genre he ever worked in, and he worked in several. I am no expert on murder-trial novels, but I have heard Edgar's *The Trial of Callista Blake* called the best novel ever written in that genre—and it's certainly one of the most heart-tearing books of any sort that I've ever read. His massive historical novel *A Wilderness of Spring* is a forgotten masterpiece, which almost seems to be a part of the *Davy* cycle in some ways. The only artistic failure of his I have seen is a very early novel called *West of the Sun,* an interesting attempt to do something genuinely beautiful within the narrow confines of formula fiction, of pulp sf. It very nearly worked.

Once Edgar found his voice he simply wrote what it

13

was given him to write, ignoring genre guidelines and following his star.

He encountered resistance. As recently as 1974, an alleged editor took it upon himself to substantially alter Edgar's *Galaxy* serial *The Company of Glory* for book publication, removing scenes that the editor reportedly found "too faggoty." (Ironically, the protagonist, Demetrios, was an aged storyteller who was run out of town for refusing to be censored. Ah, but good friends went with him: a Company of Glory.) I can of course know nothing of what went on inside Edgar's head while he was writing, but having read *The Judgment of Eve* I cannot help but believe that I know what ending he wanted to write, would have written if it had been possible to get a *ménage-à-quatre* past an editor in 1966. (It's hard to recall in these allegedly enlightened times, but three years before that a professor was fired from Illinois University for having suggested in print that there were circumstances under which premarital sexual intercourse might be condoned. Nor was his appeal successful.) None of the stories in this collection appeared in the sf magazines, because they lacked the Identifiable Hero Has Problem, Grows To Solution formula required—they were picked up only by original anthologists of taste, and in one case because their continuous background fit an anthologist's gimmick. Why, I know a man who refuses to read *Davy* because he's heard it's an After The Holocaust novel and he doesn't care for them. ("Taj Mahal? Nah—don't like tombs.")

Yet for all that I think I could make an excellent case for saying that Edgar Pangborn was essentially a science fiction writer. He said again and again in his books that love is not a condition or an event or even a state of mind—that love is a country, which we are

14

sometimes privileged to visit—and again and again he wrote of the exploration of that fantastic region, of First and sometimes Last Contact in that continuum.

His two essential themes were love and human stupidity (perhaps human insensitivity is more correct), and that sharpest of antinomies formed the core of nearly all his work. There are a few dark and anguished stories in this book. But Edgar was one of those rare ones, a writer who not only could perceive the flaws in his species, but could find it in his heart to forgive them. I think he was strong enough to bear his terrible empathy. Though he may have cried out in pain at times, he never gave in, as so many modern science fiction writers have, to screams of rage. He never attempted to renounce his humanity. Not that he could have.

"And still I persist in wondering," muses Jermyn Graz, in telling of his brother Leopold, "whether folly must always be our nemesis."

Me too.

Certainly folly was my nemesis, for over two decades. In retrospect I learn that some of the most respected editors, anthologists and critics in the field have been trumpeting Edgar's praises for years. Terry Carr, Theodore Sturgeon, Damon Knight, Algis Budrys, Jim Baen, George Zebrowski and many others have raved about Edgar, in print or in person, right along. Somehow I just wasn't paying attention. I dimly recall seeing the first edition of *Davy* on the stands, deciding from the cover painting and blurbs that it was probably dumb, and putting it back (which was *certainly* dumb—but in those days I was too poor to gamble). I missed nearly every one of these stories in their original appearances, and the one

I did stumble across I read in a hurry and entirely misunderstood.

It was in late 1975 that I finally woke up. I had taken over *Galaxy* magazine's book review column, "Galaxy Bookshelf," from Theodore Sturgeon and begun receiving literally hundreds of free review books. I ran across a reprint of *A Mirror for Observers* in Avon/Equinox's excellent (but now dormant) SF Rediscovery Series, and frankly I expected that it would turn out to be one of those Immortal Classics that looked good in the pulp days but couldn't cut it today. But I had just reviewed Sturgeon's *More Than Human* and this had won the same award in the following year, so I started it out of curiosity.

It was pick-of-the-column that month. You remember the syndrome I mentioned back at the start.

Next month I received George Zebrowski's exquisite and sadly overlooked anthology *Tomorrow Today* (Unity Press), and it contained "Harper Conan and Singer David" (included in this volume).

I was in love.

I raved about that story in the next column, and even favorably reviewed an otherwise ordinary anthology series that contained four of Edgar's Post-Collapse stories (one included here).

By now I knew that I wanted to read every word Edgar had even written, and I even knew that I wanted to meet him, to know him personally. The logical thing to do would have been to write to him in care of his publishers and say so. But I wanted to include copies of the reviews I had written, as a sort of introduction (I didn't *know* then that Edgar would have taken me off the street and fed me beer and cookies), and I decided that magazine copies would look more impressive than manuscript carbons.

Must folly always be our nemesis?

In the four or five months it took those columns to actually see print (standard lag), I did some digging, and located a battered secondhand copy of *Davy*. It took me five times longer to read it than its length indicated—I kept stopping at the ends of paragraphs, to sort of bask. When I was done I was nearly incoherent—and my column was days overdue. I sprinted for the typewriter, determined by God to *flog* my readers out into the street in search of *Davy*, and wangle Edgar's number and read the column to him over the phone, and sitting on the typewriter with the day's mail was the February '76 issue of *Locus*, the newspaper of science fiction.

The headline story was Edgar's obituary.

I have it still. Charlie Brown does a good obit. It tells me that Edgar was born in New York City on February 25, 1909. It says he attended Harvard from 1924 to 1926 and subsequently studied music at the New England Conservatory. It says he farmed in Maine some, but I'd already figured that. It says he lived with his sister Mary on the Bearsville Road outside Woodstock, and that he painted and played Bach on the piano. It gives most of the bibliographic information I've already imparted under Track Record. It includes a eulogy by Peter Beagle, dripping with true love and true respect, that still makes me weep today.

If Edgar Pangborn had only been a damn good writer, that would probably be all I know of Edgar Pangborn.

But those reviews saw print, and the response started coming back. A literal boxful, all of it heartwarming. Most of it was from grateful readers, thanking me for the tip. But a substantial percentage was from people who had *already* known and loved Ed-

17

gar's work—and almost every damn one of them enclosed some *other* work of Edgar's that I had not seen. Each acknowledged that it would be nice to see the work in question get reviewed; but each made it plain that the book was a gift, from one of Edgar Pangborn's lovers to another. One man mailed me the enormous hardcover version of Edgar's superb historical novel *A Wilderness of Spring* (Edgar once said that it "went out of print in a matter of minutes"), knowing that I couldn't review it in *Galaxy*, just wanting me to have it. Those who couldn't send books sent lists of bibliographical references, for anthologies with Pangborn stories in them.

That is the kind of writer he was.

So I acquired a complete set of Terry Carr's *Universe* series and beatup paperbacks of *Callista Blake* and *Good Neighbors and Other Strangers* (which contains both "Angel's Egg" and "Longtooth") and the recently reprinted *Davy* and *The Judgment of Eve* and eighteen copies of *West of the Sun.* I got letters from people who said that reading Edgar Pangborn had kept them from committing suicide, had helped reconcile them to going blind, had pulled them back from the Dark Place where everything tastes like cornflakes and everything looks like ashtrays. I begged Edgar Pangborn anecdotes from editors and friends (they overlap) who had known him. I felt my own writing take on depth, felt myself beginning to understand life better, with exposure to Pangborn. I began to absorb Edgar's special essence, a quality which Damon Knight, in *In Search of Wonder*, calls "very like the thing Stapledon was always talking about and never quite managing to convey: the regretful, ironic, sorrowful, deeply joyous—and purblind—love of the world and all in it."

I became myself more reconciled to being alive.

And one day it finally dawned on me that there were more than enough *Davy*-cycle stories to fill a book. I contacted Robert Mills, Edgar's long-time friend and agent, for permission to assemble and edit such a book. I told him what stories I had and asked if he had any that I lacked that ought to be considered. He didn't, but to make certain he checked with Mary Pangborn. In searching Edgar's files, she turned up a box containing everything you are about to read except the bibliography and this foreword.

Edgar had selected and retyped all these stories, written the introduction, titled the book, boxed it, and died before he could mail it in.

It happened to contain almost precisely the stories I'd planned to use, in the order I had contemplated putting them. That's irrelevant; you get what *he* wanted. He made some slight changes from the original story-appearances, mostly spelling-standardization, and the copy is so clean and obviously carefully copy edited by him that I have not presumed to touch it and neither will the publisher.

It may not even be the last Edgar Pangborn book. At this writing Mary Pangborn is preparing two final books for publication: *Atlantean Nights' Entertainments*, another collection, and *Light Another Candle*, a historical novel on which Mary and Edgar collaborated. (Mary just sold her first science fiction story to Terry Carr, and I look forward to seeing it.)

But it *is*, I believe, the finest collection available of Edgar's shorter work, superior to *Good Neighbors*, which after all had several stories that were "only" solid entertainments. I regard it as one of the high points of my life so far (as well as my career) to have had something to do with bringing it here before you.

Some day academicians will classify him, analyze him, trace his influences and effects, relate his intimate biographical details to his statistical word-choice, and in general explain to each other why anyone who didn't know how it was all done would worship him. All I can do is tell you what I told you pages ago: that I love Edgar with all my heart, and bless him for having taken on the bitterly wearisome task of writing. If love is a country, he is one of its most prominent citizens.

And so that is why I find myself writing a personal memoir of a man I never met. *I* think he is a country all his own, one I can always visit in my heart, one I share with all the people who have chanced or chosen to visit there, one I share now with you.

Welcome.

New York City,
January 1978

AUTHOR'S NOTE

We all create worlds, and writers of projective fantasy are especially prone to let them grow up on paper. My novel *Davy* developed one of these worlds—(their number of course is infinite, which is one of the advantages of living in a universe of infinite universes)—and this group of stories belongs to Davy's world. The present culture collapsed toward the end of this century in a twenty-minute war, followed by a pestilence among the survivors. The human population was cut down to minimum survival numbers; in fact there will have been many areas where the human race simply died out. (This was all most unfortunate, as well as too damned probable, so it is comforting to reflect that in a universe of infinite universes, like ours, there must be a good many where things turned out more pleasantly—good Christ, there must even be one where Nixon wasn't reelected!—why wasn't I there?—or maybe I was. . . .)

After the war and pestilence there followed what Davy's book speaks of as the Years of Confusion: barbarism, not actually "like" Fifth Century Europe because history can't repeat itself that way, but just as dark. Here and there enclaves where some of the valuable bits of the old culture survived. In some places, primitive savagery in its varied forms; and monarchies, petty states, baronies, whatever. Then through many centuries, a gradual recovery toward some other peak of some other kind of civilization. Without the resources squandered by the 20th Century.

The region for these stories is the part of the eastern United States and Canada that would be left habitable after a great rise in the sea level, a climatic change brought on by our present bungling—if this seems improbable look out your window at the smog. Along with the rise of waters there would be massive earthquakes and landslides as the earth's crust shifted in adjustment. The present New England states would become an island; so would the Adirondack country, etc. This picture is drawn in "The Children's Crusade."

"The Legend of Hombas" is set in a dateless time, perhaps 150 years after the collapse, among people reverted to the primitive, with some shreds of Christianity; in the background there are some more sophisticated communities, seen through savage eyes. "The Witches of Nupal" belongs to the new nation Katskil in the third century of a new calendar; Katskil encloses the ecclesiastical state of Nuber, headquarters of the new official religion foreshadowed in "The Children's Crusade." "Mam Sola's House"* makes a jump into the Seventh Century, when quite a stable culture has blossomed, anyhow stable enough to support a Curator of Antique Visual Arts, and brother, that is stability.

It takes a bit of time to build a world. Other pieces of this one appear in the stories "Tiger Boy," "The World Is a Sphere,"* "My Brother Leopold," and "The Freshman Angle."* In a universe of infinite universes there must be one where you could keep at it for another fifty or sixty years, or until you got tired. With infinite royalties.

* Omitted from this collection, for reasons known only to Edgar; see Bibliography.—SR

THE CHILDREN'S CRUSADE

Malachi never shunted off the children and their questions, nor did he madden them by promising they'd understand when they were older. He even asked them questions in return. If they giggled or squirmed or ran away it was not, he thought, in rejection, but because there was crisis in his inquiries:— *What do* you *think is on the other side of the hill?*— *Where does the music go when the sound stops?*—*Was there really a world before you were born?* They lacked the language to deal with this sort of thing, except Jesse Lodson, the six-toed boy, who read books and had a mind of his own and was old enough to be allowed to sit on the steps of The Store and listen to men's talk. Maybe the other kids hoped to find words by running off to search for them in green pastures; but Malachi would still be ahead of them, ready with new questions when they came running back.

Who does have patience for long labor over anything so slippery and ungentle as a question? Malachi's, and he knew it, often raised thunder out of a past that hung like a midnight shadow over himself and his people. We may scold the most appalling future into quiet by proving it doesn't exist, but the past did, once. The challenges of doubt or denial reverberate, though the cheeks that flushed and lips that curled in the passions of argument are with the leaf mold.

Born among the flailing ideologies of what we call the late Twentieth Century, Malachi Peters never admitted that children should be spared the peril of using their brains.

The red plague followed the twenty-minute war; the Children's Crusade happened some thirty years after that. Malachi's people were calling it the Year 30; one might as well go along with their chronology, for they weren't stupid, and many could remember the Twentieth Century.

Most of them also recalled the existence of a religion named Christianity. Hardly any two could have agreed about its doctrines and practice, but in this time when a technological culture was so recently self-slain, religion had come to seem important again. Among the children fantastic sparrow-arguments broke out from time to time about God and the Devil, heaven and hell and all that bit. And you could hear endless adult exegesis, logomachy, and heartburning on the front porch of The Store, or around the stove in winter. How do you ever define "religion" itself in terms that will meet the dry thorny jabs of the rebel five percent—or three percent, or whatever the minority amounts to? Up on the northeastern shore of the Hudson Sea, that minority presents an irreducible factor of serene cussedness: they're Vermonters.

(Even three percent may be too big. It doesn't imply that the remaining ninety-seven percent are too dumb or too bland to enjoy the thrills of theoretical squabblings; but they are apt to devote their energies to timely, *important* problems, such as the distinction between *Homoiousian* and *Homoousian,* or immoral-

24

ity among the heathen, or the Only Decent Way To Make Clam Chowder.)

Malachi Peters of Melton Village sometimes laid it out openly for his cronies along about these lines: Say a village of one hundred heavenbound sons of bitches like you supports a population of one sound atheist like Mr. Goudy over there; then you'll find about four who'll venture to agree with him out loud in a half-ass kind of way, in some place where nobody happens to be listening; makes a good five percent rebellion, don't it? Of course, even if you add in us agnostics the rebellion still can't so much as elect a town clerk, but we make noise. By the way, did you know it was T.H. Huxley himself who invented the word "agnostic" for crackpots like me who'd rather be truthful than sanctified?

And sometimes he went Socratic, though with caution:

What is God? Well—oh, a Supreme Being.

What is the nature of Being? Supreme over what? Why, hell, everybody knows what being is.

All but me. I'm ignorant. Supreme means infinite? Sure.

Jesus Christ was the son of God? Ayah, don't the Book say so?

God is infinite? Well, sure.

Therefore Christ was the son of Infinity? Ayah.

How does Infinity beget a son? It's got balls? You trying to make a man look stupid?

(Hearing it reach this point, old Mr. Goudy chuckles, scratches his desiccated crotch, and spits a bollop over the porch rail. Fifty-five, oldest man in town; has a patch of Connecticut tobacco and does some business in the fall blending marijuana with the chaws, packing the mixture on his back through the

25

neighboring towns. Malachi often addressed him as Messenger of Light, which caused Mr. Goudy to cackle like one of Jud Hobart's guinea hens; Jesse Lodson wasn't quite old enough to figure that one out.)

I'm just trying to find out the sex of Infinity. Man your age could get his mind off sex, seems like.

Why? . . .

Melton Village was typical of those shrunken communities on the northeastern coast of what people were beginning to call the Hudson Sea. The villages maintained a tenuous, suspicious communication with each other along the mountain trails and the disintegrating grandeur of Old-Time roads. The people did cherish a faith in a few things, but not in the dollar any more, with no central government to create one, and not in the ancient air-castle fantasy of squeezing an income out of the goddamn summer people. Weren't any.

At fifty, Malachi Peters was typical of himself. So, increasingly, was his friend Jesse Lodson at fourteen, who had the run of Malachi's library and who loved him.

Melton Village sprawls in the foothills of a green range looking down, yes, on the Hudson Sea, that long arm of ocean extending now from the Lorenta Sea all the long way to a confused tangle of islets and inlets several hundred miles south, where the Black Rocks mark the site of New York City. That tragic place was stricken by the peripheral blast of a fusion toy that annihilated the western end of Long Island, including Brooklyn and a tree that is said to have grown there. Then New York's ruins were engulfed in the rising waters, the noisy history done. West of Melton Village, the opposite shore is occasionally visible on those days of clear atmosphere that seem to be coming more frequently. Out there under windy water and skittish tides lies the bed of what was Lake Champlain. The lake was beautiful, history says, until the Age of Progress shat in it and made it, like so many others, a desolation and a stink. The waters climbed; years of earthquakes, cloudburst, landslide crumbled the narrow watersheds. The ocean, itself a universe in torment, perhaps renews itself in long labor, healing the worst afflictions of the human visitation.

Malachi Peters was in the habit of sprawling on his own elderly front porch, when he wasn't tending his garden and chickens or doing his fastidious bachelor housekeeping, or mending a kite for the kids, or describing the universe to Jesse who had (Malachi thought) a rather too dewy-eyed view of it even for fourteen. Or arguing, of course, down at the venerable shanty that retained the name of The Store.

Trading was negligible: all the nearby communities were in the same fix as Melton Village. There was in theory a sort of state government still at Montpelier but you never heard from it—sometimes an excellent thing in governments. The overland trails into Massachusetts or New Hampshire got more snarled up each year as the rise in mean temperature transformed temperate zone forest into subtropical—a few degrees are enough. A visit to New York meant a sea voyage through tough waters by a people who had scant taste for recovering the art of sailing ships. Bud Maxon maintained The Store as a public service; he couldn't support himself and his family with it, but managed like everyone else with a knee-scrabble garden, chickens and goats and pigs, and hunting. He owned the town bull; his brother ran a bit of a dairy. Bud learned archery, but kept his old rifle oiled just as if he thought there'd be cartridges for it again some day. The Store's front steps and porch in summer, its stove in the softening winters, drew the lonely in their hunger for talk, that limping substitute for love.

Malachi could also watch the sea from his own front porch. To older generations of his family Lake Champlain had gleamed more distantly, where the Lamoille River ran into it. In that time a group of islands stood out there. Mr. Goudy remembered hunting and camping on Grand Isle when he was a boy. Watching the ocean, Malachi could let his thoughts ride free, as he might have if a world had not ended.

Fifty now, he had been twenty, with two years experience of Harvard, when civilization encountered the Bang, and presently the red plague that made the Fourteenth Century Black Death look like a cold in the head. Destroying civilization, always a task for fools, was relatively easy with the tools constructed for the purpose in the Twentieth Century. To recreate one you need something stronger than divine guidance.

In the Year 30 the residents of Melton Village numbered about a hundred adults (the red plague having wiped out the old as you wipe chalk squiggles off a slate) and eighteen teenagers and children. The population before the war and the plague had been three thousand.

Malachi Peters numbered precisely one. Six-feet-two, weighed 160 pounds. Standing erect he resembled a weedy figure One, with wind-wavering hair already ice-white.

Of the children, thirteen were physically normal except perhaps in their genes. The village had no statistical information on the incidence of radiation-induced birth deformities, fetal deaths, and stillbirths. Many good souls were inclined to blame the trouble on the infinite wisdom of God (after all, it's been blamed for everything else ever since we invented it). The village did try to cherish the children. Some of the mues, as they began to be called about that time, were hard to cherish, especially the brain-mues who could only sit where they were put, smile and drool when they were fed, cry when they were cleaned. Others, like Jesse who had no physical oddity except his six-toed feet, were not yet regarded with superstitious terror. As for Jesse's peculiarity, as Malachi told him more than once, such things weren't too uncommon long before technology started monkeying with the sunfire—except that his extra toes were functional. They gave a special buoyancy to his walking and running. Jesse was slim like a marsh reed, dark-haired and faun-eyed. At fourteen he could outrun anyone in the village and not even be winded.

Most of the adults could read, but books were few—some volumes that had been in the tiny public library in the Year Zero, as many more privately owned in houses that survived flood, fire, night-raiders, and abandonment in the worst of the bad years, and Malachi's library of maybe three thousand at the Old Peters Place where he had lived most of his years alone since the crash. Except for Malachi's lot, a high proportion of the surviving books were less than useful to a society that might have liked to recreate civilization, or anyhow Vermont, if it had known how. But to understand that one shall see no more *new* books, ever, is a horror even to some of the illiterate, like smashing blind into a stone wall.

A little school limped along under good Miss Seton, whose resources were near to nothing. The greatest difference the old lady noted after the death of American culture was that in the new age she was treated with some respect even by the children. Especially by the children.

Malachi knew (but seldom said to his neighbors except for Tad Doremus the blacksmith) that the rise of waters was engulfing the dry land because of the determined blundering of expert technological man in the recent past. What else but man-made fumes, particularly those of humanity's dearest buzz-toy, had heated the atmospheric greenhouse the critical few degrees that hastened the melting of polar ice? And choking on atmospheric garbage meant Progress: so choke. All toward what conclusion—who tried to know? Not the engineers—it wasn't their job. They were earnest and righteous about that: it was never their job to foresee anything beyond the immediate achievement and immediate profit. They could only build and grow—one says that of cancer. "We climbed Mount Everest because it was there!"—that was the Golden Cliché of the Twentieth Century, mock-modest bombast quite as banal and unthinking as any Nineteenth Century godsaking, and like most popular swashbuckling it went unchallenged.

It was an exhausted world—beaten, raped, robbed, mutilated by industrial greed and political stupidity, and left for dead. Malachi himself knew exhaustion, hours when his head could hold little except despair at human folly. He looked then on Jesse, the boy's uncalculating goodness, simplicity, power to love and to wonder, and could only think: *This is the world they left you. The rain itself as it falls on your head is poisoned.* Sometimes instead of *they* he said *we;* but Malachi was not given to wallowing in unearned guilt. A yeasty college student at the age of twenty, there wasn't much he could have done to prevent the idiot

30

from pushing the button. If burning himself with gasoline in front of the White House would have had that effect, he was just the sort of ardent youth who might have done it; plain reason told him it wouldn't: the Juggernaut is mindless. The danger would remain simply because those in power had not the intelligence nor the good will to remove it, and what had been representative government had given way to the corporate state. To say these things in the Twentieth Century usually seemed like hooting down a rain-barrel. In the pig-scramble to be good consumers for the blessed state, honor and virtue and reason could not be heard; it was natural to assume that they had died.

In the Year 30 it seemed likely to Malachi that not enough survivors existed to renew the species. Within a generation or two there would be a lights-out, somewhere a last man perishing. Hadn't a critical moment arrived when the dinosaurs became dry bones without issue? He could see his contemporaries as like insects crowded to the high end of a piece of driftwood and going out on the flood. He would have been happy, if only for Jesse, to invent God and a heaven, but he couldn't do it. For a mind once honestly wedded to reason there is no divorce.

And yet, mercilessly comparing grown-ups, the children said of Malachi: "Tshee, he never acts *bored!*"

Jesse's father had been a veterinary who somehow retained the conscience of a specialized profession through years when the complex drugs, antiseptics, antibiotics, all that, were no longer obtainable. No immunology, no anesthetics, nothing that depended on the vanished Twentieth Century laboratories and the huge complex of supporting industries. Lost or broken

31

instruments could not be replaced. No more scientific journals—no more science. For the blunder, the incomparable brassbound goof, is one thing that *homo quasi-sapiens* can carry off magnificently: out goes the baby with the bath-water, and what's left (if anything is left) is an astonished and very naked primate.

Dr. Lodson did what he could, with herbs, observation, common sense, memory, and that mixture of hunch and sympathy which is justly called "a feeling for animals," through years when probably no one understood his difficulties except Dr. Stern, who was in the same fix with his human patients, and Malachi Peters who liked to play chess with Dr. Lodson and who was inclined to take all Melton Village troubles as his own—for no good reason except that this was Malachi's way. It was not meddlesome, nor particularly aristocratic, this concern of Malachi's for his own people. The village had an exasperated, partly loving name for it. They called it Malachi's Thing.

In the Year 24, when his son Jesse was eight years old (this was the same year Dr. Stern died of intestinal cancer with none to succeed him), Dr. Lodson got momentarily careless while treating Bud Maxon's priceless Jersey bull for a leg ulcer. With the lightning-flash of an act of God, the brute wheeled and gored him to death.

In that year Jesse began to see that love and mercy, like hate, are man-made. He had adored his cheerful, unexacting father. He was there when it happened, though Bud got him out quickly. The death was a hurricane smashing a door inward—maybe the house can't take it. He learned later that the world is also beautiful—"*sounds, and sweet airs, that give delight and hurt not*," as two-faced Caliban murmured to him in the peace of Malachi's library—but on your life, expect no conscious mercy except from merciful people! The bull can turn.

God's will, said Jesse's meek mother. Jesse wished at eight—and at nine, and ten—that he could discover what she meant. Couldn't God have stopped the bull? At eight he was only beginning to learn he could ask questions of Malachi, and this one was too difficult. By the time he was ten Jesse had acquired a stepfather, and Malachi's library was not only a haven but a necessity.

The stepfather, a hardworking religious man who took over Dr. Lodson's haphazard little farm and improved it, didn't like to have Jesse go barefoot. Knowing a little about leather-work, he cobbled a pair of shoes that fitted Jesse's broad feet, more or less. He said it looked tacky for the boy to go barefoot, as if his family was no better than the heathen mountain folk. Even Jesse's mother could hardly look at his feet without her eyes brimming. Jesse wore the painful shoes except when he visited the Old Peters Place. There he slipped them off at the door, and walked with his friend.

His earliest memory of Malachi dated back to a time when he had been small enough for Malachi to take him up in his lap. He remembered a long hand curving over his bare feet, and some remark—he did not retain the words—that made it seem a potent distinction to possess twelve working toes.

Love is a wordless thing in childhood and maybe ought to be. Grown-ups forget this at their peril.

Mr. Goudy brought the first word of Preacher Abraham to Melton Village, a casual profane mention of one more end-of-the-world preacher spouting hellfire and resurrection—only this guy, he said, is appealing to the *kids* for God's sake. Stuff about a pilgrimage to found the New Jerusalem. Them golden streets, said Mr. Goudy, spitting over the rail. All our troubles over, or some shit like that.

Abraham was a great tall man with flame-colored hair and a voice of thunder, said a traveling tinker who hadn't seen him—heard about him, though, from an old woman at Pittsfield Ruins who told fortunes. Abraham was come, she says, to prophesy the Messiah just like John the Baptist. The tinker himself didn't buy it, much.

Later came another man through Melton Village, a burly gentleman leading a caravan—three wagons which once had been half-ton pickups and pulled easy on the rims if you knew how to get the work out of the mules. This gentleman, Homer Hobson, and his henchmen were heading for the open country north of the St. Lawrence—might start a colony, he thought. They were foreigners from the south—New Haven. That's in Connecticut. There he had seen Preacher Abraham, talked to him and shaken him by the hand.

No, he said, the fella wasn't nine feet tall, just average or a mite under. Big voice though, that part was true, and you could say his beard was reddish like. No Goddamn hippie, talked like a gentleman. Peaceful-looking, said Hobson, thinking back over it—peaceful till you stared him straight in the eye, and then you felt maybe a wildness. Blue eyes, and Hobson admitted he generally couldn't remember the color of a person's eyes. Bright blue—stuck in his mind, sort of.

"What does he *say*, about the New Jerusalem?"

That was Jesse Lodson, talking out of turn and annoying his stepfather, but Hobson gazed down on him without reproach, knitting his brows and trying to remember. "Well, boy, he says the New Jerusalem will

34

be—be a place where the earth is so cherished that God will return and live among men." Then Hobson seemed surprised, and added: "Why—don't sound so bad, you say it right out like that."

At the time Hobson saw Abraham, the Crusade must have been barely started. Hobson saw no large crowd with him, only a couple of dozen children between ten and fifteen—yes, quite a few mues among them—who might have merely gathered there in the New Haven street out of curiosity to hear the red-bearded man talk.

Time passed, and word came that Preacher Abraham was healing the sick with prayer and laying on of hands. Word came that in New Providence he raised from the dead a poor man who had perished of small-pox and lain two days without life. Elsewhere the Preacher blessed a woman afflicted by an evil spirit, and the devil passed out of her.

Word came that a thousand children followed Preacher Abraham, foraging, taking care of their prophet with certain miracles.

These tales lit fires. Until even Jesse Lodson, fourteen and never foolish, began to wonder: *Can God after all exist? Mother believes in him. Not all-benevolent, or the bull—but Mother says we aren't wise enough to understand. . . . Should I place so much faith in my own power of reason? Can there be miracles? Then what becomes of the natural order? A New Jerusalem, "where the earth is so cherished"—but the books, the books! Or have I (and Malachi) been mistaken all this time? I pray, and it's all silence.*

He hungered to believe in the marvelous. (Who doesn't?) For most of existence in Melton Village had a flatness, a sourness partly generated by adult despair, and he was lonely in spite of Malachi. The other

35

children had little to do with him, put off by the strangeness of an original mind that is not willing to hide itself or has not learned how. He was aching and changing with the needs of puberty. There was a coolness in Malachi, a steadiness that Jesse Lodson sometimes felt as a child because he could not yet share it.

His mother and stepfather of course distrusted the love of an old man. Still, they did not forbid him those many hours with Malachi. Miss Seton herself said there was nothing more she was capable of teaching him, and Malachi was, in a way, important to Melton Village, like a monument or a natural force.

On his side, perhaps Malachi expected too much. He needed the freshness of youth with the companionship of maturity.

And word came that when Preacher Abraham entered a village and preached and asked who would help him found the New Jerusalem, the mue-children were first to forget their afflictions and follow him.

He was coming from the north. People talked now not only of Preacher Abraham but of "Abraham's Army." Or "the Crusaders."

They had gone north, rumor said, through the Maine and New Hampshire wilderness. Most of this had already returned to the rude health of nature, but it was still possible to follow the roads of the old industrial culture, the skeletal remains that demonstrate the articulation of the original monster, and its indifference to the welfare and beauty of the planet that endured it for so long a century. The Crusaders had taken one of the highways into Canada, and soon headed south again, but instead of coming by the Connecticut River they marched north of Lake Memphremagog to the Hudson Sea. They were at Richford. They were at St. Albans.

A thousand were coming, said rumor—uprooted, exalted, dangerous. Whatever was not freely given, these children took, rumor said. Melton Village stood next in their line of march.

On the porch of The Store—it was summer and robins were nesting in their wonderfully increasing numbers—Bud Maxon grumbled: "By God, them Crusaders better not come thisaway! We got to feed 'em when we a'n't got a pot to piss in ourself?"

Malachi asked: "You about to stop 'em, Bud?"

Maxon looked old and frightened, a Twentieth Century man hating every other way of life. Big Tad Doremus, who made out as a blacksmith in what had once been his father's filling station near the Old Peters Place, sat on the top step whittling applewood. He was always at some bit of art work that would have a woman's buttocks in it, though he might not be up to sculpting the rest of her. Mr. Goudy spat over the rail. Jesse Lodson sat on the bottom step and kept his young mouth shut and his young ears open.

"Eating up the Goddamn country!" said Maxon. "Grasshoppers!"

"Hippies is what they be," said Lucas Hackstraw. His face was like a worm-chewed windfall, and he was married to the saddest woman in town. "Boys and girls jumbled up together."

"How else would they travel?" Tad Doremus asked.

"And some of 'em pretty well growed," said Mr. Goudy, who liked to keep Hackstraw mentally goosed. "Exceedingly well growed and also sprightly, I'm told. Lively times in the hay pile."

"They got no moral sense," said Hackstraw.

"I've always taken a great personal interest in the moral sense," said Malachi. "By the way, does anybody

37

know what it is, to relieve my ignorance? Would you define the moral sense, Brother Maxon?"

"Up yours too, Malachi," said Bud, but his heart wasn't in it.

Tad said to his sculpture: "Anyway we got Malachi going."

"I don't suppose I'm going anywhere, Tad," said Malachi. "Doubt Preacher Abraham is either." Jesse looked up at him, unhappy, both remembering a recent conversation. "He's just traveling."

"Malachi," said Bud Maxon, "sometimes you don't make sense."

Tad said to his wooden woman's rump: "He's making sense."

Jesse heard, before the others, a high murmuring as though a thousand starlings had settled up the road on the far side of Maxon's woodlot. He thought at first it might be that, a gathering of little birds. But Malachi said: "Ready or not, gentlemen, here they come!"

Jesse watched the road. Yesterday in Malachi's library the talk had turned to Preacher Abraham, and Malachi had dropped some casual sarcasm. Driven by swift unexpected impulse, Jesse had stumbled into an awkward defense of the preacher as startling to himself as to Malachi. Maybe in making his remark Malachi had taken the boy's agreement too much for granted. Unused to anything resembling antagonism in their relation, both had been wary, puzzled, and hurt. "You know evangelists have promised to save the world before, Jesse. All they do is drum up faith in magic. This one's no different."

Supported by nothing much but his own unease, Jesse had demanded with too much passion: "How do you *know* he isn't?"

"Ah—'scuse it, I suppose I don't. I went off half-cocked. We wait till he shows up and see who's right, okay?"

Now from afternoon shadow Malachi watched Jesse's intently listening face. Some airy voices up there beyond the woodlot were singing, and with sweetness. Malachi had felt no such fear since a long-ago morning when he discovered ten-year-old Jesse walking cheerfully along the ridgepole of his house, arms out, six-toed feet proudly sure of themselves, miserable death or injury waiting on either side, and Malachi had not even dared to yell. *Who will deliver him from evil?*

The holy man came around the turn of the road with one of his disciples on either side of him. These were scarcely older than Jesse but almost as tall as the Preacher. Both were graceful, slim, yellow-haired, gray-eyed. They were twins, Jesse would learn later—Lucia and John. The Crusaders rejected last names, to signify they had given up home, family, everything, to follow the Lord.

Preacher Abraham advanced slowly, a smallish man with shoulder-length sandy hair, straggle of reddish beard, lowered head of thoughtfulness. Like his followers, he wore grass sandals and a shapeless knee-length white smock; his bony legs were muscular, toughened with journeying. Malachi saw in him the simplicity of a man prepared to walk through a stone wall in the trust that the Lord would turn it to vapor and let him through. By such singlehearted fantastics are the legends made; the Red Sea divides at Moses' command. *How am I to contend with this for the life of a boy?*

The Crusaders marched four abreast. They had ceased singing. The watchers could study the symbol they wore on the fronts of the shapeless, sexless white smocks, done big in crude red paint on the unbleached linen—a spoked wheel crossed out with two zigzag lines. Rumor had explained this symbol—the wheel stood for industry, mechanism, the things of the marketplace, all the Crusaders conceived the old civilization to have been; and God had crossed it out, utterly abolished it. Henceforth God's people were to live by the labor of their hands without machines, without enslaving animals or hunting: no meat, no money, no trade. Greed and cruelty would end forever in the kingdom of heaven; God and the angels would return.

The children matched the slow pace of Preacher Abraham, even the little ones and the lame keeping orderly in the ranks. When the Preacher was in speaking distance of The Store, the last ones had marched into sight. Malachi estimated there were not more than two hundred of them: the rumors of a thousand were like most rumors. He noticed a few considerably older men and women in their twenties—a dozen of them perhaps. There was no one older than the Preacher, who looked about thirty-five.

And Malachi brooded on Melton Village, a lonely society from which all the old had vanished, in which many of the children were stillborn, sickly, deformed. There had been serious talk of stockading the village; Malachi favored it—maybe it ought to become a part of Malachi's Thing. A few years ago the people had suffered brutal raids by the mountain people on their shaggy ponies. These had ceased after a party of young men, skilled at archery and equipped with swords contrived by Tad Doremus, had pursued a band of marauders and wiped them out—an unpredictable fury that might not have happened if Malachi

40

had gone along. They had strung up the bodies on the trees and come home not quite the same youths they had been, having tasted the style of a world that was bound to come. For this reason Malachi had not condemned their action too severely: in a world going back to violence perhaps the village could not survive without violent responses. Turn back the clock and run the bloody course again!—if there's no help for it. The mountain people might forget the lesson. And other creatures prowled the encroaching forest that had not been known there in the old time—black wolves, giant bear. A great tawny cat had been glimpsed twice, with faint tiger markings of dark yellow, no puma certainly, maybe something escaped from an Old-Time zoo, or the descendant of such an escape. Melton Village was beset with strangeness within and without, full of trouble, and tired, and excited, and afraid.

Preacher Abraham stopped in the sunny warmth of the road with his two beautiful disciples. He said: "God keep all here. We're come to promise you the founding of the New Jerusalem."

Malachi unfolded his spidery legs and went down the porch steps, squeezing Jesse's shoulder in passing. He stepped forward alone to greet the Preacher. "We can't do much except wish you well."

"Why, that's a great deal," said Preacher Abraham. It was a great voice to come from such a common-seeming, middle-sized man. "Your good will, something to feed the children, opportunity to give you our good news—that's all we ask. We'll be gone tomorrow."

"There's been a scarcity of good news lately," said Malachi, and Jesse sat in amazement: *Malachi* was the one to give the Preacher friendly greeting, while the

41

rest including himself sat mute like lunkheads? "Little news of any kind. We did learn that a civilization died."

The Preacher's gaze was level—searching for his soul, Malachi supposed. "Are you the mayor, sir?"

"Why," said Malachi, "we haven't rightly got one of those, unless it'd be Bud Maxon over there. How about that, Bud?" He tried with a backward glance to pry Bud off his butt and fetch him down to share the chores, Bud wasn't moving. Jesse's face was inaccessible; the Preacher had possession of Jesse's troubled eyes. "About all we have in that line is a Board of Selectmen, and they don't meet too regular. I'm just Malachi Peters, been around since the flood. We're a sort of Sleepy Hollow, Preacher, a wide place in the road."

"It doesn't matter. My children can camp here, I suppose? And I hope they may go about among your houses to ask bread, flour, a few vegetables, whatever can be spared."

"This man is a scoffer," said the girl, the beautiful disciple.

"Why, I don't think I am, my dear," said Malachi. "History has done the scoffing. If you need a camp site, Preacher, you can use the field below my house. Over there—you can see my roof from here. There's a stream, a pool where the children could bathe."

"Lucia," said the Preacher kindly, "maybe you are too quick to judge." The girl flushed and looked away. "I thank you, Mr. Peters, in the name of all of us. We are happy to accept."

Hackstraw rasped: "Them kids got anything on under them smocks?"

"Why, yes," said the Preacher, "they have." One of the shining young who had gathered close pulled up his smock, showing a trim loincloth. The flirt of the cloth and jerk of the boy's hips amounted to more than an answer to the question; he even tossed a wink toward Jesse. "No need of that, Simon," the Preacher said.

"Well, it didn't look like they had," said Hackstraw, but he was routed, and subsided into dithering and grumbling.

Mr. Goudy sighed, saying to the air: "Malachi's Thing."

"I'll show you the path, Preacher," Malachi said. "It's been getting overgrown with the munificence of nature since the old lady foreclosed the mortgage on her most heedless borrower."

"You have an odd way of expressing yourself," said Preacher Abraham, "but I understand you. You say nature when you mean God."

"Or you may be saying God when you mean nature. If we don't understand each other now we might arrive at it. This way, please."

And Jesse went along.

So did Tad Doremus, who hadn't spoken. He tucked his sculpture in his hip pocket and slouched down the single file path behind Jesse, followed by the multitude; he could hear them breathing, and the brush of young feet in the grass. It occurred to Tad that the back of Jesse's neck looked thin and lonesome. Tad too was a friend of Malachi Peters, and wondered whether the old man was slipping from grace, if it's possible for an agnostic to do that.

Jesse stepped to one side when the path entered the meadow. He usually came this way when going to Malachi; his home was in the village on the dull Main Street and it made a short cut; his feet had done more than any others to keep the path trodden. Countless

43

times he had entered the meadow and seen Malachi, white hair and raggedy gray-brown clothes on the porch two hundred yards away, and waved, and made a game of his progress across the field where now and then a dip of the surface would hide him. In such a hollow he'd pause, for the obscure thrill of teasing the old man, and then when amusement reached bursting point, bounce over the crest and run like a whirlwind, arriving flushed, queer-in-the-head, wondering what to say.

Paths move in time. This was not the old one, now that these strangers were filing past on it curious-eyed. He stood apart, letting them fill the meadow. The wave of them was murmuring, breaking up into separate faces, bodies, voices curiously soft. It dazed Jesse to remember that they came from everywhere—Connecticut, New Hampshire, Massachusetts, even Maine. Maybe they didn't all speak English. In a thirty-second daydream he taught one of the girls English, and how she loved him!

Malachi looked back, finding him for a long gaze, then walking on, matching his stride to the Preacher's as a taller man should.

The countries of love and terror border each other here and there. Jesse became a small boy alone in a crowd.

Most of these people were older, taller. They were following a pattern familiar to themselves. Every third Crusader carried a rolled strip of heavy cloth; these were being joined in pairs and pegged into long pup tents, big enough to hold three at each end with some snuggling. Within ten minutes the meadow had blossomed into a camp. Some of the Crusaders brought water from the pond, others searched under the bordering trees for fallen wood; a young woman with flint

44

and steel went about lighting small campfires. Never a whine or argument or quarrelsome voice. Jesse shuffled off those shoes, tying them together at his neck. He worked his feet in the grass, swallowing something bitter, not panic exactly. Not merely loneliness.

He was the only one not bound for the New Jerusalem. The only one wearing brown instead of white. Shirt and loincloth, no tunic.

He walked up the meadow toward Malachi's house in a dark passion of aloneness—*touch me not, touch me not, take heed of loving me!*—silently passing these friendly souls, some of whom would have spoken to him but for that blind, unhearing look. He was thinking: *I could outrun every single one of you.* Then one of them did speak, a girl with a warm voice, a mouth like a geranium. "Hello—aren't you the son of the man who's letting us have this field?"

Jesse fell in love. "No, I'm not his son." He was lost for more to say. She did not press for more, just waited, smiling without mockery. "I'm his friend."

"Oh," she said, interested in him, not in Malachi. "I'm Philippa."

"My name's Jesse Lodson."

"If you come with us you'll be just Jesse. We give up family, and home, and all things, for to follow our Preacher to the New Jerusalem." And she was so happy about it—that afternoon anyway, in that place and time, the sun choosing gold lights in her brown hair and blessing the freckles on her honestly chubby cheeks—that her speech was a singing and her innocence like fresh cream.

If you come with us—but of course! They expected it, took it for granted; that was supposed to be the purpose of their pilgrimage. And Jesse longed to say: "I'll go with you." He could not, quite.

The town hall bell rang five o'clock. Almost time to go home for heaven's sake, lend a hand with the chores, wash up for supper. To be home not later than half past five was the understood price of being allowed to tag around after Malachi.

Malachi had found that bell three years ago in the ruins of a back-country church. Its village had been emptied—a raid by mountain people, or pestilence, or both; forest was reclaiming everything; bones were whitened, scattered, gnawed by wolves. As Malachi had told the story to Jesse, the bronze bell lay there among charred timbers and rubbish, gleaming like a great open mouth of suffering. Malachi and Tad Doremus had brought the bell home and installed it in the town hall. Then Malachi had persuaded the Board of Selectmen—there really was one, Malachi was sometimes president of it, and it did provide about as much local government as well-behaved people ought to need—to employ half-witted Jem Thorpe to ring that bell every hour through the days. In return for this and a bit of easy janitor work, Jem got enough to eat, a place to sleep, and something to worship. He adored the bell, and the wonderful clock which he had been taught to wind and which told him when to pull the rope. He would have happily died to protect the bell, or the ritual, or Malachi. Just another part of that complex of the unpredictable that followed Malachi Peters like a leitmotif through the orchestration of these years of sadness and perplexity. Malachi's Thing.

"I have to go home."

Philippa nodded sweetly. "But the only real home is the New Jerusalem, Jesse."

He knew her words came from Preacher Abraham, yet her sincerity made them hers too. She had a warm

46

strange smell; her breasts were big enough to push out against the formless smock, and she carried them with no slouch. Jesse realized he was staring, and flushed. But she put her hands on his shoulders and kissed his cheek, bumping again his dangling shoes. "We want you with us," she said. He knew she had glanced down at his bare feet. "Our Preacher says, Let all who are strange and lonely come with us, for we go to build a place where none shall be lonely or strange."

Part of Jesse's mind protested that without loneliness and strangeness this world would not be this world at all and maybe not worth having; but it was a formless protest: he knew he would have grass sandals and a white tunic, and go with Philippa to the New Jerusalem.

Malachi felt silence around him as he climbed the slope to his house. The children's voices had fallen behind them. The Preacher had sent off those attending him on various errands, all but two young men in their early twenties whom he called Andrew and Jude. Andrew seemed cheerful—thoughtful too, plainfaced and kind. Jude's young face was already cut with worry lines and the start of a chronic frown.

Tad Doremus kept quiet—a natural occupation, almost a life-work.

Malachi asked: "Where will you found the New Jerusalem?"

"I think I shall know the place when I see it," said Preacher Abraham. "We turned south in Canada because Andrew here brought me word of a place called Nuber on the west shore of the Hudson Sea. I must go there—it may be the place."

"Nuber? There was a town, Newburgh," said Malachi. "I drove through it the summer I was eighteen. But that area of the Hudson Valley was destroyed, you know, in the floods and earthquakes."

"This place is on higher ground, ten or fifteen miles inland."

"You're a New Yorker, sir?"

"I was born in Maryland. I have almost no memory of the old time. Barely five, the year of the war, and I spent my youth in witless sin and folly until I was given light. Andrew is my right hand," he said, and smiled at the young man as they climbed the steps of Malachi's porch. "We separated a few months ago so that he could explore western New York while we went through New England. Then he rejoined us in the north. Tell Mr. Peters about Nuber, Andrew."

They settled on the porch, for the Preacher wanted to watch the preparation of the camp site in the meadow. Andrew spoke almost bookishly. "What they call Nuber is an area fifteen miles by twenty—say three hundred square miles—where there were wealthy estates in the old time, and some arable land too, not spoiled by commercial agriculture. Long before the last build-up of political tensions in 1993 the rich people of that region were running a private oligarchy, nominally within the American political framework. They had a little bit of foresight, enough intelligence to see that the commercial-technological rat race couldn't keep up much longer—raw materials were running out for one thing—and they may have been wise enough to fear the end result of political insanity in a world with atomic power. At any rate they were much concerned with survival—their own, that is. According to their cult, so far as they had any beliefs, altruism was a bad word, and they had always considered their society as not much more than a source of loot and personal power. They dug in against the storm. They built underground refuges, hoarded enormous quantities of food, fuel, arms, ammunition. They couldn't make new guns, but even now, I understand, there's a miniature subterranean factory in Nuber that turns out gunpowder, and usable cartridges for the old weapons."

"Nice people," said Malachi.

"It is after all," said Andrew sententiously, "a primary preoccupation of any dictatorial state."

"Yes," said Malachi. The Preacher watched the meadow.

"They shall be humbled," said Jude, his voice sudden and harsh. His white hands knotted in front of him. "It is in Ezekiel: *Moreover the word of the Lord came unto me, saying, Son of Man, when the house of Israel dwelt in their own land, they defiled it by their own way and by their doings: their way was before me as the uncleanness of a removed woman. Wherefore I poured my fury upon them for the blood that they had shed upon the land, and for their idols wherewith they had polluted it.*"

"Amen," said Andrew mildly. He might even have a sense of humor, Malachi thought, but his devotion was complete and obvious. Intelligence and literacy he possessed, both wholly at the service of Preacher Abraham. He continued: "They hired a lot of laborers, technicians, and a police force. Also a great many more personal servants than was usual among the rich at that time, paying high for them. Mostly they seem to have been following the advice of a man named Bridgeman, one of history's little Hitlers. Before the world blew up the police were called security guards—I suppose nobody asked, security for what? Then the world did blow up, they did survive, the po-

49

lice force was an army, some of the technicians were a palace elite, Bridgeman was king in everything but name, and the blue-collar people and servants were slaves. Specifically, Mr. Peters. Nuber today makes no secret of being a slaveholding state. Bridgeman had a mint, turning out pretty gold and silver and copper money: trust him to think of that and grab control of it, among people who had thought all their lives that money was a paper fairy tale told by themselves."

"He must have known a little history."

"Yes, Mr. Peters, but not enough to do him any good. His official title, by the way, assumed right after the twenty-minute war, was—" Andrew smiled, his young face pleasantly professorial. "Guess."

"Couldn't."

"Secretary," said Andrew. "Secretary of the Nuber Historical Society. Well, in a year or so he began hankering after something more like imperial purple, the name as well as the game, and somebody eager for his job stuck a ten-inch knife in his back, taking the job *and* the name of king. Bridgeman should have expected it: it was the kind of political operation Nuber was built to understand."

Malachi asked: "Preacher Abraham, do you propose to advance on a vicious military state, with a horde of defenseless children? How? How and why?"

"I will first explain the why," said Preacher Abraham. "Because it does seem impossible. Mr. Peters, the world cannot be saved unless we show God's power in us by doing the seemingly impossible."

"Oh," said Malachi, "the world is sickened of attempts to save it. The world is saving itself now in the only way it has or ever can—by small, brave individual efforts at recovery now that the storm's over. It will take centuries. Institutions have never done it and

50

never will. Well, I see you don't agree, you're not hearing me."

"To God nothing is impossible," said the Preacher, as if he truly had not heard. "As to the how, Mr. Peters, we go there under God's guidance. As I have been assured by his very voice." His face was glowing. "Do not tell me this is a subjective experience—those wise little words! I know, Mr. Peters, I *know*! If we fail, then the failure itself is God's will: we can only die in the Lord a little sooner than the natural time."

"Have the children asked to die young?"

"You seem angry. The children understand, as perhaps you do not yet, the meaning of eternal life." The Preacher rose. "Thank you for the meadow, Mr. Peters, and for this little time of rest."

But Malachi had risen too and grasped his arm. The Preacher gazed back unmoving. "Preacher Abraham, will you allow me to come with you? Will you give me your light, as you see it, and perhaps—perhaps—"

"No one who wishes to follow me is refused," said Preacher Abraham.

"I think he has no faith," said Jude.

"If some follow me for the wrong reasons," said Preacher Abraham mildly, "perhaps right reason will come later. We shall break camp early in the morning. Come to me then if you will."

"Will you—stop in now and have something to eat?"

"Thank you, sir, but I see you keep goats and chickens. We must no longer exploit the captivity of living things. But thank you for the offer, which was kindly meant."

Malachi sagged, watching the Preacher depart with Andrew and Jude. Tad sighed harshly. "I don't think you sold him, Malachi."

"Come inside, Tad. The elderberry's near-about the best I've got. I distilled her some, see, and exploited her captivity in a bottle, sort of. Maybe she ain't a living thing, though."

"Seemed like one, time I sampled her last." Tad reached for the glass, drank, and nibbled his lips. "She's living." Malachi dropped in his big armchair by the hearth, the armchair where Jesse discovered Shakespeare and Mark Twain and Melville. "You look a mite bushed, Malachi."

"Am."

"I a'n't exactly making you out."

"Could you look after this place a while, Tad? Feed the stock—and help yourself naturally. Keep an eye out the public doesn't go off with the books for luck charms?"

"Could of course, Malachi."

"Place'd be yours, come to that, I'm not back in a reasonable time. I'll write that in the form of a will, tonight."

"Jesus, Malachi. I don't see you in one of them fucking nightgowns."

"Maybe I'll be let to keep my pants." Malachi refilled his glass. "Jesse," he said, "I believe Jesse is hooked on the New Jerusalem."

Tad reached down a blacksmith's hand to Malachi's bowed scrawny shoulder. "Ayah. Uhha."

"Why do we love?"

"I don't know," said Tad. "I'll mind the house. No trouble."

"*Jesse,*" said Malachi, and drank his glass empty, and flung it against the fireplace stones.

There are many new islands. Wherever the land was low to the west of the Green Mountains the climbing waters intervened, carving them into new solitude. Little islands, maybe good for a family and a farm if anyone chose to come; larger islands, where deer could breed, and brown bear, and the newcome coyotes, and wildcat. The toiling waters were fresh in the first few years except for flood rubbish and other pollution, then brackish as the vastly expanding Sea of St. Lawrence (but it was becoming easier to speak of the Lawrent Sea, or sometimes just the Lorenta) swallowed the Richelieu River. The earthquake that destroyed St. Jean, Rouses Point, Plattsburg, a hundred other towns, brought southward the taste of ocean. In a few years another earthquake, another adjustment to the fearful stresses of the new weight of water on the land, flung together Lake George, Sacandaga, the upper tributaries of the Hudson, in a muddy boiling confusion. The Ontario Sea breaks through along the country that once knew Lake Oneida and the Mohawk River; some now call that passage Moha Water. Where the Lorenta and Hudson and Ontario Seas come together at the southeastern corner of the great Adirondack Island, outrageous complex tides tear about in a crazy Sabbat of the elements, and scour an unknown bottom. In the Year 9, they say, steam hung for six months over four hundred square miles of that tidal country; there was no one to go in under it and search for the cause. No volcano—none known, that is, not yet; but today there are hot springs along the southeastern coast of Adirondack that certainly did not exist in the old days.

At a place called Ticonderoga small sailing vessels can often make fair passage to and from Adirondack Island, passing out of sight of land for hardly more than an hour if the wind is right. Where the sea is narrower up in the north there's too much jungle and,

53

they say, malaria or something like it; the Ticonderoga crossing is the best. Then, if you must go south, there are several places—Herkimer, Fonda, Amsterdam—where Moha Water can be crossed with not much danger except from pirates. Amsterdam, to be sure, is a little too near the tidal country and its frequent mists, which the pirates are apt to understand better than the ferry captains do. The devils come nipping out from the heavily wooded shores in their canoe fleets—true savages, reversions to the Stone Age, many of whose grandfathers must have sold insurance, real estate, and advertising just like anybody.

As for crossing the Hudson Sea in the far south, that's for professional heroes. Those tidal waves are treacherous and frightful. The pirates there have all the advantages, and they can do things with a lateen rig and a shallow draft that no decent sailor would think of doing unless he'd sold his soul to Shaitan. There, in fact, modern piracy may have developed; the canoe operators up north are imitators, amateurs. That corner of the world south of the Catskills needs more earthquakes. "The Crusaders will have rough travel, if they mean to go as far as Nuber."

"Yes," said Jesse, who had come to Malachi dragging his feet after Tad Doremus went home. Malachi was back on his porch; bats were darting in the cool air; at the far end of the meadow some of the children were singing. "But Andrew came north by way of Fonda, and he didn't have any trouble. Malachi . . ."

"Get it off your mind." Malachi patted the step beside him, and Jesse sat there. Malachi could feel his warmth. Wisdom, or fear, or that dismal blend of the two called caution prevented Malachi from putting an arm over the boy's shoulder as he would have done an evening or two earlier.

"What does it mean when—when all of a sudden everything changes, like upside down—I mean, you start believing one or two things different, or even just try to think how it would be if you *did* believe those things, and then a hundred other things change, and—and—"

"Your syntax is slipping."

"I know. I got excited."

"Like turning the Kaleidoscope?"

"Man, yes—it *is* like that, sort of."

"I guess," said Malachi presently, "it means you have to look at the new pattern. . . . Do your folks know you're thinking of leaving with the Preacher?"

"I haven't been home," said Jesse almost sullenly. "Gah, you always know everything. If I told 'em they'd lock me up till he's gone, you know they would. . . . Are you going to tell them?"

Malachi brooded. "If I intended to, I would tell you first. I don't think of you as a child these days, Jesse."

And Jesse thought in panic and misery: *But I'm not ready—not ready to be anything else. Oh, it's easy for you to be wise, Malachi!* "Malachi, I—oh, I wish to *God* my old man—the—the bull—"

Jesse was lost in a sudden agony of weeping such as Malachi had never seen. It was easy then to take hold of him and cherish him as if he were still a child. "I know," said Malachi, rocking him lightly. "I loved him too, your father. We used to play chess. He was a wonderful man, Jesse. Everybody knew it."

"So how can you believe he's dead? There *has* to be a—a—the Preacher—yes, I talked to the Preacher for a minute, and he—blessed me. Don't say anything, Malachi, just don't say anything for a while." He gasped and blew his nose. "I'm not going back to the house tonight. I'm to sleep in John's tent. They're going to have sandals for me." He took the leather shoes from his neck, and set them inside the porch rail, his hands saying: *So much for my stepfather.* "Can I leave them there, Malachi?"

"Yes."

"I guess you're pretty disappointed with me."

"No. . . . Jesse, I am considering going with Preacher Abraham myself, for my own sake. I even spoke to him about it."

Jesse started and turned his wet face to Malachi in the dusk. *"You!* Why?"

"Oh, let us say that sometimes I too find Melton Village to be a kind of dead end. I have worked for the town, and you might say loved it—an ugly duckling—ai-yah, Malachi's Thing. But I need to learn what's happening in a bigger world. I've got in a rut. Why, man, for more than your lifetime I've had no news of the world except what's trickled in as gossip from the occasional traveler or tramp, most of it worthless, I expect. It's shameful. I needed something to fetch me loose. Besides, Preacher Abraham interests me, and he said that no one who elected to follow him was refused. He has his own kind of wisdom. It's not my kind, Jesse—I won't pretend. But perhaps I can be of some use to him, who knows?"

Jesse's stare would not let him go. "You've got other reasons. You're not quite leveling with me, Malachi."

"Maybe not. Not crooked either. Some things I find hard to explain, even to you. Suppose we just let it work out."

Jesse relaxed. "All right." One of the natural surges of affection that made him what he was brought him back to Malachi, warm and close. He sat still with his head resting over Malachi's heart, and said at last: "Well, I'm glad you're coming along." Then he was gone, walking down the meadow to the little camp-fires.

Malachi carried the shoes indoors and put them away in an old trunk already loaded with history—the ancient kaleidoscope for instance, given to Malachi by his grandmother long before the Year Zero and still miraculously unbroken for Jesse's brief pleasure and amusement; and his father's diary that ended in the old year 1972, when the extinction of the Republic was obvious; and a photograph of a girl who had died with so many others in 1993.

The company of two hundred started in the early morning, marched east two or three miles to reach the old mountain road, and followed it south. They camped for the night where they could look toward distant Burlington Ruins, an old wound of flood and earthquake never healed. Malachi slept alone that night under the big dark. He had brought on his back a rolled blanket and change of clothing. He contributed a sack of potatoes to the general supply and whatever else he could find that seemed innocent in the Crusaders' terms. He also wore at his belt his old hunting knife, which Preacher Abraham deplored. "I cut my food with it," said Malachi, "and sometimes I whittle. And no, sir, I'll decline the tunic for the present and just wear these." They studied each other, antagonists not too unfriendly; Malachi perhaps had an advantage in knowing where the true conflict lay. "Now if you can persuade me of the existence of God, Preacher, I will wear the tunic and throw away my knife. But don't rush it, sir. I'm inclined to make up my mind on my own time. Meanwhile let me be the oddity among you. I wash and I don't eat little girls." The Preacher brooded and then smiled, and surprisingly patted Malachi's arm before he turned away to more important matters.

At home Malachi had often slept outdoors, in his back yard or out in the meadow. He knew the Pleiades, and the wandering of the planets and the stars. He had found his strength more than equal to the day's march, and was healthily tired. The campfires burned low; Malachi noticed Jude and one or two others taking up sentry duty out at the fringes of the light. Then someone—Malachi could not see him in the dark—sounded on a bugle the ancient army music of Taps. How did it happen the Preacher had resurrected that, and did he have any idea of the far-off associations of ideas? After the music died slowly—no one can hear it unmoved—there was a rhythmic murmuring all through the camp; it ended all in the same moment, and Malachi understood it was the sound of the children praying. Somewhere among them, Jesse, snug in a tent with the disciple John and three or four others. It would take Jesse no time to learn the words and rituals: he was always a quick study. Malachi sighed, and after less pain than he had feared, he slept.

In hilly country Preacher Abraham did not demand of his children more than twelve to fifteen miles of marching in a day. A majority of them, Malachi guessed as the march resumed in the morning, would have been delighted to exceed that. But an army, and sometimes a civilization, must proceed at the pace of its weakest marcher. Some were very young. The mue-girl Dinah, twelve years old, slight and small with the patient look of sainthood, had a defect in her knee structure that made her stiff-legged and slow. Whenever she tired Jude carried her. These were the only times when his haggard face lost its frown and became tender; but with that frail burden he could make no speed himself.

On the second and third days Malachi stayed most of the time in the rear, knowing that to all of them, even to the Preacher and Jesse, he must seem monstrously old. But the rear was a good vantage point. He could see whatever happened. He could watch Jesse's dark head, and know at least who his new friends were, and read whatever was told by the set of the boy's shoulders. And sometimes Jesse dropped back to walk with him. Though in a too exalted, precarious way, Jesse did seem happy, and full of a natural interest in the new country.

Reading history, Malachi had noted that throughout most of the past the counsel of the old had been valued, even sought for; it was not until the Twentieth Century that old people were declared obsolete and swept under the rug; and the Twentieth Century itself was now merely one more lump in the record.

On the third night out the company reached the settlement of Shorum, where the ferry sails for Ticonderoga now and then if the captain considers it worth his while. He has been known to stir his stumps for one old woman with her cat in a basket who wanted to get over to Chilson Landing and see a new grandchild; and once he made the mayor of Shorum wait a week on account of a few cross words. About transporting two hundred kids from here to nowhere to found the New Jerusalem, he was not pleased, pointing out that it would take four trips, two days' work considering the tides, and even with four trips the crowding would be somewhat much. "We are patient," said Preacher Abraham, "and used to material difficulties."

"It'll cost you a dime a head," said Captain Gibbleson.

"Dependence on money is the death of the spirit. What can you buy with it?" asked the Preacher. "The old system's gone, Captain."

"State gov'ment says the old coinage is still money. Naturally I wouldn't take no paper."

"I've hardly been aware you had a state government."

Very much the wrong thing to say. Malachi intervened deprecatingly: "We sort of invoke it, Preacher. Some claim to've seen it." But his wink at the Captain did not restore the peace.

"Got no money," said Captain Gibbleson, "you can swim."

Andrew took over. "Captain, I see you have quite a miscellaneous log pile, there along the bank."

"Ayeh, driftwood, some of it." Captain Gibbleson chewed on his plug and eyed him unhopefully; the plug smelled as if it had been sold him by Mr. Goudy. "You wouldn't believe what high water fetches in sometimes. Got a whole cabin one day, with a dead man in it. Blowed up like a punkin he was, you should've seen."

"I offer you two alternatives," said Andrew. "We will stack that wood for you, and split any that's worth splitting, in return for our passage. Or, overriding your wishes as it were, we will simply take whatever wood we need to build a raft." Behind Andrew's back the disciple Simon explained further by sticking out his tongue.

"Why, you'd drown," said Captain Gibbleson, chewing. "Like bugs. I can't have that on my conscience. Stack the Goddamn wood and it's a deal." Later, hunkered on the pier and watching Andrew oversee the labor, he confided to Malachi: "Sometimes I almost halfway like a man that don't mind being a damn fool." His back turned to the Crusaders, Malachi slipped him five bucks in 1984 quarters.

The gray-blue reach of the Hudson Sea proved not unkind. Preacher Abraham and Andrew went with the first group on the ferry, a flatbottomed barge with a crude square sail. Her name was *Pug*, after Gibbleson's third wife, and he claimed she was too squat and wide to turn over—in a hurricane she might go straight up or straight down, but she wouldn't tip. Jude was in charge of the group that would go on the fourth sailing; Jesse lingered for the transparent reason that this group included Philippa. Malachi observed that he won no profit from it beyond a staring and a few choked attempts at conversation. Philippa, Malachi thought, was managing Jesse's compulsive adoration rather well. Malachi had also seen the look that Philippa had for Andrew only: an ancient story, one who loves and one who is loved; maybe a constant in the human pattern, the exceptions shining only for a most fortunate few. But it seemed to Malachi that Philippa might be not without the rudiments of compassion. Before Shorum, Jesse had brought her to Malachi, saying with glazed casualness: "This is Philippa."

"How do you do?" said Malachi. The freckles were appealing.

"We are sure to do well in the Lord's grace," said Philippa.

Now Malachi, loafing in the stern with Captain Gibbleson (almost a friend), watched the clumsiness and grace of youth. The scow crept torpidly across a placid sea toward a gray excrescence of rock on a hillside; there's water all around it now, a few people and goats inhabit the island, and it is still overlooked by that mountain which General Burgoyne's artillery found so convenient once upon a time. Malachi heard Jesse offering some news, up forward: "They restored the old fort in 1909—" *What's he done, memorized the Britannica?*—"but it probably isn't true that Ethan Allen demanded its surrender in the name of the Great Jehovah and the continental Congress." Except for a passing uneasiness Philippa looked quite blank.

Then up on the wharf and goodbye to Gibbleson, and on into the perilous world of Adirondack Island. There would be nearly a hundred miles of it as the trail winds from Ticonderoga to Fonda, following the roads of the Old Time whenever they seem practical. Nature is trying not unsuccessfully to heal those scars. The busy vine spreads across with sucker rootlets, the innocent seed reaches down through any crack in the dreary concrete or asphalt and is sustained.

Already at many places the easiest route will be a new earthen road with no decaying metal hulks or broken slabs of rubbish. (But the automobile corpses that held their shape so persistently, when overgrown with cool Virginia creeper, are of benefit to rabbits, weasels, ground-birds, and such folk, who know how to make honest use of them.) In this Adirondack Island country you are better off with a guide, if you find one you can trust.

There is for instance the matter of bandits and large wild animals. If one of the outlaw or savage groups does come after you on those burr-shaggy mountain ponies, bent on loot or women or violence for its own sake, the guide isn't much help, and whatever happens will be soon over; but the guide is expected to know the latest rumors about those devils, and find you the safest routes. Guiding is an honorable profession, at least in theory. A guide must know the animals too, and steer you right if you need to hunt. Some of them of course are no damn good.

A long day's march from Fort Ti brought the Crusaders to Brant Lake, and they camped beside it. Here in the morning a guide offered his services, a small brown smiling man in the skimpy G-string of a savage. (We already begin to hear something of the Cayugas in the central part of what used to be New York; they are a difficult people, with old grievances rooted deep.) He wore a more civilized belt above his hips to hold a steel hunting knife, and he carried at his shoulder a quiver of brass-tipped arrows and a short bow unpleasing to Preacher Abraham. Andrew tried the man with sign language and grunts, transmitting the message that he apparently wanted no money in return for showing them a safe way southward, but just their company as far as Moha Water and a roll of the linsey cloth their tunics were cut from.

"The knife and bow will be his living, Preacher," said Malachi. "No one has taught him any better."

Preacher Abraham sighed and said: "I know. Grace does not come unsought, nor overnight unless the Lord wills." Then he looked deep in the guide's squirrely brown eyes and inquired in simple English whether he believed in God. The guide nodded with solemn reverence.

A few hours later, when the brown man had led them down a wood road that became a pleasant sun-speckled green trail, Malachi ranged ahead to walk beside him. Jesse came too, evidently wanting just then to reestablish closeness. Speaking too softly for those behind to hear, Malachi asked the guide whether he believed in Satan and the ideological solidarity of the capitalist class. The little man nodded again several times, delightedly.

Jesse smiled too, but the smile wiped itself out. "Malachi," he said, "why do people always make such a tremendous thing about words?"

Malachi worried over it for him, and presently said: "They are clumsy, and often unnecessary. But I think they may be the best means we have for probing certain kinds of darkness. As for communication, Jesse, we might survive for a while without it, but I'm not sure the survival would be worth having. Words weren't invented *only* to conceal thoughts as the old wheeze has it. They create thoughts, give thoughts, and are thoughts. People live by honest words and die by the other kind."

Frowning and still bothered, Jesse said after a while: "Yes, I guess that makes sense."

There was no denying the guide's usefulness. When they camped beside the Sacandaga River he found early mushrooms for them and showed them edible marsh plants, so that the grim diet of cornmeal mush and potatoes and soggy wheat cakes could be a little varied. It puzzled Malachi that he should have apparently known the Crusaders' vegetarian principles without being told, but no one commented on it. At the music of Taps the little guide bowed his face to the ground.

All the following day he led his charges along firm earth through a region of brackish swamp where the Sacandaga once comfortably paralleled a Twentieth Century road. Dark country here, too close to that outrageous great tidal pocket of the Hudson Sea. Mists float unexpected through the more open reaches of the woods. It is quiet. No snowmobiles nor snarling chain saws nor bulldozer flatbeds shuddering uphill.

Wind sometimes or the other sounds of storm, or of a deer dying to feed panther or wolf or brown tiger. You may hear a coyote desolately howling, or a loon in the marsh. No transistors.

On the morning of the ninth day after leaving Melton Village, an inquiry from Andrew about Fonda drew from the guide the gestured response that the place was two sleeps away, meaning perhaps anywhere from twenty-five to forty miles. The black flies that day were a torment. The Crusaders marched four abreast, a cloud of needling misery all about them. It was one of the old highways, in fair condition. Forest stood oppressively deep on either side; imagination provided glimpses of motion in the heavy green, hints of pathways not to be followed. But the march was bringing them into open country, and shortly after the second rest of the morning—scant rest it was with the tiny black demons whining and settling, nothing to do but slap and suffer—they came out into it.

The deep woods lay a few hundred yards behind them when Malachi saw another road up ahead, a simple line of reddish dirt emerging from thick tree cover and snaking down a long slope to meet their highway. The guide flung up his hand. The company halted as Andrew dutifully repeated the motion, and stood raggedly, slapping at the flies, two hundred children wondering, murmuring. Preacher Abraham called out: "What is it? What's the matter?" Andrew shook his head don't-know.

The guide was running forward bent over as one might do to evade a stone or arrow from behind; in his stooping haste Malachi saw a thing turned suddenly feral and vicious. At the end of his long rush he flung up his arms and sent to that wooded summit a sharp yell, the word *"Here!"* His mission achieved, he crouched then, smiling and ugly, holding an arrow leveled toward Andrew as the horsemen plunged out from under the trees.

Andrew shouted: "Scatter! Back to the woods!" Malachi shouted it too, and he saw Andrew crumple and fall, the guide's arrow in his chest. Jude had already snatched up Dinah in his arms and was running with her. John too shrilled at the company: "To the woods! *Hide!*"

Too many of the children were slow to grasp it, and stood in a sick daze until the Preacher added his urgent voice. Then they began to go, stragglingly and late, staring over their shoulders, maybe not quite believing any of it until they saw Lucia snatched up and flung across a pony's back, and John leaping at the rider's leg, falling back with blood spurting from his throat.

The riders were not more than a dozen, and strangely silent except for a gurgle of excited laughter. Naked but for loinrags and moccasins, they rode bareback as if they had spent half their lives that way, and they were men of any breed, all breeds. They did not trouble to draw their small bows, seeing (or knowing in advance) that the victims were unarmed—their servant might do as he pleased. They wanted women, but young girls would do very well. They rode their fiery little horses in and out among the fleeing, now terrified children, and picked them off as they chose, each man as soon as he had secured his captive riding back up the long hill. It was over in minutes. Europe's Fifth Century would have been proud of them.

Malachi looked at the knife in his hand. He could have used it, if there had been time, and anything in reach. Maybe the sight of it was what had made the

66

riders circle clear of him and Jesse. Philippa had been with them when the storm went by; now she had run to where Andrew was lying and flung herself down. Malachi saw the last rider disappear up the hill and into the woods, and behind him scampered the busy small figure of their smiling guide.

The Preacher was saying: *"Resist not evil.* This was the word of Christ: *Love your enemies, bless them that curse you."* Was the Preacher counseling himself? The disciple John was dead, Lucia and eleven others gone; Andrew whom he had called his right hand could no longer serve or hear him, though Philippa with her clutching hands and crying voice was trying to make him live.

"For he maketh his sun to rise on the evil and the good, and sendeth the rain on the just and the unjust."

"Philippa." Malachi knelt by her. "You must come away."

"Come away," said Jesse. "Come away, Philippa."

"Be ye therefore perfect even as your Father which is in Heaven is perfect."

Philippa rose and brushed past them. She stood before Preacher Abraham and said: "You did this."

"Forgive me then," said the Preacher.

Philippa stared at Andrew's blood on her hands. "We were going to marry, in the New Jerusalem." She turned her face to the woods, and Malachi felt Jesse tense with readiness to run after her, bring her back from that suicide. She took a few sleepwalking steps that way and halted, looking about her, saying: "But I have no place to go."

"Philippa," said the Preacher, "there *is* the New Jerusalem."

She did not answer.

* * *

67

They carried the bodies of Andrew and John down the road, and made a burial place in the open country; that wooded hilltop stood vague in the north. The day was still, no sounds but those of peace, and the Preacher spoke to them. "I will go to Nuber," he said, "and preach there the founding of the New Jerusalem as I am commanded to do by my Father which is in Heaven. I will wear on my breast this image of the conquered wheel, and I will testify."

Malachi wondered: *Does he know who he is, in his own mind at least and in the minds of many of us? Would he have us know?*

"But I am weak in the vessel of the flesh, and do not always see my way clearly, and at times I may have been deceived and unwise."

Well, Christ would not have said that.

"It may be, my children, that it is not for us to build that city, in Nuber or anywhere, by the labor of our hands, though I still hope it will be so. Therefore I do release from the vows any of you who for any reason no longer hear the call of God to follow me. There are other ways you may serve his purpose, many honorable ways. From our beloved disciple Andrew I learned more about the sorry kingdom of Nuber than I have told you. Perhaps I understand why it is that God plainly directs me to that place, but I will not try to explain it. Nuber is a city of the damned, a place of greed and cruelty, smallness of the spirit, evildoing and blindness. So it may be that I go there to my death, and God's purpose in this may not be understood for a long time to come. I will demand nothing of you that is not freely given, and so God be with you."

He said no more that day, and he did not preach at Fonda.

Sympathy and friendliness were strong in that lonely village, but cooled somewhat at Malachi's suggestion of an armed search party to rescue the ravished girls. He was talking to the mayor of the town, and the good man said nothing about resisting not evil, but pointed out that those bloody bandits would now be fifty or a hundred miles away in their own kind of country, by trails nobody knew. They were a familiar plague; it had happened before. Who could deal with it except the kind of police force no town nowadays can support? Be reasonable, man. Shortly thereafter the townfolk took up a collection of pay for the transport of Abraham's Army over Moha Water.

Here a maternally minded citizen intervened, protesting the exposure of these children to the perils of such a journey. Others before her had felt it, but this was a sensible woman with tact. She talked long and amiably with the Preacher while the two ferry captains were waiting on the tide, and then with his permission spoke to the children, praising their devotion, their hope of the New Jerusalem (a hope she shared), adding almost like an afterthought that if any of them felt unequal to the task, or wanted more time to think about it, why, she and some of her neighbors were prepared to give them shelter, or help for a journey back home if that was what they wanted.

Sitting on the pier with Malachi, Jesse heard him murmur: "Bravo!" But he noticed the old man was gazing at the Preacher, not at this good Samaritan who looked as if she wanted to cuddle the whole company in her lap. "We ought to stay with him, Malachi?" And Jesse studied the Preacher, trying to find what Malachi had been observing with surprise and respect.

"This woman is blessed," said Preacher Abraham.

"Again I say, you who wish to remain with her are released from your vows." And when he asked for a sign from those who elected to leave him, more than half the company raised their hands, Philippa among them.

"He believes it," said Malachi, "even to the cup that will not pass. Yes, I think I ought to stay with him, Jesse, in what time he has left before death or disillusion. I have heard about Nuber too. Once or twice he has found it possible to talk with me. But you yourself are first with me: that is how I've always loved you."

Jesse looked down at his feet. The grass sandals had never fitted; he carried them, like the old shoes, at his neck. "It was to have been a city for the mues, among the rest."

"You're not even a mue." Malachi shook his shoulder. "God, Jesse, I hope you'll marry some time and replenish the bloody earth with a pack of six-toed children. Think what it would do to the ski industry!"

"The what?" Jesse was bewildered.

"Never mind," said Malachi, and kissed the top of his head.

Nuber, a city of wealth (which is always relative) and poverty (which is basic hell), surrounded by a dutifully toiling countryside with plantations of slave labor, felt in those years no foreign threat. Life could be a little relaxed. To enter the borders you had only to convince the commandant of the post that you nourished no pernicious design against the stability of the realm, and to convince him might cost no more than ten dollars. Malachi still had a mite more than that; or the band of Abraham's followers, less than fifty now, might even be admitted free.

The very location of the border posts was subject to

70

the commandant's caprice. He might move his little establishment a mile or so down the road if something that way caught his fancy—a juicy melon patch, or a farm family with a goodlooking daughter who might be more contented as a citizen of the Republic. (It is after all something of a distinction, Malachi remarked to Jesse: not every republic has a king for a dictator. And Jesse had been laughing some that day, a kind of half-choked outbreak, maybe a new Jesse trying to crack the chrysalis of a very solemn boy.)

To the camp at Trempa, a day's march from the nearest border post of Nuber, came an old peddler—at least he was dressed like one, and gnarled like a fellow often exposed to the seasons, but he never opened his shoulder sack, nor paid much heed to anyone but the Preacher himself, beyond a few puzzled glances at Malachi. "You ought to go back, Preacher," he said. "Oh, you ought to go back, let it pass from you. I come from Nuber and I know."

"Who are you?" asked the Preacher.

"A tinker, an old man, a nobody. I come and go. I've been called Ahasuerus—in jest I suppose, for never did I despise Christ and his kindred; the old and slightly wise become used to the jesting at their expense, it's only natural. You ought to go back. Oh, they are saying in Nuber, there's a wheel for you, you that condemn the wheel and wear that handsome symbol over your heart. Why, they've found a great steelbound wooden wheel, something maybe from an old-time farm wagon, I don't know." He muttered and flexed his arthritic hands, tired from carrying the sack and from age. "They are saying that if you come to preach your sedition at Nuber you shall carry the wheel on your back to the marketplace, and it shall be set up there for the multitude; and they speak of nailing your palms to the spokes. And oh, Abraham, there will be one to betray you and one to deny you, and one to judge you and wash his hands."

"Why do they hate me?" asked Preacher Abraham.

"Because you speak of the good that all men dream of as if it could be real."

At these words the Preacher was troubled, and when the peddler had received his blessing and gone away up the north road he came to Malachi and asked him: "Why have you remained with me?" He shook back the hair from his shoulders, a young man's motion, but looked tired and old as he rubbed his fingertips over the frown that would not leave his forehead. The painted wheel on his tunic bore the dark appearance of blood. "You have not faith, Malachi, yet you are faithful to promises, and have served me and my poor children with devotion. I watched you helping Jude care for Dinah at Coble, when she was dying. And in the weeks at Gran Gor, where the smallpox was, where so many died, you were tireless in caring for the sick, those of the town as well as our own. If only for these things I'm bound to love and respect you. And now it seems you are prepared to go with me, though I cannot ask it, even to the end of the journey."

"Or perhaps I will deny you," said Malachi Peters, smiling, and the Preacher presently smiled, in his own fashion. "It's my belief that human beings choose their own ends, Preacher Abraham. There is no purpose under the heaven until living creatures on earth create it. And there must be few indeed who don't cherish a faith in some things, because all knowledge remains incomplete; even though faith is only the fantasy of things hoped for, the invention of things not seen. I have faith in the good will of myself and certain others, faith in the rightness of love and virtue and mercy. That faith will sustain me as it has in the past, while I live."

The long weeks lay behind Jesse like a year of difficult growth. This was beginning autumn. The border post of Nuber stood only a few steps down the road. Tomorrow they would pass it, and that would happen which was to happen. Tomorrow would be the day that Nuber celebrated as the Day of Coming Forth, the day when according to their history and legend they came out from underground after the twenty-minute war and found that the Earth still lived. Jesse's memory brought him like a remote music some words from the Gospel of Matthew: *Ye know that after two days is the feast of the passover, and the Son of man is betrayed to be crucified.*

Still and sleepless under his half of Malachi's blanket, Jesse gazed toward the south horizon where a few strong stars cut through the haze of the night. Malachi had said it would rain before daylight. A huge roadside oak spread over them, big enough to shelter most of the Preacher's little company, and Malachi had pegged a strip of canvas over their heads.

How did one learn the ways of earth and sun and sky as the old man knew them? It was more than observation. Observing the natural world, but also continually knowing himself a part of it. *He could speak like Saint Francis (though he doesn't) of "my brother the sun." Here am I, says he (or is it myself speaking for him?), a unique pattern briefly arranged on this earth for my only time to think and feel and see. So may it not be that what I do to and for myself and others is more important than what I believe? Belief governs what I do—yes, partly. Well, I can be mis-*

*taken about many things and still be happy if there is
happiness. I can even be good. But I can never do evil
without evil consequences, no matter how pure my intentions. Who taught me this?—I've discovered only a
little bit of it just now. Why, Malachi. Malachi and the
books. . . .*

*Tad will be taking good care of the books. He'd
better!*

He shut away the southern stars beyond his eyelids,
and tried to measure the time since he had last attempted to pray as Preacher Abraham had told him it
ought to be done: "Relax, Jesse, and think of nothing
directly, it's not a matter of words. Open your mind
and give yourself to God." He could not measure it—a
long time, he knew. Maybe he had not attempted it
since Dinah's death.

Senseless. *"As flies to wanton boys are we to the
gods—they kill us for their sport." Lear,* said Jesse's
complex, accurate, toiling mind—*the Fourth Act, and
spoken by Gloster after his blinding. "I have no way,
therefore I want no eyes; I stumbled when I saw. . . ."
But the true religious will have us believe God is
merciful.*

A senseless death. Some hidden lethal thing, perhaps in Dinah's deformed bones, had stricken her
with a sudden paralysis. For two days she could not
lift herself, nor relieve her bladder, nor even breathe
unless supported. Her twelve-year-old face remained
sternly patient, asking no favors, but she could not
hide the evidence of a racking pain. Then a fever
when she no longer knew even Jude, and death. When
it was over, the thing in Jude's face was not the ap-
palled misery that Jesse had seen in Philippa, but
hate, a hate that brooded and grieved and would not
declare itself.

74

And while he yet spake, lo, Judas, one of the twelve, came, and with him a great multitude with swords and staves, from the chief priests and elders of the people.

Jesse sighed, in need of sleep. The Preacher's advice concerning prayer gave him nothing. *At the last came two false witnesses, and said, This fellow said, I am able to build it in three days.*

And Jesse remembered the talk of Malachi, recent talk and some from long ago, when the first rumors of Preacher Abraham came to Melton Village. "How often, Jesse, how often has Christ been crucified! The old grim story so many times enacted—for the poor human race has always longed for a Redeemer to take up the burdens that human people themselves alone must carry. Once he was a dying god on a spattered altar. This Preacher Abraham will make it plain that he must be crucified, and there will be those to do it as blindly as the rabble and the Roman soldiers. And maybe we learn a little, century by century; or sometimes we forget too much."

Nevertheless tomorrow they would go into Nuber, the end already known, carrying the dream of the New Jerusalem, "where the earth is so cherished that God will return—"

No, thought Jesse—*No. I have no wish to give myself to God, even if God lives. Human love is greater than divine love*—he looked for the southern stars again but the rain had taken them, and was falling in light haste up there on the October leaves; with care he shifted the weight of his head on Malachi's arm—*divine love is at worst an illusion, at best a dream for some imaginary future time. Human love is here and now.*

75

HARPER CONAN AND SINGER DAVID

Donsil village stands inland sixty miles from the Hudson Sea. About twenty families, a good inn at the four corners where West Road meets South, a green with an open market, a town hall and a church. Conan the Hunter, son of Evan, Master Silversmith, was born in this small hamlet. Binton Ruins, which Conan visited in later years—that's forty miles off down the West Road. Word of them—rumor, legend, gossip—had reached him in childhood, and they possessed their own dark place among the creations of his mind. When he learned to play the lyre his father made for him, one of the first of his own songs was a fantasy belonging to that place: his mind saw desolate ground, fields of tumbled rocks that had once formed the bones of houses, the stubs of once great buildings like blackened tree stumps after a fire; but since his eyes had never seen Binton Ruins, Conan's poem spoke of all ruins everywhere, all the loss of Old Time. Later, much later, when David led him into the neighborhood of the actual Binton Ruins in pursuit of a fabulous rumor, Conan understood the direction of the journey he was making. The west winds cooled his face; his hand was spread out on David's shoulder for communication, or it was grasped by David's hand;

for at that time Conan the Hunter had become Harper Conan, and he was blind.

In his eighteenth summer, already well known for skill with bow and spear, for his endurance and courage and acute vision, Conan had gone on a bear hunt out of Donsil with three or four young and turbulent companions. It was the Month of Strawberries, of June passions. After the killing the young men rejoiced, and sang praise of the bear's bravery and for propitiation of his gods. They wrestled in the early summer air, and bathed in a pool where they found exciting diving from a high bank—delightful and treacherous diving. Since Conan was stronger than any of them, taller, perhaps more eager to discover and display the outer limits of his strength and skill, his last dive carried him out where a rock lurking under water cut his skull. Terrified and heartbroken—one of them had been daring him on—his friends got him out on the bank and found that he breathed, slowly and harshly. Breathing so but aware of nothing (so far as we know, so far as he could ever remember) he lay at home for ten days before recovering awareness of his surroundings, and then he was blind.

Evan the Silversmith his father was praying. Evan was a valued and formidable man in the village, his work known well beyond it: a proud and religious man, now frightened and humbled. "Deliver back to me, O God, my true-beloved son who does not know me, whose soul is wandering the outer fields before the natural time! Deliver him back to me, and I will offer up—"

"Father, I know your voice. I'm here. Will you light a candle?" Conan understood, by the smell and feel of things, that he was lying on the bearskin of his room at home.

"Now God be thanked! Oh, a thousand candles! I am answered. But look at us, Conan! Look at your mother and me!"

"Why, I can't see you. Isn't it midnight?" The air stirred before his face. He knew his father's hand had passed in front of his eyes. He heard his mother weeping. Presently, his father's trembling embrace, and a long trouble of words. Midnight remained.

"Conan," his father said—weeks afterward, when the boy had begun to learn his way about in the dark country, to develop the careful, not quite heartbreaking art of seeing with his fingers and ears and nose—"Conan, son, it's not so great a thing to be a hunter. I was skillful in it once; I taught you. But when I learned the mystery of making good things from metals, I found I cared much less for other work. Of course I was pleased when you became the best of the hunters, but something else has been closer to my desires for a long time. There's something all good men do, and we call it making the most of what happens. I don't know whether that means accepting God's guidance or merely taking whatever comes and thinking about it, examining it, more deeply than a fool can do or a sorrowful man can find the patience to do." He set in Conan's grasp a cool framework, of silver by the feel of it. Conan's exploring fingers found a base that could rest on his left arm, or on a table, and a mechanism that could be studied. Most admirable was the waiting presence of taut cords and wires, which murmured to his touch as though a god had said: *I am here to become a part of you.*

"This lyre I made," said Evan Silversmith, "under the guidance of Harper Donal of Brakabin. He tells me that one comes to the great harp later, after learn-

78

ing this. But one never abandons this first instrument, he says, if one has the fire for it, the voice to sing with it, the heart to speak through song. Harper Donal came here once, and you won't have forgotten it. But I remember how even before then you made songs for yourself in childhood. I think your ear is true, though I'm no judge. You shall go live a while with Donal at Brakabin. It's arranged—he wishes it, he remembers the listening child you were. He's very old. You'll find ways of being useful to him in his feebleness, and he'll teach you all he can. You may not possess what he calls the fire: he will know."

"My father, if I haven't it I will find it."

"A brave saying, possibly an unwise one. Harper Donal spoke to me of the many who waste life trying to find it, only to learn it's not for them. And then, he says, it may blaze up in some who haven't the strength to bear it. Dangerous country, Conan."

"I must explore it. I think I can do that."

"Go then with my love and blessing. Learn to give people music as I give them the work of my hands."

Therefore, with the consent of Chief Councilman Oren and the other Elders, Conan went north and lived with Harper Donal at Brakabin for four years, learning first the art of singing with the lyre. Donal himself had learned this from one of the Waylands of Trempa, who may have learned it from Esau of Nupal, who could have learned it from a musician born in Old Time whose name is lost. That legendary one survived the Red Plague and lived to a great age, traveling through Katskil and teaching music (also something called philosophy) to the children at Nuber, Cornal, elsewhere, as far north as Gilba, as far south as Sofran. Some say the Old-Time singer and visionary was one Aron of Penn. Others claim this legendary figure was a woman, Alma of Monsella, who composed the best of our hymns in praise of God and his Son and Prophet Abraham. Look also on a bothersome contradiction that intrudes here: not one of the Old-Time books we possess mentions the art of singing to the lyre in connection with that period they called the Twentieth Century. In other words we're in the habit of believing numerous lies, and nobody knows much, and every civilization has bloated itself on vanity, and most of them have died of it.

As he studied and grew, it appeared to Conan that although the fire burgeoned in his heart and hands, it was absent from his voice. His singing, in his own judgment, was good but never more than good, which is the devil of a thing—any artist will know what he meant. However, nobody can hear the timbre of his own voice. Harper Donal told him he sang rather well, which from Donal was next to the highest praise. (The old man's highest was to say that a student had done not too badly.) Then at the appropriate time Donal taught him the handling of the great harp, which is to the art of the lyre as the ocean to a brook.

Conan took to his study with a brilliance that dumfounded his master. Harper Donal's maidservant, a kindly taciturn woman of Moha, noticed that because Conan could not see it, Harper Donal grew careless about his face, something she had not observed in thirty years of worshipful service. A teacher must maintain his mask of varied uses, but Donal's lessons with this boy were frequently illuminated by smiles, astonished frowning, starting of water to the old man's eyes. A marvel like Conan's rapid learning of the harp is not unheard of. Donal had taught many other fine players and singers; he remembered and loved them all, and followed their fortunes. Technique is in itself no mystery. Donal himself used to say so, and to him it was a commonplace. The mystery prevails in the mind and heart that bridle technique and ride it out beyond the morning mist.

A time came when Conan heard his teacher declare he was playing not badly. Moments later the maidservant touched Conan's shoulder. He was then playing, at Donal's request, the rowdy joyful dance *Elderberry Time*, composed by Donal in his own youth. She told Conan his teacher had smiled, nodded, and ceased to breathe.

This was Harper Donal's passing, as Conan knew of it. No doubt there had been the usual sad small indignities of dying, while Harper Donal's own merry music was making nothing of them.

At the funeral Conan played and sang the laments and other traditional music, in the company of two or three others whom the Brakabin Town Council found fit for the honor. And at that time the Council told the blind youth that the will of Donal bequeathed him the golden harp thought to have once belonged to Alma of Monsella. Donal had already spoken of this intention to the boy, so he was prepared with acceptable words and able to speak them with the graciousness expected by the Council. They were old men, wise, kindly, and rather stuffy. But then—(etiquette required, by the way, that he ask the Council's permission; greater fires than grief were burning in Conan, and he just forgot it)—Conan played and sang his own lament for his ancient master. The golden harp was in his hands. Part of the *Lament for Donal* came as an impromptu, born that moment, and a few of his hearers were disturbed.

* * *

81

Donal is dead, who sang for the morning.
Out of the gray cavern his song bore us the glow,
the warmth of fruitful daytime.
Out of the stillness music he wakened;
out of the winter gloom his song brought us the
   green
and gold of fruitful springtime.

   Sing for Donal as I cannot, waking birds!
   Sing for Donal as I dare not, waking winds!
   Sing for Donal, jonquils and violets delivered
      from the snow!
   Sing as I cannot,
   for Donal is dead, who sang the morning.

I fear long life, knowing now that song perishes
and the earth lies still, unloved.

Donal is dead, who hymned the sunny roads,
sang for the sweet dimness, sang the tale of the
   deerpaths,
the hush of summer clearings.
In loveless age the music of companions
rang in his song, telling of loyalty and love,
of summer journeying.

   Sing for Donal as I cannot, wanderers!
   Sing for Donal as I dare not, true companions!
   Sing for Donal, lovers delivered by his music
      from the dark!
   Sing as I cannot,
   for Donal is dead, who sang the high noon.

I fear great love, knowing now that song perishes
and the flesh lies still, unkissed.

Donal is dead, his melody the evening.
Out of day's melting his song draws on the stars

that stir in the harbor of the hills.
Out of the evening, music he wakened.
Out of the summer and the winter night his song
harbored beyond the Pleiades.

> *Sing for Donal as I cannot, constant stars!*
> *Sing for Donal as I dare not, autumn winds!*
> *Sing for Donal, mountains that knew him,*
> *streams that cooled his feet!*
> *Sing as I cannot,*
> *for Donal is dead in the world's evening.*

I will live and love, knowing that no song perishes
while one soul lives to hear.

Certainly there were those whom the *Lament for Donal* disturbed. They believed, those nice old men, that blind Conan might have been more concerned with his conscious art than with his dead teacher. It never occurred to them how immensely this would have pleased Harper Donal himself, who might have snorted that he thought there was already grief enough on earth without the customers complaining about short measure. But the Council was generous too, and gave the young musician a safe escort out of Brakabin, all the way home through the forest and hill country with his golden harp.

Thus Conan in his twenty-second year returned to his father's dwelling at Donsil. After four years in the house of Donal of Brakabin, this was one way of beginning his journey into the world. Evan the Silversmith, whose obscure talent for fatherhood amounted to genius, didn't ask the boy what he planned to do next.

* * *

Donsil enjoys the many annual festivals of music, and takes pride and pleasure in accommodating them. That inn at the four corners is rather large; several private houses, especially the communal types, also invite paying guests at festival times. Other visitors can camp a few nights in the town's groves that spread out from the green like the wheel spokes, if they mind their manners. Since they have come for the music, they generally do, even to the extent of picking up their own trash and using the public latrines. A village of hospitality is worth a bit of kindness.

Donsil makes a good thing out of festival times financially, but that has little to do with the emotional climate of the place. History tells of a school of Old-Time sociologists, safely extinct we may hope, to whom the dollar value of the music festivals would have provided the full explanation of Donsil Village. But good nature is one of those stubborn activities of the mind and heart which can be made an end in itself—like love and honesty—if human people so choose and if circumstances aren't too persistently clobbering them. Having never heard of Twentieth Century sociology, and possessing a small enclave so far only moderately oppressed by a developing feudal tyranny from above, the Donsil villagers were free to be pleasant folk. Somehow, at least in this one little spot of the world, after the long dark of the Years of Confusion when savagery ruled and most remnants of civilization were forced to shelter behind wooden stockades relearning the primitive arts (and forgetting much)— somehow the sick money-greed of Old Time had diminished to a manageable intensity. Human beings were still as a rule greedy animals—of course. But the bloated hugeness of Old-Time society, and its ghastly illusion of success, had favored piggishness at every turn, often openly making a virtue of it. Not in Donsil.

Since we create our own ends and purposes, whether or not we invent gods to blame them on, it would be astonishing if we didn't create plenty of stinkers. But a survival society, unless it is content with a pretty flabby and boring goal of day-to-day eating, security, and copulation, actually cannot afford the perversion of piggishness. Donsil had discovered music.

The incursions of visitors at well-spaced and predictable intervals had also encouraged, even driven Donsil's citizens into developing the art of composting to a remarkable degree of efficiency. In the best of human societies as well as the worst, one thing does lead to another, and we do all get to learn a few cute tricks. Culture, anthropologists call it.

To Donsil, several times, while Conan was away at Brakabin, had come the young singer David Maplestock, at first with a traveling choir for the festival of Midsummer Eve, celebrated in this country on the fourth day of July. He did not sing alone that time. It was merely noted how brilliant the Maplestock Choir sounded in the tenor section—too brilliant for the rest; in fact for that reason the famous choir only won second prize, nosed out of first place by the Nupal Glee. Later that year, before the Harvest Festival—not any special occasion but the will of his own wandering—David came to Donsil alone, and drew crowds to the green for three days before he moved on. He could have stayed another three and repeated his repertory; the crowds would not have diminished, for when something like that occurs, word goes around the countryside.

A wanderer by nature was David, at any rate he said

so, claiming not to know where he was born. It might have been in a gyppo wagon heading north from Moha, for his first sure memories belonged to the deep forest and mountain country of Adirondack Island. He had adopted the name "of Maplestock," he said frankly, just because he'd lived in the town a couple of years and liked it well enough. His manner suggested that further questions weren't invited. The gyppo part of his tale was clearly absurd. He couldn't be a gyp with such fair hair and gray eyes, to say nothing of a touch of accent that sounded like Penn or even the southern country, and nobody around here nowadays believes those stories about the gyppos stealing babies.

He was ugly, some felt, with his pug nose, big flexible mouth that made his eyes appear small, a jagged scar on his left cheek that could have been acquired in a knife brawl, heavy shoulders and neck and chest seeming too big for the rest of his short frame. Now and then, though rarely, a quick smile revealed good nature, a quality Donsil village always recognized, and redeemed what some thought of as his ugliness. It was never a confiding smile, just a friendly way of saying: "Give me no trouble and I'll give you none; give me some and heaven help you." He possessed an unremarkable lyre with a light frame of bronze nicely polished, and he played it well enough to accompany himself, just respectably.

When he sang, nothing else existed—no crowd, no weather good or bad, only a surpassing voice that searched out and touched every element of response in the hearer's nature, as if the singer had studied and cherished that one particular person all his life. So clear and blessed was this illusion that some felt the presence of magic and made the sign of the Wheel over their hearts. Good magic of course it was, though not of the kind they meant. Any critic would have been torn apart if he had chirped while they were under the spell: a significant hazard of the profession which has an indirect bearing on Darwinian natural selection.

David's voice was rich in the baritone, and spread through some not quite believable tenor range beyond two octaves—up to a treble C if you care to believe me; I am not by profession a liar. Through that upper range the tenor quality was sustained; no hint of falsetto, no loss of power. C-sharp maybe. What mattered was not the tonal but the emotional range: no nerve of human experience that David of Maplestock could not touch.

Certainly, certainly it was magic, the magic not of hush-hush and spookery but of art, which grabs hold of any available science it needs as a carpenter reaches for a saw. It was the magic that derives from intense long labors toward a perfection admitted to be unattainable, carried on by one with adequate endowment for the art, the patience to endure, the vision to discover a goal and the road that runs there. At some early age, perhaps fifteen or sixteen, when all boys must start threading the obstacle course of booby traps that the community mindlessly dumps in their path, David had simply told himself: "I will make myself the best singer it is possible to be, given my body and my intelligence."

Councilman Oren of Donsil remarked, during those first three days when David of Maplestock visited Donsil alone, that when this young man was singing a person dying in agony of a mortal wound or illness would hold off death until the song ended. The Councilman was an honest old fellow not thought to be very imaginative, and since at that time he was suffering an illness that did prove mortal, his words were remembered with a bit of keenness.

Magic: one element is courage; another, strange though you find it, is good sense. If you happen on a genuine artist who is also a kook, that's for fun, or an accident, or because the public is in a mood to gobble it down and pay for it: under the fuss, somebody inside there knows what he's doing, otherwise the art itself would be of the sort that wilts on a second look. This form of magic was the only one possessed by Alma of Monsella, Donal of Brakabin, Conan himself.

David, by the way, was no sort of kook, just a rugged young man who minded his own business. He never tried to be flamboyant. As a matter of course he wore the mouse-brown shirt and loinrag and sandals that have come to be like a uniform for itinerant minstrels. His singing inevitably drove women insane. In this matter he tried to conduct himself with good manners and kindness. What great singer could go to bed with all of them? They don't *make* that kind of bed.

David was heard of from distant places, word drifting back on the tongues of other wanderers—from Moha, Vairmant, Conicut, the Bershar mountain land, even from Main. Yet he returned to Donsil—drawn to the town and its inn, he said, by Mam Selby's corn fritters, and he was indeed observed consuming those culinary poems with the vigor of a starved farmer. Donsil had come to expect David's frequent returns, and his name was much in the common talk on the spring days after Conan came home.

"He is truly one of the great singers, my father?"

"So far as I am a judge," said Evan the Silversmith.

Others might, and did, make the dull error of belittling David of Maplestock with the notion of soothing the jealousy they imagined the blind youth to be feeling; not Evan. Conan since his homecoming had sung a little, and played, and his music was praised not on its merits (he felt) but merely because he was one of the town's own, originally Conan the Hunter. His singing, as he knew himself, was no great wonder; the power and strangeness and harmonic discoveries of his harp playing seemed to be over their heads, and probably were: no one had told Donsil village that there was anything uncommon here to admire. He was just Evan's boy, and had made himself a fine harp player—very nice. "When David of Maplestock sings," said Evan Silversmith, "one thinks and cares about nothing else except to hope that he will soon sing again."

"I can never become a singer of that kind. But I am a player of the harp. In another year or two I shall be a great one."

"And you compose new music."

"Not as I wish. One or two things. In the rest, so far, something's lacking, my father. I mean to learn what it is, and how to bring it into my music."

"Conan, I think I could find someone with the art of writing down your music. That ought to be done."

"Not yet. As for my songs, other singers remember them from hearing—we're trained to do so. The harp music—well, some time, but not yet. . . . This David of Maplestock will sing tomorrow?"

"He came to the inn today, they tell me, dusty and tired, and Mam Selby restored him with corn fritters. Yes, he'll certainly be singing at the green tomorrow, if the day's fair."

"My father. . . ." The Silversmith's hand on his arm

told him to continue. "The fire is in me. Donàl of Brakabin believed so. In the music of the harp, not in my voice, which can obey only so far as nature allows. Music is—a world in itself. I have no other way to explain it, maybe I need none. I am finding ways to explore that world, ways that I think no one has discovered, unless it was done in Old Time and then lost. New avenues. They open slowly."

Next day in that time of afternoon when the height of town hall and church hold the village green in comfortable shade, Conan with his father and mother went down the slope from the house of Evan the Silversmith to the village. Town folk and visitors were gathering; Evan described them for his blind son, who already sensed their presence. And as Conan's footsteps began to tell him of level ground, a song passed him on the air, one of the old airy love lyrics of Esau of Nupal, with the freshness of breeze and bird wings.

> *My love is fair like summer leaves,*
> *like autumn fruit my love is fair.*

But when this trifle of delight had gone on its way—one could only love the singer, without need of thought—Conan halted in astonishment, hearing the voice, to an unknown simple accompaniment of the lyre, sound a plangent outcry—

> *Donal is dead, who sang for the morning.*
> *Out of the gray cavern—*

Clearly someone who heard him at Brakabin had remembered, as the minstrels of today are expected to do. But David of Maplestock broke off the *Lament* after only a few lines. At Conan's side his mother exclaimed: "Why, he's coming to us, Conan! Do you know him?"

"In a way I do, Mother."

Then his hand was grasped, the voice was coming to him with warmth and assurance: "I was afraid you might not be here, Harper Conan." One doesn't use "Harper" as a title unless the person one speaks to is an acknowledged master; the silent, friendly-breathing crowd around them knew this. "Man, where's your harp? I must sing this with the music they heard at Brakabin and couldn't remember for me, the music none but you can play. At best I'm only a singer." The crowd rumbled a bit of laughter, but Conan knew he had spoken with no thought of jesting. "Where's your harp?"

"I will bring it, Singer David," said Evan of Donsil, Master Silversmith. Conan in his daze heard an unfamiliar happiness in his father's voice. Relief too, if that is the just word: the relief of one who sees the sun come out on a day that had promised gray sadness; for Evan was another of those incalculable eccentrics who do not build their lives on jealousy.

They played and sang together that afternoon, as wind and bright cloud belong together, or sea and sky, arm and hand. Some listeners later said that until that day they had scarcely been aware of their own man, Conan son of Evan. The quiet, the hushed, almost diffident quality of the crowd's reception derived mainly from astonishment at what happened when these two musicians came together, without rehearsal, without having even met before. The applause, though not loud, was persistent, entranced; it was long before the villagers permitted the music to end. Then Conan and

91

David, allowed to be alone, walked across the fields together.

It may seem strange that a village noted for good nature should also excel in tact. Some of it the people might have picked up from Evan Silversmith and a few like him; but Donsil is an uncanny place in its own right. Not fantastic; not out of this world exactly. One dreads to use a term so long and bitterly abused as the word "civilized," but maybe there's no other.

"I twice heard you play alone," said David, "when you were with Harper Donal of Brakabin. It was at the student concerts he arranged so rarely. I was in the crowd, and learned only that you were of Donsil. That's why I returned here several times—no reflection on Mam Selby's corn fritters: they drew me too. There's a tree root here." As if he had performed such little services all his life, he touched Conan's arm and guided him past the obstruction.

"I wish you had spoken, at Brakabin."

"Harper Donal was rather peppery—maybe you knew—about others making contact with his students while they were in his charge. Afraid of patrons and such-like taking them away before they had learned enough. And also, the listening crowd—what I wanted to say to you wasn't to be said in a crowd. It may surprise you, coming from a singer who's won a bit of popularity, but I'm a shy man, Conan. I suppose we all live too much in our skulls."

"Most of the time it's necessary, isn't it?"

"Yes, but not in this hour. Here's high sunny ground, let's sit a while. I must tell you first about a rumor that came to me less than a year ago—and God forgive me if I raise false hopes. It may be nothing but rumor—trash talk, deception. But I felt so much possibility of truth in it that, now we are friends, I must pass it on for what it's worth. It reached me when I was traveling the Twenyet Road, and I stopped overnight at an inn near Onanta, a dull place. One of the guests, a bright old man, was on his way home to Skendy in northern Moha. I thought him sober and sensible. He was telling about his experience with a group of healers who have settled, it appears, right in the middle of Binton Ruins. You may already have heard something about them?"

"Not of any healers. Word might have reached Donsil, but I have been at Brakabin until only a short while ago, and Harper Donal, as you say, didn't want the world coming close to his students. Even here at Donsil news from the west is slow in reaching us. Most of our festival visitors come from the more civilized parts—Nuin, Conicut. I know of Binton Ruins, however. They say it's very desolate."

"It is. I've never gone inside the limits of the place, only skirted the fringes, and that's dreary. I went there from curiosity after meeting that old man at Onanta. From Skendy southwest to Binton Ruins, the way the roads twist, must be well over a hundred miles. The old man couldn't afford a litter for that. His back was in such continuous pain that he couldn't ride, and dreaded the jolting of a cart, the only vehicle he owned, more than the ordeal of struggling along on crutches. His wife and daughter and one old friend made the pilgrimage with him, so there was love to help him walk. If the healers had failed him, he told us, he would as lief have lain down and died there at Binton Ruins as anywhere else—the pain was that severe, and had been with him so long that it was shoving everything else out of his life. It disgusted him: he had no desire to exist as a creeping bag of pain. . . . They healed him, Conan. As he told us the story the

93

old boy kept getting up on his feet, grinning and proud, to show us how well he could walk."

"They healed him."

"Not long after this came the first time I heard you play, at Brakabin. It never occurred to me you were blind; no one told me. The second time, someone did, but I feared—oh, false hopes—and I may be raising them now, doing harm when I only wish—"

"Whatever comes from your heart is good, David of Maplestock."

"Conan—probably these strange people at Binton Ruins *can't* do anything for blindness. It's only a mad hope. All I know about them comes from what this old man said, and some—some talk I've picked up since then in my travels, bits and pieces that I don't really credit. I value the old man's story because he was so intelligent, because there seemed no doubt that they had cured him of a great trouble. But when it comes to—oh, curing the smallpox, making the dead walk—ach, who knows? For example, his wife and friend and daughter never talked directly with the healers, and they were convinced it was all a blessed magic, or maybe not so blessed, anyhow something they didn't want to inquire into closely. Rumors from other sources will have it that the healers are wizards of Old Time who've been living underground or off on a cloud somewhere, praise Abraham, amen—damned nonsense. They say the healers have something called a generator, a machine that creates the Old-Time marvel of electricity, whatever that was. They say they can regenerate lost organs—arms, legs—"

"They say that?"

"Rumor does. They say, they say."

"But they did heal the old man's pain."

"Yes. According to what *he* said—and he'd talked

with them, listened, asked questions that I'm sure were intelligent—according to him they don't even call themselves healers. They describe their work as inquiry, themselves as seekers. The old man said they have books of method and knowledge—neither he nor his family could read, by the way—and it seems to me they must have kept alive or rediscovered some of the wisdom of Old Time. They used no drugs on him except a little of one of the common harmless herbs—I forget which; all the cure-women and herb-women know it—marawan?—well, I don't remember. But he said they knew a great deal on that subject, and talked with him freely about it, and about everything they did for him, in a very clear, friendly way. None of the hocus-pocus and puff-puff show that most of our ordinary doctors make to conceal their bloody ignorance. They gave him massage—better than what a Skendy cure-woman had done for him, but the same kind, and they kept him a fairly long time in a cool, quiet room with nice meals, and frequent visits from several of them, not very many from his family. All this right there in the middle of those haunted ruins, in a few of the Old-Time buildings that they've been able to make useful. They have an area out near the fringe of the ruins where friends and relatives of sick people can camp, and food comes in from farms in the neighborhood. The old man lost count of the days. He had rest, and a few simple exercises, and in time the pain just faded out. They warned him it might return, and told him how to care for himself if it did. They inquired what he could afford to pay, and asked half of that. . . . He said only one thing, Conan, that suggested a hint of the supernatural, and though it did so to him, it might not to you or me. He said their faces had a distant, close-listening look. But surely we've all seen that look on someone who's concentrating on a problem and needs to shut away the immediate surroundings. I suppose it was the circumstances, the coming out of his long ordeal of pain, that made the old man find something remarkable in it. I believe the healers were just listening to their own thoughts as we all do."

"Will you go with me to this place, Singer David?"

"With all my heart, and we'll make music on the road."

"How can this be?" said the blind harper. But he spoke like one who says: *How strange that the sun rises!*

"Since I first heard you play, Harper Conan, I've desired to go with you, and be your eyes, my voice reminding you how the fields look under the sun, wherever you go and as long as we live. I am only a singer; I had never imagined the country you explore with your harp until you made it known to me: there you must be my guide. But if there were no music in the world, in a world of the deaf and blind, Conan, still I would love you."

The mother of Conan had been and still was a true believer in the near and constant presence of God, a faith that Evan's skepticism never attempted to assail, though now and then he used the defensive weapon of silence. Her faith made her vulnerable to bewilderment at the stark happening of her son's blindness: it had come on him so like God's punishment!—but what had he done so terrible as to deserve it? Surely she knew all his sins great and small! And she would count them over, and try to measure them against a lifetime of darkness—yet God cannot err—and so on and so on around a circle, with no result except that chronic bewilderment, embittered now by seeing how blithely Conan went down the road in the company of a stranger, when she had only just welcomed him back from the long absence at Brakabin. He walked with a swing of the shoulders she had not seen since the days of Conan the Hunter.

Except for this inevitable pain for which there was and is no healing even within the power of Evan the Silversmith, the young men were allowed to make a quiet departure. Just a bit of a westward journey (they said). They would practise making music together, and explore the countryside for the devil of it. Without even discussing it between themselves, neither mentioned Binton Ruins.

"How can you trust that—that Maplestock man so lightly, Evan? It isn't as if they *knew* each other. And if Conan's to go haring off like this at the first whim, how will he ever get himself a decent girl and settle down the way he must?"

"I don't know, Ella."

"You sit there. You sit there and say you don't know! Where do I find the patience?"

When the friends set out for Binton Ruins it was again the Month of Strawberries, a season that love must have for its own whatever the rest of the year may do in the way of sorrow and confusion.

Between Donsil and Binton Ruins the roads at their best are not much more than expanded deer trails, even where now and then some fragment of Old-Time blacktop appears and runs a little way, not yet quite crumbled into lifeless black mud. The trails together with these bits of ancient road describe a shallow northward curve through a country of small hills, and turn again south toward Binton, serving on the way

97

nothing larger than a few stockaded villages, surrounded by poorly protected fields of rye, wheat, buckwheat, corn, and hay. Everywhere between these lonesome villages stands heavy forest. More pine and mixed growth, less hemlock here than in the hill country to the north, but Conan smelled the hemlock sometimes and felt its presence. Occasionally David found a spruce tree exuding a mild resinous gum that he liked to chew, finding it good for his singer's throat. These were warm days, of trust and pleasure and the making of music. David's most cherished burden was a thick sheaf of fine paper purchased long before in Maplestock, on which with quill pens and good oak gall ink he could capture his friend's harp music and the new songs that were almost daily born of Conan's mind; thus in future time they might become known, played anywhere in the world, without the loss that we know occurs when memory, even the best, is the sole means of preservation. Whole worlds, in fact, have been lost that way. It is a pity.

I see the road where you part the branches
and run toward the sun's heart, yourself new gold in
the divided light.

I see the brook where you stand in beauty
and lift the bright stream to cool your flesh
in the still-shining day.

I see the night where you hold the shadows
around me like a shelter: your mouth is sweet
with deep-forest spices.

"Ah, Conan, who would know you were not singing of what your own eyes tell you?"

"As I shall be soon. As I shall be."

"But Conan, Conan—" there was great fear in David's voice, remaining when Conan told him not to be afraid; but Conan grasped his arms and wrestled him laughing to the ground, and then nothing more was said that touched on the healers of Binton Ruins until a day when the two came out into open country drenched in sunlight, and Conan heard distant voices and clatter from the campsite at the border of the dead city. David said: "We have come to it. The camp is bigger than when I saw it less than a year ago. O Conan, remember—"

"That it may be useless, certainly. But here is no illusion," said Conan, and kissed his cheek.

On the edge of a mighty field of rubble stood a three-story building of ancient style, stark and alone, a fragment of Old Time not quite submerged. From the structure a fence ran in both directions to the surrounding woods. Everywhere on the ranch ground, among slowly disintegrating heaps of plaster, brick, metal that could not rust, indestructible plastic garbage and other rubbish of every sort, vegetation had found small footholds of available earth and declared the intention to live. Behind the fence the same sort of desolation continued until hidden by a rise of ground, but beyond that here and there the ruined upper parts of tall structures appeared, hazy and meaningless. All this David described to his friend. The fence, he remarked, looked sturdy and forbidding, while those shut out by it showed no resentment, no notion of defying it. The building looked like a place under invisible siege, asserting property rights to a section of the calamity of history. "When I came here before," said David, "only a few dozen people were camping here, and they were all relatives or friends of the sick,

99

who were being cared for at some place deep in the ruins. Word must have been traveling, Conan. I remember this isolated house, but there was no fence then. Now, by the look of it, there must be two or three hundred in the camp, with many sick people among them, waiting."

"Then we must wait too." Conan smelled the crowd, a dull stink of people who had scant facilities for washing or caring for themselves or disposing of their own pollutions. A little dog barked stupidly on and on—*ack-ack—ack-ack—ack-ack*—nerve-rasping and unappeasable. With the same persistence, a baby unanswerably wept.

Two men were posted at the entrance of the house, and a woman with a book. She sat at a desk. Since her face invited them, David led his friend to her. Casual and kind, she asked: "What is your trouble, sir?"

"I have far less trouble than most people," said Conan, "for I am a minstrel, and we rejoice in our work. Music comes to me, I love and am loved, my friend is a singer like no other. But it is true that my eyes are blind."

"Were you born blind, my dear?"

"No," said Conan, and he told her of his injury, of the ten days lost out of his life. Her friendly quietness made it easy to speak. When he had finished, the silence was long and thoughtful; David's hand on his arm counseled patience. The quality of the woman's voice had told Conan that she was of middle years, herself patient.

"Come," she said at last, and he heard her rise.

"My friend with me."

"Wherever he goes," David said, "I am his eyes until his own eyes are healed."

She hesitated, but then said: "Of course. I hope we

can help you. If we can't—and there are many we can't help at all—you still have the greatest of all forces for healing."

They understood her. They followed her into the building and up a flight of stairs to a room at the rear which held a pleasant scent of dried herbs. Here the monotone discomfort of the crowd was hushed to a murmur no more intrusive than the sound of a waterfall off in the woods. A man's cordial voice exclaimed: "Why, Sara, surely nothing ails these handsome cubs? What a beautiful harp! They must have come to entertain the old man."

"Your voice isn't old, sir," Conan said.

"My voice—oh, I understand." Conan heard the woman Sara going away, and David guided him into a chair and stood by him, his hand on Conan's shoulder communicating in a language that had been growing wider and more fluent with every day that passed. The cordial voice continued: "I am Marcus of Ramapo. Do not call me doctor—it would have been fitting in Old Time; not now. Not healer either, as so many insist on calling us—there are too many we cannot heal. I am a member of our small society of inquiry. I have some knowledge of sickness and health, ancient and modern; not very much. Tell me who you are, so that I can look intelligent and write something in a big book."

"We are Harper Conan and Singer David."

"Singer David of Maplestock? Why, I heard you, sir. I heard you at Albani in Moha a year ago, but I was far out in the crowd and could hardly see your face, or I'd have recognized you. I have never forgotten it, Singer David."

"When you hear Harper Conan play, you'll never forget that, Marcus of Ramapo."

101

"I believe it. Well—now tell me what happened." And when Conan had done so he sighed, and Conan heard the soft tap of his fingers on the edge of his book. David's hand said only: *Be patient. I'm here with you.*

"Do you have headaches?" asked Marcus of Ramapo.

"Sometimes. Not always very bad, and when they pass all's well."

"When was the last one, as near as you remember?"

"It will have been the day after I came home from Brakabin, a little over two weeks before I met my friend, and we have been more than a week on the road, lazing along. We spent two days in a good place, not traveling at all. A month, say, since the last headache that was bad enough to remember."

"And before that one?"

"Two months, about."

"Headaches like that before your injury too?"

"Why, in those days I scarcely knew what a headache was."

"Any suggestion of vision returning?"

"Not real vision. Flashes—like light, perhaps, but— well, like what anyone sees if he bumps his head or presses his eyeballs, only the flashes come with no cause like that."

"Nausea?"

"Nay, hardly ever. I eat like a hog."

"Like a thin hog," said David.

"Drowsiness when you should be wakeful?"

"Once in a while."

Marcus of Ramapo asked a number of other questions, his voice brooding and mild; and David later told his friend that the lean, sad, bearded face of Marcus had certainly shown a listening look—but as David had guessed, it was the look of a man listening with all his powers to a thousand books and a thousand years, and the magic of it was simply the magic of a human mind reaching for light in darkness. At length Marcus of Ramapo said: "Gentlemen—I will not say that we can never help you. If you come to us again in a few years—who knows? Our knowledge is growing, very slowly. In a few years it just might be possible to attempt some of the simpler kinds of brain surgery that were practised in Old Time. We have some of the books—a few, never enough, but we search all the time. I myself have tried some easy surgical techniques on little forest monkeys and other animals—with not much success. Do you understand, gentlemen?—there is no body of experience, no tradition to support us. Only what we can win from the books. No industry—no chemistry, physics, engineering, nothing at all of the great interdependent disciplines that Old-Time medicine and surgery could take for granted as part of their environment. All gone down the drain, and so long ago! Two hundred years some say—I would guess more than that. We don't even understand asepsis enough to be successful with it—that's the technique of preventing infection; we know most of the principles and theory, but we haven't the chemistry or the practical experience. Look at the rubble out there, and this one creaky building that somehow managed to stay upright long enough for us to come shore it up. A good monument it is to Old Time, a civilization wrecked apparently by the old, old union of politics and stupidity. Come, boys—I'd like to show you our—hospital and laboratory, let me call them; I suppose nobody will dispute my use of the nice old words. If you see what we are trying to do, perhaps a thought of it will come into your music now and then, Conan and David, and that way a little something of us will continue even if we fail altogether or are destroyed."

"Destroyed, sir?" said Conan. "Destroyed?"

"At least a third of those people out there hate us for not accomplishing the impossible. Oh, they would far better go to the famous shrines of the saints, and some would be cured too, seeing how great a part imagination plays in it—I can say that to you because of what I see in your faces. Yes, we've been attacked by the angry once or twice—our reason for the fence. Harder is the desperate expectant staring of those who never get angry, but simply insist in their thought that somehow we *must* be able to lift a stick of magic called science, and heal some walking shell already half dead. Gentlemen, I am certainly talking too much—so seldom we meet anyone here who is fresh and brave. Seldom anyone even young, for that matter—except the mue babies, except the mue babies—oh, I talk too much!" But as he spoke he lifted his book, with deliberate care to make no noise with it, and turned it outward so that David must read: *I recognize your love for him. He may have several years or only a few; or I may be mistaken. Never, never leave him.*

Then Conan and David left the building and followed Marcus across the rubbled area, up and over the rise of ground and into what must long ago have been the center of a large city. Endless blocks of houses, most of them fallen and covered with creeping vines but not all—some were upright, as very old men and women might lean into each other's shoulders if they were trying to stand against a wind. They crossed broad squares still partly paved, and David was alert

104

that Conan should not stumble. Once Marcus said: "Feeble attacks, hardly even mobs, you know, but soon they'll be around us in greater numbers. We live strangely, gentlemen. We heal a few, we learn—but then, how can you tell them not to spread the word? How could we make them understand that the recovery of wisdom takes a long time? I'll tell you something, knowing it will be safe with you. Our group—we are only fifteen—has decided to move again, this coming winter. Three times we've been driven out by hordes of the sick we could not heal, many of them hating us. We began in Penn, moved out to the edge of the wilderness country, moved again south, then here. After this month we'll admit no more to the hospital except those we could take with us. Seems harsh?—well, it's decided so. Next year we shall be near the coast of Adirondack Island. Come to us again, on the far chance that I shall have learned enough to help you, Conan. A small chance, but I shall work toward it."

"What brought the blindness on me, can you say?"

"Oh, the injury. Our eyes see through our brains. In some manner your injury damaged the connection of eye and brain. Sight may return—don't hope for it, I only say it may. I can do nothing now, Harper Conan—if I attempted it, you would die. But next year, or the next—who knows?"

"Then I will live with blindness," said Conan, "and I honor you for telling me the truth. It's not hard—I have my love and my music."

"This building was truly a hospital in Old Time," said Marcus, and they entered a place of stone walls and floors. "The old machines are all useless—depended on electricity. If there was iron in them, there's rust, and anything adaptable for a weapon or

105

tool was long ago stolen." They passed some open doorway; Conan heard muted voices, and someone whimpering. "In here—" Marcus greeted someone passing and opened a squeaking door—"here we have a toy that we put together from an ancient book. I have crazy hopes about it, gentlemen—you know, in our group they sometimes laugh at me for hoping too much. The thing's called a generator. There's the remains of a big Old-Time generator in the cellar, along with a thousand other gadgets, covered with dust—no fuel even if we knew how to repair and operate them." Something buzzed under his hand.

"Describe it for me, David." But David only made a harsh noise in his throat, startled by the contraption, Conan supposed.

"He's stepped over to the window," said Marcus, and touched Conan's arm peacefully. "Some things in this place are a bit grim for a newcomer. Well, this generator toy—God, the thing hardly has the power to galvanize the leg of a frog." The buzzing ceased. "And yet, Conan, an electric current no stronger than this was once made to do marvelous things. Believe this, I *know* it to be true: in Old Time there was a device for sending a tiny wire down through the great vein in the throat, as far as a heart that had ceased beating, and the light push of an electric current made that heart beat again, and sometimes the one who would have died lived for years afterward in quite fair health. Also—" but his voice sagged, and Conan felt his hand shiver as he took it away— "also there's word in the writings of bringing about a regeneration of entire lost organs through the stimulus of a weak electric field. Experimental work was being done on that when the world blew up. Well, carry it in your imagination. Find a song in it, if songs are made that way—

I don't know. I suppose I shouldn't take up your time with this any more. Your friend is disturbed because down the corridor we passed a room with some very sick patients, and the door was open."

"I'm all right," said David, returning. "Wasn't expecting it, that was all. They didn't look so bad."

"Are they too sick to enjoy a little music?"

"Oh," said Marcus, "no, they are not. Would you do that for us, Conan? David?"

David cleared his throat. "I am not disturbed, Marcus of Ramapo. I will sing, and Conan will make music with me. Conan, let's give them *Jo Buskin's Wedding* and *Elderberry Time*—then your tarantella for the harp, and—and the new song I learned from you yesterday evening in the woods."

The legend says that Harper Conan and Singer David never played and sang as splendidly as they did that afternoon for the sick people in Binton Ruins. It is not known whether the two were able to come the following year to Adirondack Island; it is known that they traveled widely all over the eastern nations, and were loved. Since it was long ago, and all records confused, it is not known when Conan died. He may have lived a full lifetime: Marcus of Ramapo is said to have assured David that this well might happen, in a later moment when they spoke out of Conan's hearing; or that could be another story.

It is known (to some) that by dwelling in the present, conceding what is necessary to past and future but no more than is necessary, it is quite possible to live happily ever after.

By an interesting chance, one of the sick people in the hospital at Binton Ruins was a musician, Luisa of Sortees, with a true minstrel's memory, and she recovered and returned to her good life; for this reason the new song Conan gave them is remembered by more than legend.

> In sleep I could not find you—
> only the winter blurs of dreaming
> desolate, not you, not you.
>
> My morning sought you
> over the reddening hills
> and down steep shadows.
>
> You with summer breath
> found me and restored the day,
> and I am content.
>
> One yellow leaf falls
> unrescued, undefended
> evening is blameless.
>
> Winter shall be our portion,
> but in the flow of foreign voices
> your music known sustains me.

THE LEGEND OF HOMBAS

Hombas was wiser than his people, but not stronger than Death, who makes no exceptions. Several times, even before the departure of the Spring Caravan, when the day's-end prayers had been spoken and he sat at the fringe of the night fire in the compound, Hombas had seen the red bear Death approaching through the flames.

Hombas had also seen Death in the woods by daylight, the presence so like a true red bear that it would have deceived anyone else. He knew the truth, being Shaman and Chief Elder of the Commun. He had observed the red shadow, the Unanswerable, the Well-Intentioned, following one or another of the people. Unaware, the objects of Death's study continued their evening tasks, preparing the Commun to survive the night—stacking wood for the fires, making a circuit of the stockade, rounding up and counting the goats and children.

Trailing older members of the Commun (or the children, the timid weaker ones) and snuffling at their heels, the red bear might lift a black nose to savor the air for the scent of mortality. And now and then Death stood in front of them, obliging them to walk unknowingly through what only Hombas saw, the core of the mystery.

Hombas knew that Death had so far reached no decision.

Many times the red bear Death had risen to overwhelming shaggy height, twice the height of a man, and stared at Hombas himself across the village street, small red eyes noncommittal like a pig's and sorrowfully wise like a man's. And now and then, when Hombas had been fasting or smoking the marawan pipe to invite wisdom, the red bear Death had drawn very close to observe him, vast russet head swaying back and forth barely an arm's length away. The last time this happened Hombas had said, quietly so as not to excite the small fry who enjoyed their evening romps around his hut: "I will go and wait for you in the open place when I must, but I am not ready." Death made no response to this, and he spoke again: "Or, if it will not offend you, I should like to wait until the return of the Spring Caravan, which must be soon (Jesus willing), so that I may bless the young men and hear for the last time what they tell of the out-world."

The red bear sighed hugely and went away, but only two nights later returned, standing close over Hombas, rising up on mighty hinder legs and gazing down, blotting away the night and the fire, and youth and age and time, the village and the world. The Spring Caravan was now shockingly overdue. Fear of disaster was chilling everyone. Hombas prayed once more to the red bear: "I ask you to allow me to remain until after the Ottoba harvest, for my people have always needed me when they were frightened."

At this appeal—Hombas hoped he had avoided loss of dignity in making it—the red bear Death showed neither anger nor assent, but shambled off to lie in the grass of the out-ground, under Hombas's eyes, until the stockade gate was closed for the night. Head on great flat paws, Death dozed, or looked toward the south when the children squealed or the little blattering goats walked through the presence.

Death lives in the south when at rest. The warm wind-spirits flee; that is why the south wind is hurried and soft like the touch of memory.

Hombas's people were wealthy, owning two other commun sites and prepared to defend them. It was nearly time, even in the usual order of affairs, for the people to move to the next of these locations—Flint Hill—after the necessary sacrifices and housecleaning. The people should never remain too long in one place. The ground sickens; squash, yam, and beans come to a puny harvest; the goats give poor milk. Men also sicken of sameness, just as they dread too big a change; then the gods are offended. Hombas saw in the eyes of his people that the move ought to be made soon, and all except the children would guess that on this occasion Hombas was not to travel with them. But he had not yet spoken, and one does not hurry the Chief of Elders.

They possessed other wealth, including a treasure of Old-Time coins for trading with the mad foreign city of Malone (some say Mayone), a four days' march toward the sunrise side of the world. In the spring, loaded with a winter's take of furs, or after the Ottoba harvest with handsome stacks of new-woven baskets, wood carvings, bows, necklaces of painted clay, doll toys of soft pine or plaited straw for children, the young men of the Caravan would gather for the good-luck prayers and Hombas's blessing. Then some skylarking, brag, and horseplay—boys are like that, and young men may now and then be allowed to act like

111

boys—and in good time the Caravan would sort itself out and march in excellent silence down the dense green trail.

Those foolish people of Malone have no notion of commercial values. For a stack of fewer baskets than the fingers of one hand, they may pay a whole nickel coin, or even a penny. Apparently they don't know how grand a polish these red-brown things will take, nor how easily you can pound a hole in one of them with a steel point, and thus wear it for protection against smallpox and the malare. A soft people, the Maloners, and often you see grown mues among them behind their great stone walls, a great evil certain to bring a greater evil upon them, if they really don't understand the necessity of destroying these dreadful beings at birth. But their weapons and magic make them terrible. (Someday, says another Shaman who has grown old since Hombas's time, Malone shall fall desolate, and we shall go there to take what we will, and be rich forever.)

In a good year the Caravan would return with whole handfuls of gorgeous coins—steel knives too, brass arrowheads nearly as good as steel, perhaps smoked fish, and soft cotton or wool cloth for the women's delight. It was a day for carnival and rejoicing when the Spring Caravan returned.

But where were they?

Hombas could remember the time, before his initiation, when the Elders had taken him aside and taught him how to measure the years of his life by spreading the fingers of both hands. You can measure days in the same fashion. He recalled how, after the circumcision and knocking out of an eye tooth and other agonies of passage, there came a year when his age was told by both hands together and one more hand. Thus

112

on and on, adding a finger with every return of the moon of spring, until the joy was gone from it, and such counting became a reminder of stiffening in the joints, fading of sight, waning of all powers. He remembered the spring moon of nine fives, long ago, when he became a Shaman, and with the following winter moon an Elder. His age now was hardly to be credited: he numbered it by opening both hands together six times and then showing two fingers. Few but the gods can live to such an age. The people believe that when a Chief of Elders journeys over the waters marking the boundaries of life he becomes a god, and joins the divine Council of Elders in the country beyond the mountain Marsia.

The hands of Hombas counted far too many days since the Spring Caravan had gone. The red bear was walking in the firelight.

The red bear comes for all, but only the wise can observe the presence; only the wise remember that the red bear Death will take from them even wisdom. That is why we should listen to the wise, but not too much.

The Spring Caravan never returned. One young man at last crawled naked up the trail, gasping and torn. His right leg was broken; flies clung to the gaping festering wounds; he could not number the days he had spent in hobbling and creeping home. Once, driven off the trail by the smell of black wolf, he had lost his direction, and found it again, he said, only by the mercy of Jesus, Shaman of Shamans. He was brought to Hombas, and in the dust before the blanket where Hombas sat he collapsed, digging clawed fingers into the dirt and beating his forehead on the ground, broken with shame that he should be the car-

113

rier of such news. But Hombas was gentle in speech, saying only: "You may tell us now, Absolon, son of Josson."

The young man told how the Spring Caravan, returning with rich goods from the trading at Malone, had been ambushed not far outside the walls of the city. Of the seven young men, only Absolon had survived. Him the ravagers had left for dead under the pile of other bodies, after stripping them of every smallest thing, every rag, bead, coin, ornament—even the wild parrot's feather that Absolon wore in his hair because the White Parrot was his patron.

The enemy were Sallorens, Absolon was sure, from the Ontara coast country, squat black-haired men who took no scalps. The savages of Eri in the southwest, or the red-haired Cayugas, would certainly have taken scalps and probably living captives, too, for the entertainment of their villages. These Sallorens, or anyway dark men tattooed just like them, are often seen at Malone, Absolon declared, wearing Mohan clothes and acting in other ways like Maloners. Then Absolon lifted his torn head and cursed Malone in all its days and years, for he believed there had been a conspiracy, Malone sending word to the Sallorens of the Caravan's coming.

"Do you know this, Absolon? Perhaps they were lying in wait for any caravan that might appear."

"It may be," said Absolon. "Before the Chief Elder's wisdom I am a fool and a nothing."

The women wailed and scored their breasts; they pulled out their hair and raved. The other young men who had not been chosen to go with the Caravan smeared their faces with dung, and wept, and sharpened their knives. Then all became still, for after Absolon had been taken away to be cared for and if pos-

114

sible healed, Hombas called a Council of the other four Elders. When the old men discuss what is to be done, there should be no speech or foolish noise.

The Elders grouped by the night-fire. Hombas said: "My brothers and my children, this calamity was foretold. But I, Hombas, Chief of Elders, failed to read the signs truly. I am in sorrow. For many days and nights I have seen the red bear."

Isaia, second in age and virtue of the Elders, asked: "The red bear, the Well-Intentioned, has not chosen, Chief of Elders?"

"He has not chosen."

The Elder Isaia said: "The Chief of Elders is burdened with years and long service to Jesus, Shaman of Shamans."

And others: "Jesus, Shaman of Shamans, knows what is to be."

"The people shall move to Flint Hill," Hombas told them, "as soon as the bodies of the young men have been recovered, if that may be. They shall be given as heroes to the burning. After this, Jero, and Adam, and the Elder Elahu, shall go to Flint Hill and see that the stockade is in repair, the ground fit, the dwellings clean and sound, the wood gathered, and the night-fire restored."

"It shall be done as the Chief of Elders explains."

"I, Hombas, shall not go to Flint Hill."

"The saying of the Chief of Elders is hard."

"I have lived six tens and two."

"Make us to understand the will of the Spirit."

"I foretold a safe journey for the Caravan. Now the young men who went with my blessing are dead, my head is covered with ashes, the women tear their breasts."

Isaia said again, as was proper, but with the noise a

115

voice makes when ambition mixes uneasily with kindness: "The Chief of Elders is heavy with years and godlike in long service."

"Before the sun rises ten men shall go and recover the bodies of the young men, if that may be, if the forest has not taken them. But now the people must understand a hard thing: Without these men we have not the strength to carry war against the Sallorens this year. After the winter moons perhaps it may be done, under the guidance of another Chief of Elders, when I have journeyed over the waters that mark the boundaries of life."

"Amen, amen."

"At your departure for Flint Hill, I shall go out to the open place and await the Unanswerable. Let none look back."

"Amen, O Hombas, Chief of Elders."

"And now, O Lord of Hosts," said Hombas, "deliver us from evils and evildoing, in the name of the Father, the Son, and the Spirit! May the wombs of our women bear, may the earth bring forth, and the white-scut deer be plentiful. And may my children and my brothers dwell with one another in justice and mercy, amen."

"Amen."

After quiet, the Elder Dorson said: "Hombas, Chief of Elders, the fourth child of the woman of Jero turns blue in the face and scarcely breathes. The child is, to be sure, a girl."

"I will carry her with me to the open place, in Jesus' name."

And the Elder Magann: "Hombas, Chief of Elders, an earthen pot in the house of Adam cracked last night for no clear reason as it stood by the fire."

116

"Let it be broken in small shards, for exorcism. The fragments may be left with me in the open place."

The Elder Isaia said with respect: "Hombas, Chief of Elders, I have a sleek male kid not yet weaned of its mother."

"This I accept as first offering to the Unanswerable. Let it be tethered in the open place at the time of your departure. Should the people ratify you, dear and well-spoken Isaia, as Chief of Elders, may you live long and continue to love justice."

Then Hombas, who had lived for many years without women, entered his hut and laid across his eyes the white cloth that brings prophetic dreams. In the village, no loud talk, no more wailing, out of respect for the rest and sleep of him who had been Chief of Elders and who would not go with the people on their next journey.

And Hombas dreamed of his own journey to come, over the waters that mark the boundaries of life.

He stood on the bank in his dream, while the Ferryman approached through fog like one reluctant. By the mystery of dreaming, Hombas was able to observe his face—calm it was, devoid of anger and joy—as he could not observe the face of a companion who stood beside him in the heaving vapor. It was proposed to Hombas by this companion that he might not be ready for the passage. To him Hombas replied: "I am ready in years, ready in weariness; my joints pain me, my memory mocks me like a naughty servant. In other ways, can one ever be ready, my companion? Is not life too sweet to abandon even when the stream widens and moves sluggishly with a burden of memories? What more must I do before I rest with my fathers?"

The reply of his companion was not in words, but Hombas understood that some further labor might indeed remain—meanwhile the Ferryman approached—but it would be for him to discover the nature of it. And as though he had come to Hombas for no purpose except to offer a troubling communication, the faceless companion was now gone—all along he might have been no more than a heavy part of the mist. In his place the red bear stood half-seen, surely too vast to accompany Hombas in the little boat, but ready perhaps to swim in the black water beside him, or to drift through the obscurity as a phantom. As one who had loved and served his fellows a long time, Hombas understood how the most immense and inescapable of forces may well appear unreal to human beings—they always have—until these forces sweep them away: flood, fire, war, pestilence, human folly, or that death which is merely the end of living.

The Ferryman was poling an oarless boat. This might mean that the waters marking the boundaries of life are as shallow as they are slow. It was an instructive, amusing detail that he could have told the village children who liked to tumble and chase each other around his hut, climb his legs, sprawl in his lap and fall asleep, tease for some little present or a kiss—children are not repelled by the truly wise, only by the half-wise. But the red bear stirred and sighed, and Hombas remembered it was not fitting for him to think of seeing the children again, nor the village, nor any of the faces of his own kind.

The Ferryman grounded his boat on the gravel margin. Hombas offered him the coin of passage. But the gaunt naked fellow said: "This is only metal. From Hombas, Chief of Elders, more is expected."

"What must I pay then?" asked Hombas. "The wise

are poor in the world, Ferryman; their chief reward is not much more than uneasy tolerance."

"Will you pay me your hopes?"

"If I have my hopes no longer, can I rest among my fathers? I see that perhaps I might, and—yes, rather than stay here on this bank among these homeless vapors, I will pay you my hopes."

"It is offered grudgingly. It is not enough. Will you pay me your visions and your memories of human love?"

"Without them, Ferryman, how shall I be better than this broken rock and sand, which has no will except the water's will?"

"You are not ready for passage," said the Ferryman. "Go back in the world a little while, Hombas, in your tattered loincloth and nakedness and pride. Go back and labor again, if it is only the labor of learning humility."

And Hombas woke, putting away the cloth from his eyes and seeing the tranquil night-fire outside his hut. He heard muted voices with other village sounds, the desolate laughter of a loon in the marsh, a night-hawk, a wolf's howl from the midnight hills. Up in the maple leaves a wind was rippling in the current of spring. The dream disturbed him in his heart. Before first light—he knew the ten men were about to go and recover the bodies of the slain, if that might be—a boy came softly to tell him the messenger Absolon had died in the night, of fever and the festering of his wounds.

Hombas wished he might consult a wiser head as to the meaning of all that was happening, but he knew, as sober truth, that however imperfect his wisdom, no one wiser than himself was in the village or perhaps anywhere in the world; unless it might be the children, who have no time to transmit the virtue of their simplicity before it is gone—that is why we should listen to children.

The bodies of the young men were brought back, what the Sallorens and the forest scavengers had left of them, and were given as heroes to the burning. All that day Hombas sat on his blanket in the compound fasting, his eyes in pain from the smoke of the pyre. It hung sullen over the village in the windless hours. He was aloof, as was proper for one lately Chief of Elders, unapproachable and old. He thought of the young men, prayed for them. He thought too of the older days, of the years outside his experience but spoken of by his father, who had known himself to be a great-grandson of the West Wind. When at last the funeral songs were done and the blaze not more than heat remembered, evening was coming on again, while in the village certain quiet preparations were being made for departure in the morning.

It was not fitting that Hombas should pay heed to these. He meditated through another night on his dream of that shallow river marking the boundaries of life, of the Ferryman's hard sayings. He did not see the red bear.

At dawn the younger wife of Isaia brought him goat's milk, and the kid that was to be tethered near him in the open place. As he drank the milk and blessed her, the Elder Isaia came also to kneel before him, and said: "Hombas, venerable Shaman, the Elders have chosen me to hold the office that you honored, in Jesus' name. I pray you bless me to this service, Hombas."

They say that Hombas smiled as he blessed Isaia, who was not a cheerful man, and placed on him the sacred deer-bone necklace that confers courage and quickness of mind. They say also that Isaia, in his time as Chief of Elders, governed well, though sometimes hesitant and anxious, and that the precedents upholding his decisions were very often the judgments of Hombas. "Be content, Isaia," Hombas said. "It is a brave journey between midnights." This has been remembered, though few agree on all that Hombas meant by it.

Then there came to him the aging warrior Jero; he had taken from his woman the infant girl five days old whose face turned blue and who could not breathe except with difficulty, bringing her to Hombas; behind him his woman watched dry-eyed, and did not speak. The baby, as Hombas received her in his arms, curled a fist around his finger and for a while her gasping breath came more quietly. The people remember this, not as a miracle but as a certain evidence of divine grace. And when Hombas rose, holding her in the hollow of his arm and leading the unweaned kid with his left hand, it was seen that the kid followed him without any tugging at the leash of leather, and that the child had fallen asleep. Hombas said then to the woman of Jero: "Be content, Rashel, with what no power can change. If she is not to know joy in living, neither can she know sorrow."

Hombas went out beyond the stockade of the village, through the pasture where the goats were being herded together for the journey to Flint Hill, and up a winding path in the long grass, among juniper and scattered boulders and tangles of wild raspberry canes, to the open place, a wide area where flat granite covered a shoulder of the hillside; at the western end of the outcropping of rock grew a thick spruce that held away the wind. Near this tree the good man

121

Adam had brought the shards of his broken pot, and a sound jar filled with spring water. Hombas blessed him, and sat here with the still sleeping child, gazing over undulant hills in the south, and toward the mountain Marsia in the southwest, distant under the sky of spring.

The little goat he had tethered somewhat below the open place out of his sight. It was necessary that it should bleat and call, being a first offering to the powers who would come for Hombas himself when the time was right. The small creature might feel desolate and abandoned for a time, until the gods of the forest came and released it; but they would do so. It would not be fitting for Hombas to witness their coming. The forest gods ought not to be drawn by trickery, or against their will, into human observation. They are lonely ones. That is why the bats, who are the gods of those night-thoughts that flutter past too quickly to be questioned, never appear by day. Or if one does, a good man will help it to a tree-hollow where it can wait on the return of dark.

Holding the infant, Hombas meditated on death, and found it strange that all he could remember of his people's thought on the matter, including his own, had been concerned not with the thing itself but with hope or legend or speculation concerning some life beyond the incident of death: as though death were no more than a passage, an opening in the woods. *But what if it is not so? What if death is no passage at all, only the termination of thought, feeling, presence? Who has seen the soul that is to board the Ferryman's little boat and cross the waters that mark the boundaries of life? If none has seen it, can a wise man accept a belief in the existence of it?*

Was it my soul far wandering that spoke with the Ferryman, and with someone faceless, in my dream? All people dream, and most dreams are ridiculous. In sleep are we perhaps not wandering away from the body into the country of the spirits as the wise men of the past have taught us, but merely lying still and thinking fantastically in our sleep? . . . Now this might mean that there is no soul, and even that the wise men of the past were not quite wise.

The morning drew on with quiet, in springtime coolness. Hombas sensed that the people had gone, and his mind traveled a little way with them on the obscure trail to Flint Hill, and let them go, returning to the open place. The child did not wake; her breathing was very shallow, her pallor more waxen than bluish, with pinched tiny nostrils. Now and then Hombas waved away a hovering fly. It might have been more fitting, more pleasing to the forest gods, to set her out now on the rock or where the kid was tethered, but Hombas preferred to hold her fading warmth against his own until her small, foredoomed struggle for continuing life should end. It would not be long.

He meditated on the tales and fancies and histories of the Old Time, the Age of Sorcerers. It was darkly long ago—five generations, even two fives, who can say? Hombas's father when he was young had met a very old man in Malone who said that as a boy he had seen one of the Old-Time death-sticks of heavy metal, in possession of an ancient redheaded Cayuga. That savage had told him how there used to be pellets made by the Sorcerers, each containing a devil, which could be placed inside the hollow stick. Then, by command of the stick's owner, the devil would burst forth at the other end with such frightful power that

123

anything in its path was instantly killed. Catrishes, those pellets were called. The Cayuga assured the boy they had all been used up and swept out of existence in Old Time—at least, he said, looking sly, he *thought* they had. He broke open the stick at the large end so that the boy might look through the hollow passage inside and see the strange regular spirals cut into the metal, and then made him jump out of his skin by slamming a foot on the ground and shouting *"Brroom!"* Cayugas never had any manners. The boy, telling the story as an old man, was said to have said that the Maloners who saw the stick had no belief in the powers of it. They claimed it was just a hollow iron bar with wooden fittings, part of one of the Sorcerers' miraculous machines; or perhaps the Sorcerers had used it to beat their servant devils and make them obey.

Hombas knew other tales. In the Age of Sorcerers, myriads of magicians rushed about all over the earth in wheeled carts that moved of themselves by a horrid magic. Hombas himself, when young, hunting with two companions and following a wounded woods buffalo too far to the south, dangerously close to Cayuga country, had come upon one of the enormous roads built by the Sorcerers to serve these hell-carts. Straight as a spear the road ran and level as a stream, cutting a valley from hilltop to hilltop with mighty disdain for any lesser rises or hollows. Vines had been able to cross it here and there, especially the poison ivy and jinnacreeper, with their countless busy rootlets. Elsewhere the road stretched bleak and clear, pitted with cracks and holes but nearly lifeless, a track of desolation through the green. Seeing this thing, one could understand how the curse of the good Jesus had

124

fallen on the Sorcerers and destroyed them and all their works.

Hombas and his friends had known better than to venture out on that horror. Yet, the young men do say that the Townfolk make some use of these roads, near Malone and those other places where they have their clustered dwellings, and impregnable high walls to hold off brown tiger and black wolf and red bear. The feet of their horses and oxen cannot endure the surface of the ancient roads, of course, but the Maloners and their kind, with leather shoes and an unlimited store of foolishness, walk out on them and apparently take no harm.

The Sorcerers rode in machines that climbed through the air beyond human vision. They could make the air vibrate, too, and so talk magically with each other across many miles. And they traveled back and forth at will between the earth and the moon.

The moon is a globe that the god Jehova set spinning many centuries ago along with the sun, in such a way that the two run a strictly ordered course above the earth and below the earth. The heat of the sun is life and day; the light of the moon is wisdom and night. A long time from now, the force of the god's original cast will run down (according to his own foresight) and then both sun and moon will fall into the sea that runs all around the field of the earth. In that time will be only starlight; there will be no day. The earth will stand without heat or wisdom. The people, all of them, will have crossed the waters that mark the boundaries of life.

In the time of the Sorcerers the moon was larger in the skies and often red. And the impious traveling of the Sorcerers to the moon resulted in the first of their great punishments. The moon people came out of the center of their globe and made war on them. The Sorcerers fought hard, but the moon people, whom Jesus loves also, defeated them with a mightier science (that is an Old-Time word for magic), destroying countless numbers of the Sorcerers' flying craft. Before the Sorcerers' armies on the moon were annihilated by the moon people, the colossal warfare had laid waste enormous areas of that globe and created mountainous ruins.

There is never any profit in trying to tell of these things to the Maloners. They build walls, contrary to Jesus' commands, and they cherish the ugly fancy that the earth itself is a globe, and there is no truth in them. When they die, the Ferryman cannot take them because they do not believe in the god Jehova nor in Jesus his prophet, but follow the false prophet Abraham. At death their poor homeless spirits go wandering, swept here and there until they become caught in the tree branches. When the wind strikes those branches in the barren time of winter, you hear them crying.

This is how you may know the truth of what happened to the Sorcerers on the moon. When the moon is full, look on those gray marks that seem like shadows. Those are blighted areas left by the war up there, just like the desert of Eri and other places that the Sorcerers left ruined on the earth before they perished.

The child made a noise too small and fleeting for a groan. Her breathing ceased. Hombas recited the prayer for those dying in infancy, that the Ferryman should let them pass without payment of a coin. Rising stiffly with her, he felt the spring chill with sudden acuteness; his joints ached. Dizziness from the hours of fasting laid hold of him, and he staggered.

These disorders could be overcome. Presently he was able to carry the baby's lifeless body to the far edge of the rocks. There the Forest People would find her, or the well-meaning Winged Ones whose faces are not to be looked on because the god Jehova for his own reasons has made them horrible.

He had set down the little corpse and made the sign of the cross over her, when from no great distance an intolerable cry of outrage and pain rang and rang through the woods, echoing metallically from bare tree trunks and rock surfaces. Shrill it was, keening and prolonged, coming from some great chest of powerful resonance. Black wolf could not have made that noise. Red bear does not speak, except to growl or chuckle or snort a little: the red bear expects deference from everyone, except the Maloners who are foolish and sinful, and has no need of threatening or angry cries. Hombas stood paralyzed with wonder, shrinking too, for it was a sound to make the flesh cringe regardless of courage. He trembled in the certainty that he would again hear the anguished voice. He did, once more, and the sound trailed off in a long groan. Brown tiger never sent forth that roar of agony. If this were a victim of brown tiger—woods buffalo, maybe, or elk—it would have had no chance for a second cry. And what grass-eater could utter such vast rage?

There came distant thrashing noises, and a muffled pounding as if a giant's fist were hammering the earth. Then Hombas belatedly remembered that not very long ago, before the departure of the Spring Caravan, the people had built a deep deadfall near the Open Place, where they had found a trail beaten by those vermin, the wild pigs, attackers of children and raiders of the gardens. Hombas had approved the digging at the time. Presumably the swine had proved too clever to be deceived, and so he had heard no more said about it. All the same Hombas found it shocking that he could have forgotten it. High time indeed to go and sit in the Open Place.

Well—wild boar never made such a noise as that. And Hombas reflected: *In the forest live many gods we do not know. Perhaps one of them has need of me. Perhaps Jesus, Shaman of Shamans, has offered me opportunity to do some service before I cross the waters that mark the boundaries of life.*

Somewhat lightheaded but no longer much afraid, he glanced toward the sun, astonished to note how far the day had advanced beyond noon. He let himself down from the rock, moving more easily as his muscles limbered with the action, and moved off under the trees in the direction of that pounding. He heard now a heartrending moaning, muffled, high, nasal, broken now and then by a snap of jaws. So it might be bear after all, for they chatter their teeth like that in anger; but surely not a red bear. In Hombas's memory, no red bear had ever been caught in a trap or deadfall.

Hombas's foot caused a dry branch to crack under him; the moaning and pounding ceased. The noise had summoned him; now the being, whoever it was, knew he was coming, and so fell silent. Hombas was sure of the direction. He called politely: "I who come to you am Hombas who was Chief of Elders. If you are a god you may command me, a believer in the laws. If you are a forest thing, I come in mercy."

He heard no reply. But the Forest People are not given to needless speech, except for the wind spirits, and what they say is more music than speaking. He hobbled on therefore, no longer trying to move with quiet. He found the trail that had been tramped, not recently, by the wild swine. The smell in his nostrils was the feral, fishy scent of bear. He came to the edge of the pit, where the branches hiding the deadfall had been broken in. Rearing a tormented head above the surface of the ground was the red bear Death, who was blind.

With the eyes of the flesh Hombas saw him, an old and mighty male who had evidently been blind in his right eye for a long time, since the socket was shrunken and fallen in—perhaps an arrow wound, or a slash in some battle with his own kind. Now the other eye was squeezed shut, leaking tears, and in the fur of the great, round, innocent face were tangled the bodies of many wild bees, smashed by the bear's paw—but one of them must have carried a sting to the eyeball. The bear's head was turned toward Hombas, but only because he had heard the approach. When Hombas stepped silently to one side, the creature did not move in response to the action.

With the sense of his flesh Hombas heard, some distance up the trail, the still furious snarling hum of the hive. The bee warriors had not pursued the ravisher this far, or perhaps had lost sight of him when he fell into the pit in his pain and blindness.

Hombas smelled the bear's blood. In falling he had pierced a hind foot on one of the sharpened stakes in the pit. He had torn the foot free, but other stakes prevented him from winning a purchase with his hind claws on the dense clay walls. He had pounded at the edges of the pit, without aim in his darkness, trying to break down a passage to freedom, but the clay was tight, the pit dug deep and wide by the people with good steel tools from Malone. Now the bear had ceased that effort.

Smelling and hearing man, he roared in despair and agony. He lunged toward Hombas, bringing down both forepaws tremendously on the edge. But then his blind head dropped between them, and he let it remain there, as if he prayed.

With the senses of the flesh, the knowledge of a hunter, the wisdom of a Shaman, Hombas observed and understood all this, and feared the tortured beast, and pitied him.

With the eyes of the spirit, Hombas knew that the red bear Death might be about to die.

Hombas asked him: "Has the god Jehova decreed that Death shall die? Is it possible?"

He won no answer. In the faintness from his age and long fasting, he believed the waters that mark the boundaries of life must be flowing not far from this lonely place in the woods, and without sight of him he felt the presence of the Ferryman. Poling the little boat (perhaps) nearer to this shore, expecting that Hombas might by now have discovered what labor it was he ought still to perform. *What will become of the Ferryman, if Death is about to die?*

Hombas moved away, disturbed by an inner rejoicing not altogether candid nor genuine. Death was to be no more—why, if so, all the Forest People should be singing, and every leaf should smile with an inner sunlight. But he, Hombas, was the only one who knew it yet—he alone among all the wise men. Soon all would know it. *No more dying!* (*But if flowers do not fade, how shall new flowers grow?*)

He walked feebly down the trail, unwilling to look back although the blind bear might be silently calling him. *I shall not die. I shall live forever.* (*With these*

130

aching joints, this weariness?—oh, even that way, is life not dear?) I shall enjoy the night-fire, the changes of life in the compound, the children, the meditation, the sharing of wisdom, the tenderness of returning spring. (But if flowers do not fade, how can there be rebirth, how can there be spring?)

I must go to Flint Hill and tell my people. I return to you—hear me! There is to be no more dying. I, Hombas, Chief of Elders, have permitted Death to die although he prayed to me. I bring you life eternal—rejoice, rejoice! Your children shall not perish! Never shall your beloved die!

He found laughter, running down the trail, stumbling, weeping and shouting: *"Life eternal! Hear me, my people! Life eternal!"*

But in this clumsy ecstasy he tripped on a root, and saved himself by clutching at a branch, and stood there wavering, dizzy and gasping for breath. His eyes cleared. He stared along the branch. A fat greenish blowfly lit on it not far from his fingers; she was ripe with eggs and bloated with carrion meals, and he saw her accept the mounting and penetration of a male. The two squatted there linked in copulation, seeming to regard him. *No dying?* . . .

Hombas returned to the pit. He spoke a little to the red bear Death, but the legend does not say whether this was a true conversation or only the voiced reflections of a man with a difficult task to perform. He searched the region around the pit until he found where his people had cut an ash tree to use in making the deadfall. They had left the long butt on the ground, wanting only the flimsy upper branches. Moving this fourteen-foot log was surely a task for two men in their prime, yet Hombas accomplished it, levering it with small sticks we suppose, and resting often.

He worked it to the edge of the deadfall. He said to the blinded beast: "It is well that we met, who have need of each other." And then he slid the log down so that an end rested against one of the stakes, a bridge on an easy slant for the bear's escape. And he sat by the trail waiting.

That is how Death became blind. But the people who know the legend call Hombas blessed, because of his mercy to us.

TIGER BOY

Bruno perceived, but his vocal cords were missing or defective. He could not moan or murmur; as a baby he shed tears without vocalizing. The parish priest Father Clark had declared him to be not a mue but a natural human child, implying that anyone who put Bruno out of the way would face the disapproval of the Church.

Bruno could listen and was permitted to do so even among the Elders. If the old men lapsed into foolishness, could Bruno tell? He would squat outside their circle, soft intelligent eyes wide awake; now and then he smiled.

Baron Ashoka, a few of the Elders, the monks of Mount Orlook, Father Clark, Town Clerk Jaspa, all possessed the art of writing, but never attempted teaching it to Bruno—how could a child without speech be taught? And did not his dumbness and illegitimacy mean that God intended him for ignorance and humble service? Once when Bruno was seven he broke away from Mam Sever, who was minding him, ran up into the pulpit and made as if to grab the Book of Abraham from Father Clark. For that he had to be whipped. At Father Clark's nod Mam Sever attended to it at once with the flat of her shoe.

Bruno's mother had been the woman of Yan Top-son. Yan put her away because the infant was none of his. When Bruno was born, March 20 of the Year of Abraham 472, Yan had been in the south country, believed lost, at least nine months. He returned scarred and gaunt, and entered the Karnteen Hut for the five days of ritual purification; when he emerged his fey woman Marget confronted him with the baby. Town Clerk Jaspa was present, Elder Jones, Marta the Cure-Woman, Hurley the Ironsmith. Yan took the baby—it was dark like Marget, and Yan a bright blond with cutting blue eyes—and gave it to Elder Jones. Then he struck Marget across the face, an official declaration that the child was not his but a public charge, and she no longer his woman.

Because the child's hair was earth-dark, his skin tan as a sandy road, his eyes brown as a trout pool, Father Clark named him Bruno. He grew up living here and yonder, wherever there was food and a place near the hearth. Mam Sever, a bountiful woman whose newborn child had died, nursed Bruno after Marget drowned herself in Lake Ashoka—and they say, Father Clark begged a dispensation from the Holy City of Nuber itself to have her buried in consecrated ground, and was refused. Later Marta the Cure-Woman, Marget's half-sister, often gave Bruno food and shelter during his growing up. He may have picked up fragments of her learning.

Thus it was that Bruno was allowed to listen—big and powerful at sixteen, apprenticed to Hurley the Ironsmith—when the Elders were discussing the rumored approach of Tiger Boy, whose music of the pipes was always sounding in the woods and meadows for many days and nights before his terrible appearance.

In time he would show himself (it was said) in

some open region near the village he had chosen, and play his music, and sometimes sing, incomprehensibly—the words were true words, but no one had ever managed to write them down. A youth, according to the stories, with hair falling to his shoulders. Because of the huge brown tiger that walked with him and lay at his feet when he played or sang, no reasonable person dared approach him, and it was generally understood that he was a manifestation of the Devil.

No reasonable person would approach. But when he ended his music and walked away into the woods— this would always be early evening (they said) and the sunlight making long shadows on the grass—one or two foolish or miserable people might run after him; and not return. They'd be sick people, or very old, or strange in some manner and so thought to be suffering a malady of the mind. When the appearances began—a few years ago, ten, twenty, few agree—children ran after him before they could be prevented. These did return, full of totally incredible tales: the nice young man told them funny stories (which they couldn't remember), and let them pet the tiger's fur (but not pull it), and showed them where wild red raspberries were growing, and played music just for them, and then saw them safe to the edge of the woods where they could find their way home. Thereafter children were kept closely guarded indoors at the first hint of Tiger Boy's presence.

"There's plenty whopmagullion into it," said Elder Jones in the Store. Bruno was there. "Lies, lies, people got no conscience the things they tell. Like about him raping twelve women up to Abeltown."

"If it was only six," said Elder Bascom, "you'd still got to call him supernatural, I don't care how young and pert he be."

135

"Same and all," said Elder Jones, "there's something to it, something out there that ought not to be."

"All mahooha," said Elder Bascom. "Somebody dreamed it up out of the lonesome itch, and now it goes on and on."

"No," said Baron Ashoka, "I agree with Elder Jones. And the thing is against Nature." He had ambled in, tethering his horse to the rail himself in his democratic way, wanting no fuss from servants as the storekeeper Jo Bodwin well knew. A fine old man in his yellow shirt of Penn silk and loinrag showing his family colors of brown and orange, he stood with one well-shod foot planted on a chair-seat. Genial, this whitehaired squarefaced old gentleman who owned most of the valley land, the mill, the pottery, the flax fields. As President of the Maplestock Corporation, he could also have been said to own the sheep ranch and fulling mill; in the Corporation's name he exercised the right to impress four days' labor each month from every able-bodied villager. He represented the township of Maplestock at the Imperial Assembly in Kingstone, and spoke out there against slaveholding in the western provinces. His family dated back more than two hundred years to the reign of Emperor Brian I, who made the knight Ian Shore the first Baron Ashoka, for services rendered in the Penn War that established our southwest border from Binton Ruins down the Delaware to the Atlantic. The family had grown in wealth and importance also during the glorious War of 435–439, when we absorbed the old republic of Moha, so that now, except for a strip of land border with Penn from Binton Ruins north to the Ontara Sea, we are bounded altogether by water—the great Ontara, the Lorenta and Hudson Seas, and the measureless Atlantic where no one ventures, though men are said to have done so in Old Time. And here was Baron Ashoka chatting with the Elders like anybody. "If it comes on this village," he said—"God forbid, but if it does we know how to deal with it, eh, Jo?"

"My lord," said the storekeeper, agreeing heartily with no notion what the Baron might have in mind, "I'm sure we do." Jo was a transmission line. The labor tax usually took the form of an order to Jo: I'll have so-and-so many men on such-and-such a date; as one might say over the counter: I'll have a pound of raisins.

"Standby posse, that's the thing," said the Baron. "That's what I stopped by to talk to you about. No labor tax, boys—take off that worried look." The company laughed as required, and Bruno smiled, perhaps at the resonance of laughter. "Special guard round the clock in four-hour shifts, Army style by God. You pass the word to Guide Lester, Jo. Five men, three shifts of 'em, four hours on and eight off, ready to go out and *take* him." The Baron checked as if he had bumped into an obstruction. "Hm. . . . I want the first shift to start tonight, tell him that."

Jo Bodwin nodded, tactfully silent. Elder Bascom in seventy years had never learned tact. "My lord, what with the smallpox last year, fifteen able men took off their regular work is going to make one almighty hole in things."

"I know, Elder. Yes—well, Jo, tell Guide Lester to get nine men, three to a shift, and I'll send three archers of my household. He's to have the first shift assemble outside the Store here, not later than eight by the church clock. And they're not to go out for any silly rumor about somebody tweedling a pipe in the woods—only for the open appearance they say he always makes. We're going to deal with it once and for

137

all, gentlemen." Another slip: the Elders were not the Kingstone Imperial Assembly, and they weren't gentlemen. Gossip might mutter that the Baron was feeling his years. He nodded to all, mounted his mare stiffly and was gone.

Bruno sometimes woke whispering. In early childhood when he tried to form words with no sound except breath, nothing good happened: the few who noticed were unaware of anything like words in the hissing noise, and it bothered them. Mam Sever, more kindly, was also rather deaf; she noticed the stir of Bruno's lips but thought he was expressing hunger, and so stuffed him with food and frustration and patted him and went on with her perpetual busyness. By the time he was sixteen Bruno had learned to hold his mouth quiet—except for that rare smile, fleeting as the passage of wings, of which he was not conscious. But often, in the crumbling cabin adjoining the forge where he now lived alone—he was a useful watchman and could be trusted not to steal—Bruno woke whispering. And sometimes when wide awake, if certain that he was alone, he allowed himself the indulgence of it, the hurting half-pleasure.

For his head was alive with words. Magicked by words, their agile intensity, words that soared and swooped and darted about him until he felt himself among the swallows or crossing the hills on hawk wings toward a forever. His words could rush together, go chiming in love together down a long golden rolling morning. And they responded to his wish—a little. He could urge, instruct, tease them until they leaped from thought to thought so clearly that between two pinnacles he could find the rainbow bridge. They would play games with him—ah, it was all a game, he supposed, only a game, something to be doing when not eating or sleeping or messing around or listening to talk-talk or working for goodnatured Hurley in the goodnatured sweat and clang of the forge. Only a game—

> Woodthrush, woodthrush, I follow to your city
> by the alone way
> where you say the fountains are forever playing.
> I'm hungry, I'm tired—
> why do you cease calling when I was so near?
> How can I find your city now
> by the alone way?

It was a game of invention, with the tickle of untasted pleasure—

> Back into the brush smiling scared, naked,
> like a trout to his safehold under a stone,
> but it was the trout I hunted.
> They're gone.
> My fish-line hangs limp-silly in the stream.
> The girls are all gone.
> What am I hunting?

Once he had indeed come on girls bathing in a pool in the woods, sparrow-voiced and delicious, but it was Bruno who had hidden. No matter: words can drive one thing into another, flow everywhere, pierce all mysteries at least once. Bruno was often not unhappy.

Anyway Bruno had a girl. His fertile loneliness had created her out of the visible figure of Janet Bascom, daughter of the baker, great-granddaughter of Elder Bascom. Janet as the village knew her was a modest mouse soon to be married to the farmer Jed Homer, who held his land directly from the monastery of St. Benjamin on Mount Orlook; Jed's second wife had died and he wanted to collect Janet and her plump dowry before he or she became any more overripe. She had smiled pleasantly at Bruno once, perhaps for no reason except that she felt like smiling, and had forgotten it ten minutes later. Henceforth Janet as Bruno knew her was a woman-spirit of air and fire. In the sun her hair became as the halo of the blessed St. Jacqueline in the stained-glass window in the south wall of the church. Her voice rang in his brain, gently, as sometimes the church-bell music reached him across two miles of fields when he was at the forge. Her hands—oh, surely kind if only because such beauty dwelt in them whether they moved or rested. Sometimes Janet even glanced at him again. Should he have known that he did not want her any nearer than she was?

Sometimes when he woke whispering in the dark, especially if the moon was riding clear and jubilant, especially in this sixteenth year when he was beset by the troubles and wants that all youth knows (especially if youth must remain silent), Bruno might go wandering.

He would close the door of his cabin softly. No other house stood near, but he felt such a night as a state of being perfect in itself, not to be marred by noises that are no better than blundering, and heedless. He would slip away across Hurley's pastureland by routes his feet could follow without requiring thought: sometimes toward the village, where all the dogs knew him and did no more than snuffle a greeting as he drifted along the sleep-filled streets and marveled to see what broad rivers of moonlight pour from slanting roofs; sometimes into the woods, under the hemlock and maple and pine. His night vision was a little better than the human norm. He liked to follow the happenings of moonlight where its pattern lay broken on the ground. Now and then when the soft air itself became a challenge he would walk silently for a mile along a certain wood-road, a passage that made him think of the church aisle leading toward Father Clark whom he feared and loved. At the first turn of the wood-road stood a massive rock; here he would leave the road to follow the tunnel of a deer-run that led into the open at the base of a grassy mount. No tree grew on this knoll. Ancient thoughts quickened here about a broad flat rock at the summit; merely one of Earth's bones breaking the skin, but a sense of human presence clung.

In the night that followed Baron Ashoka's appearance at the Store, Bruno came here, moonstruck. Along the wood-road the white light created legions of night thoughts driving—where?

Even through the dense growth of the deep-run he heard the music.

Baron Ashoka meanwhile had ridden from the Store up the twisty Mount Orlook road to dine with the Abbot of St. Benjamin's. A dainty small dinner for the two of them, served by one of the Abbot's many discreet servants, who vanished as soon as the Abbot and his guest had dealt with roast goose and delicacies from the monastery garden—green peas for instance, and strawberries in thick Jersey cream. The wine was a sauterne from the province of Cayuga, unaggressive, but the Baron played safe and drank in more moderation than did the Abbot. The meal ended with a subtle golden tea. Penn merchants, the prelate confided, got it by caravan from Albama, wherever that was—another Penn monopoly. "But I thank the good God," he said with mischief in his ancient voice, "that my concern is entirely for affairs spiritual. Enough for me my little sheepfold in the hills." Over the wine he crinkled a smile at the Baron, who seemed gloomy behind that ruddy handsome face under the ostentatious white hair. The Abbot of St. Benjamin's was entirely bald and sensitive about it, also beleaguered by a host of old-age pains and frets—acid stomach, shortness of breath, swollen ankles, a vindictive prostate. Occasionally he imagined that if only his dignity allowed him to consult Marta the Cure-Woman instead of pigheaded Brother Walter he might feel better; most of the time he merely admitted that old age is like that, a necessary last trial before the tranquil joys of Heaven. "By the way, my dear Baron, I always *try* to make sure my Cellarer purchases wine from non-slaveholding establishments."

Baron Ashoka bowed. "It's a matter close to my heart, Father."

"Yes yes." The Abbot reflected on the loneliness of important people. He supposed the Baron believed in God and the Church rather cynically if at all, but quite strongly in the freeing of the slaves, whereas he himself believed deeply in the unshakable rightness of his Church and thanked God there was no other, but very little in what certain well-meaning visionaries were calling a Free Society. How can you have such a thing? Any society includes and therefore surrounds the individual, cutting off freedom on all sides. Men don't want freedom anyway, thought the Abbot—look at their panic when they get a little of it! All they want is to dream about it, and talk. Since he liked the

Baron, and since they must remain on good terms if the affairs of Maplestock were not to degenerate into a sticky mess—after the Baron the monastery was the largest landholder in the township—these differences of view required solicitous tiptoeing among the tea-cups. "Yes yes, let us hope the—ah—joys of freedom become happily extended—ah—year by year. And now do tell me!" Spectacles gleaming, little nose twitching like a rabbit's, he leaned his plump eminence toward the Baron across the table. "Our news of the world is so scant," he lied, "you must forgive my old-womanish curiosity. What is the latest on this—ah—this absurdity, this Tiger Boy nonsense?"

"Father MacAllister, I am afraid there really is such a person."

"Oh dear! I had hoped—assumed—it was no more than a country fantasy or a practical joke."

"I've ordered a standby posse at the village, with some of my men to help. We can stop the thing. We've always had good hunters here—good hunters and good poachers."

"It's really that bad?"

"Father, I got some information the village doesn't have, through an acquaintance in Grayval, a trustwor-thy man. Tiger Boy appeared there last month. It's hardly twenty miles from here, but as you may know, a very shutaway place, not much news coming out of there. He appeared—it was in the full and wane of the moon, I believe, as it always has been. His music was heard in the woods; cattle were killed, everything the way they say it's happened in other places. Then he showed himself in an open field near the village— played and sang, although my friend said it was more like reciting an outlandish poetry, and he felt he could

143

understand some of it, almost. And the tiger stood by him like—shall I tell you how my friend described him?"

"Oh dear! Your friend is an—ah—imaginative type?"

"Not in the least. My friend says the tiger, stood there beside the youth like a river of fire made flesh. And when he roared, once, the village people fell on their faces, and my friend did not hear them pray to Abraham. After the youth had done singing and turned away into the woods, an old woman hobbled after him, and that was when my friend could still see the brown and gold of the tiger slipping away under the trees."

"How it repeats! An old woman. Always the old or the halt or the sick. Oh dear! The children were kept indoors, I suppose?"

"Yes. One thing was a little different, Father—at least I haven't heard it in accounts of the other appearances. At Grayval it seems the old woman not only wished to go, but was encouraged to do so by her own people—days in advance, when the music was first heard in the woods. My friend couldn't discover that they had any spite against her; on the contrary she seems to have been well liked. And he says, Father—he says she wore a garland of May flowers."

"How's that? A garland?"

"A garland of May flowers, and when she tottered off into the woods they saw her smile like a girl going to her bridegroom. . . . Father MacAllister, it is on the way to becoming a cult."

"My God! Yes, I begin to see. Well, Baron, it won't do, it won't do. We must eliminate it before it grows."

Baron Ashoka murmured: "It seems that even in Old Time it was found very difficult to eliminate a cult—any cult."

144

"Old Time? Don't give me ancient history!—we'll have trouble enough as it is. It's got to be stopped. Oh dear. Just when everything was so peaceful—but really, Baron, who ever heard of a man walking around with a tiger? It's not in nature."

"My mare shied twice coming up the road this evening. She's a very steady little thing—hardly ever known her to do it."

"My God, Baron, you're not suggesting this monster would venture near consecrated ground!"

"Well, she did quiet down as soon as we were inside the monastery walls. Noticed the difference right away."

"What's Father Clark doing about all this? It's his parish. I hope there's no implication, Baron, that *we* are supposed to—ah—take measures? We are a contemplative order." The old man was up and pacing the room, making the sign of the Wheel on his chest. "You're aware, Baron, it's our prescribed duty to remain retired from the world so that we may praise God and the works of his son Abraham, and live by the Ancient Rule that comes down to us from days far beyond Old Time itself, a most holy thing. Eh? Well, what's Father Clark doing?"

"I've talked with him about it only once, Father. He seemed—I would say, resigned."

"Now I know that man!" the Abbot cried. "He's a do-nothing. He'll let that tiger thing move right in on you. He ought to be ready to go forth against it, exorcise it with the power and in the name of the holy Wheel whereon Abraham died for our sins! But not Father Clark. Not that I have a word to say against him, of course—very faithful to his flock, yes yes." The Abbot sat down clumsily, short of breath, and reached for the wine. "We are, by tradition, by our own law

145

and the wish of the Church, a contemplative order."

"I have it in mind to ask one thing of you, Father MacAllister. I intend to be with the posse when the confrontation comes if it does. There's been idiot talk about this beast turning arrows, about arrows passing through the youth without harming him. Soon we'll be hearing of other—huh!—miracles. I haven't patience for that sort of thing. It's a betrayal of human intelligence."

"Baron, is human intelligence so mighty?"

"I do not say it is. But I think this is an occasion when we must defend it."

"I'd be happier, my son, if you had said that enthusiasm for evil miracles, whether fraudulent or of the Devil, is a betrayal of God."

"Oh, that too, Father, that too, certainly."

"It has just occurred to me that the prior of St. Henry's at Nupal, somewhat a friend of mine though I can't altogether approve the extent of his secular activities, often goes hunting with the local nobility—it does, I suppose, help to maintain good relations between two estates of the realm; anyhow, it so happens that he maintains a small pack of northern wolfhounds some of which, I dare say—ah—at a word from me, he might be willing to lend, with their trainer, in a good cause. I do not urge it, I do not altogether approve, but—but—"

"They'd be very handy to have, Father. What I wanted to ask of you was something else. I think I must be the one to lead the posse against this—monstrosity, with spear and sword and bow; also, I hope, with the blessing of the Church and the aid of your prayers, Father Abbot."

"But of course, my son."

"It is long since I have confessed. My sins are many

146

and heavy on me. Cleanse my soul, Father Abbot, and bless me before I go."

Bruno moved toward the music with the confidence that may waken when the heart commands and the mind waives protest. A music such as Bruno had never imagined, pure-toned yet with a hint of reediness that bound it to the earth of grass and forest and stream. The melody's intervals were not alien to music he had heard in his village, and in the church where Janet's voice was clearest and truest of the choir—indeed if this music resembled any other it might be Janet's soprano when it went skylarking above the imperfect dull singing of the rest. But Bruno was not thinking, not making comparisons. He moved toward the music, to the summit of the knoll, to the flat rock where Tiger Boy sat playing and the tiger lay out beside him, tawny gold turned to black and silver by the moon, a river of fire made flesh.

Having come so far, standing by the rock under the other's regard and observing the tiger's lifted head, Bruno understood he ought to be afraid. But Tiger Boy finished the air he was playing—it had not wavered when Bruno appeared; and when it ended he patted the rock beside him: who could be afraid of that? The pipes idle in his hand were of a design unknown to Bruno, slender tubes of graded length, hollow reeds, Bruno thought, bound together with vine. The youth with the long locks and clever hands was asking him, no such unwanted questions as *Who are you?* or *Why have you come?* or *What do you want?* but only: "Do you like my music?"

Bruno nodded. Then slowly and carefully, wishing only to be understood and not required to go away, he whispered: "I have no voice. I can speak only this way." The tiger swung its enormous head to study him more intensely, perhaps disturbed by the uncommon small sound. "But sometimes I think poems."

"Tell me one," said Tiger Boy, and laid a quiet arm over Bruno's shoulders. Tiger Boy was naked and brown, dark like Bruno but with hair lighter than his skin, and he smelled of leaf mold and wild thyme.

He is white under this moon as sand
where waves have gone over it
on the sea beaches.
He is black under this moon as the mold
that pleased me when I pushed away the pine
needles
and lay breathing the spice of forest noon,
thinking of the friend who had not then come
to me.
Surely the stripes are shadows cast by marsh lilies.
when the sun smiled on him:
surely in the day he is a child of the sun
and plays delighted at the foot of the rainbow.

"I like that," said Tiger Boy, "and it's easy for me to understand you. A voice isn't everything. Tell me one more, Poet, and then no more until tomorrow, for I want to think about them, these first poems of yours I've heard, and taste them again, and have them go on speaking in me when I'm sleeping and when I play my pipes."

Bruno whispered: "I'll be with you tomorrow?"

"If you desire it," said Tiger Boy, and smiled. "I hope you do."

I am a stream in flood
with all the weight of thoughts, the fallen leaves

148

that pile in confusion if the stream is dammed
by the stone of your absence, as just now because
you looked away from me.

See how the flood runs free!
And all my thoughts have caught a thousand colors
not of my common day, because you turned
facing the flood and welcoming my presence
and looked again on me.

"Is there anything in the village, Poet, you would
not want to leave behind you?"

The question troubled Bruno for a truthful answer.
There was much in the village that he loved: Janet's
voice escaping from the choir like a breeze rushing for
the clouds; Father Clark who (he sometimes
dreamed) might have begotten him in some fierce up-
rising of passion of a kind that married people apparently lost or never knew. There were the village gardens sheltered by lilacs from the dust of the street; the
dogs and cats and goats and chickens who never acted
afraid of him when he happened by (perhaps these
animals are not as delighted by the human voice as
we sometimes suppose); the paths and good hidden
places of the woods and pastures; and he thought of
the red and gold and purple body of Mount Orlook in
the autumn under a late sun. There were the white
small beaches of the Hudson Sea less than an hour's
journey from the village, where he had once ventured
alone at night, when younger and reckless with ignorance of the dangers, in order to watch moonlight on
the water. There were all these, and many other plea-
sures and little loves. But then he considered Tiger
Boy's question, in the manner of one who loves words
and cherishes the life in them that they will not show

149

forth to those who do not care about them, and he understood: he would want to leave any place, however familiar and dear, where he would not be in the company of Tiger Boy. Therefore Bruno shook his head, and the transitory smile appeared on his mouth, remaining there longer than at any time in the past.

"Then my search is over," said Tiger Boy, "if you will go with me and be my friend forever."

"Is it true," Bruno whispered, "that some have followed you and died?"

"It is true," said the other with a quiet above and beyond sadness. "They followed me for love of death and not for love of me—except the children, and they don't come to me anymore. Since they were in love with death and merely a little shy of speaking to him, I did not keep death from them. But you would be sharing my journey for love of me. Had you thought, Poet, that this village, this nation might be part of a world so much larger that if we had a map of it the Empire of Katskil might look like a speck of dust on a sheet?"

Bruno nodded happily. Then the world's angers rushed in across his happiness and he whispered: "Tiger Boy, they are forming a posse in Maplestock, to destroy you. I've listened in the Store, where they talk-talk. From tonight on, men will be waiting there to hunt you down as soon as you appear."

Tiger Boy smiled. "I no longer need to appear there," he said, and he took up the pipes and played a small thing of amusement, an impudent, jaunty, defiant air. The tiger slanted his head and rubbed his neck softly against the youth's side. "We'll go away, Poet. I know places where forest extends for many days' journey. I know more open regions full of deer and elk and wild swine and buffalo where our tiger can feed in his natural way with no risk of a hunter's arrow. I have heard talk of a river as mighty as a sea, and beyond it wider plains—they say the old ruins of men's work stand up stark and lonely there—and beyond that, mountains so huge, so closely ranked together that surely no man ever climbed them: snow remains on the summits, I hear, through all the summer season. We shall look on them. And no more than ten days' journey from here I know a small lake, deep water blue as noon sky, sheltered by little hills. Men seldom go there now, for fear of tiger, red bear, black wolf—no, they huddle in villages, stockaded villages, and in the great villages they call cities with high stone walls to defend them against others of their own kind. Isn't it marvelous, Poet, what fools men are? But we can go to that lake. You're strong. I'll make you a bow like mine. We'll stay there as long as we please, and I'll make you a set of pipes too, and teach you how to play."

Bruno wondered why he felt no wish to ask Tiger Boy who he was, or how a brown tiger came to be his friend, or what it was he meant to do with his life in the years to come. Bruno found he truly had no such wish: if in his own time Tiger Boy chose to tell him, good; if not, no matter. Bruno waited among the multitude of words that offered themselves, until he knew he had found the most beautiful company of them in the language, and then he whispered them: "I will go with you."

Maplestock woke to the distress of Hurley the Ironsmith, who rode into town jouncing on his gray plug and his gray hair flying, too early for most folk—scary excitement comes better after settling breakfast. Bruno was gone.

If he'd been an ordinary boy prone to laziness and lapses of virtue—but he wasn't. Always loyal to his work, seemed to enjoy it too, punctual and goodnatured. Everyone knew how he wandered harmlessly at night, and hung around the Store when he had a free daylight hour. No harm in that. Hurley had never known him to be late or unwilling. Now he was gone, the door of his cabin closed, his bunk not slept in.

Shouting the news to everyone he saw without waiting on a reply, Hurley rode direct to the posse, who were making the best of Mam Bodwin's corn pone and thin tea, on the back steps of the Store. "Bruno's gone."

"Who's Bruno?" said the gaunt archer with the brown shirt and orange loinrag.

Stunned, Hurley glared, phuphing his gray moustache. "Da'say you're newcome around here," he said, and then realized this must be one of the men sent by Baron Ashoka. He looked at the others, not at their best at seven in the morning after three hours' guard alert and another hour to go. Dan Short, Barton Linz, Tom Denario—not incompetent exactly, but a scraggy lot, getting on for elderly. Jo Bodwin came out then, and Hurley spoke to him in a dry snarl betraying the truth that he rather loved the boy: "Bruno's gone."

"Well, now—the men can't go looking for him *now*, Wilbur—see, it's guard duty. Not without the Baron says so. Ain't it natural a boy might be late for work?"

"Goddamn it, Jo, you know how it is—he sleeps right there by the forge. He's *never* been late. Always there when I want him."

"But you know, Wilbur, he does kind of go wandering at night."

"Likely," said the stranger, "you'll find him dead beat in bed with some little piece." Wilbur Hurley stared, his blacksmith's hand tight on the bridle and one eyelid twitching. "Well, Jesus and Abraham, I can't seem to say nothing right." Hurley's silence agreed.

"Like to oblige you myself," said Jo Bodwin, "but you see I can't leave the Store, not with this guard duty thing, I'm supposed to keep it organized and so on and so on."

"Shit," said the Ironsmith.

"No, honest, Wilbur, I really like that boy, you know yourself there wasn't a time he couldn't come in here and sort of help himself to a bite and so on." Unknown to Jo, perhaps, his voice had already taken on a note of elegy, as if Bruno were six feet under in the churchyard. "And you'll find Mam Bodwin say the same—I bet there wasn't *nobody* really that didn't kind of like him."

"He'll turn up," said Tom Denario. "You'll see."

"Up there right now likely," said Barton Linz.

"Guts of Abraham!" said Hurley the Ironsmith. "You can't any of you lift up off your butts without the Baron says so, I'll get the Baron." And he kicked the old gelding into a shambling gallop.

Watching his receding dust the stranger remarked: "Skin my ass if I ain't just remembered, the Baron was off to Nupal at daybreak, anyhow said he intended it when he rousted me out, sent me down here."

"Do say!" said Jo. "Now I wonder—"

"It's a fact Hurley's old ho'se needs the ex'cise," said Dan Short, whose uncle had carried on a line-fence quarrel with Hurley's father about forty years back.

"I do wonder," said Jo, "what he's off to Nupal for?"

The man with the orange loinrag started his morning's chaw and spat between his feet. "When he

153

rousted me out, Storekeeper, he was higher'n a hickory tree on monastery wine, nor I wasn't truly wakeful whiles he was expressing himself, but I believe it was something or another to do with hound dogs."

Father Elias Clark, parish priest of Maplestock and long ago a graduate of St. Benjamin's Seminary at Kingstone, privileged (under supervision of the Church) to read the books of Old Time and to write after his name the rarely awarded letters F.L., *Frater Literatus*, climbed the wearisome long road to the manor under the sun of midafternoon. His broad black hat held away the heavy light but pressed its own soggy heat on the pain in his head. The village behind him buzzed and yattered at him keenly, every predictable word another spike driven tap-tap-tap into his skull.

Don't y' remember, wun't he always ready with them special favors, the way Marget couldn't do no wrong? Like the time—

Oh, I dunno—poor Bruno, always did think he COULD *be a—you know, it ain't nice to speak the word—and in that case he wouldn't be none of Father Clark's get—*

Yah, but look how quick and sharp the Father was to say Bruno wun't no—

But look, didn't he turn out to be a nice sort of kid except he can't talk? Wun't for that he'd be just like everybody, and what harm'd he ever do anybody?

It's the sin. Turns my stomach to think of that Marget you-know with the priest that's give me communication with his own hands. Disgusting, him and her, wonder the lightning didn't come for both—

Well, see, God got his reasons to wait for this p'tic'lar judgment.

154

—in his mysterious ways, amen—
But look, she's been dead sixteen years.
Do say! Been that long, has it?
But look—
Wouldn't think he had it in him, would you?
But look—

Father Clark's mind echoed: *Sixteen years!* He halted short of breath on the high ground not far below the manor, and through a gap in the hemlocks he looked out over the valley, his valley, to Maplestock, his village, his charge, his parish, his life's labor, a jewel of human making in that hollow of the hills which he had once thought of as a symbol for the hand of God. And with the village, did not God also hold and cherish that building, that white church he could see from here, and its clean spire rising toward heaven from the matrix of the sacred Wheel? *Yes, she has been dead (and not in consecrated ground) for sixteen years, and I may have lost the son I never had—to a beast, to some outrageous devilish thing, whatever it is that haunts us in these years. O Bruno, I begot you on my poor wild love, only to rob you of both father and mother, and have given you nothing in return. (The watch and ward of a parish priest is nothing?) I saved your life—no crossroads burial with a stake in the infant heart, not for my son! Saved you for what?*

He sank down by the roadside and covered his face with his hands. *How they feared your silence, Bruno, even before it was time for a child to speak! Oh, natural enough, for certainly a child should weep aloud on entering this world, if only to break the silence with a demand and a protest. But they fear silence anyway because no one ever knows what may come out of it. Not I, certainly.*

155

Out of the silence that surrounded him here and absorbed the small sounds of his trouble as the ocean might swallow one drop of blood, he heard a distant noise of hooves—Baron Ashoka, he hoped. Wilbur Hurley had ridden back to the village fuming because the Baron was away to Nupal and not expected back until after midday. Father Clark had spoken with him, and with many others in the muttering, clattering village. Everyone thought it would be a fine idea if somebody (else) got up a search party. Mam Sever, the priest thought, would have shamed the men of the village into action. But Mam Sever was dead last year of the smallpox.

And why could not I? What's happened to my silver tongue? My calculated angers? They heeded me once, they believed me a true vessel transmitting the will of God for the direction of their affairs. Now and then (O Lord, forgive me!) I believed this too. I had a vision of a great moral cleansing that would start in this small place (myself the evangelist, O vanity!) and spread—who knows how far? . . . Had I not? And what happened to it? Was my sin so great that God took away all virtue from me? But would not that be a punishment of my village for a sin that was only mine and Marget's? More light!

O God of Christ and Abraham and of the prophets, having given us life couldst thou not have enlightened us, if only a little, how to deal with it?

It was the sound of horse's hooves, but blurred as though other feet scuffed along in the dust. Baron Ashoka appeared around the turn of the road on his beautiful roan mare, and behind him a foul-faced man with matted hair—a black tangle of it never combed and doubtless full of lice. This man seemed to be slouching along in his excellent, immensely dirty moose-

156

hide moccasins, but the slouch was an illusion given by his overdeveloped mass of shoulder and arm muscle; actually he was moving in a quick buoyant stride that matched the mare's pace without effort. His left hand held two stout leashes, a finger hooked on each; his right grasped a vicious, heavy-butted whip—easily, lightly, like an extension of his arm ready for immediate use. His arms and knotty legs were marked as if by smallpox, but a second look showed the dents to be the scars of a hundred old bites. Father Clark remembered Kingstone and the wild animal dealers, feral creatures themselves, who brought in wolves and black bear (never the red bear!) to parade them through the city streets before delivering them to the Arena.

The leashed brutes who followed this man, if he could be described as a man, did so not meekly, but with that savage resignation which is only a waiting for the chance that never comes. They were northern wolf-hounds, probably from the Saranac country, long in the snout, shaggy, gray as stormclouds and fast as the brown tiger himself. The Baron halted, and as the dogs raised their heads to stare in iron cruelty at Father Clark, he saw that their muzzles were level with the trainer's waist.

The Baron dismounted courteously. "On your way to the manor, Father?"

"I was, yes. This is a fortunate chance—now I can get back to the village immediately. I came to tell you, Baron, that the boy Bruno has disappeared. There was strange music heard in the woods night before last and the night before that. Most of our people think the tiger has taken him."

"Oh, that's bad, that's bad."

"Some, Baron, are for going in search of him." Father Clark tried for a neutral voice. "Others are already saying that the tiger has accepted the—the sacrifice, and will now go and leave us in peace. . . . I must know which course you favor, Baron Ashoka," said Father Clark, remembering and half regretting the long years of his dislike for this man whose image tended to submerge itself in the image of abstract power, this man whom he seldom met at all except in the formalities of Friday mornings, when the Baron in his pew was making all the correct motions and would shake his hands correctly after the service with the correct small talk and never offer anything beyond that. Seeing the Baron now sagging with fatigue and his square face gritty with road dust (and in the background that infernal trainer with his dogs waiting like a little company from Hell) it seemed to Father Clark that he could almost like the Baron—if there were time for any such trifles. "The village, Baron, will go according to what you say, not by what I say."

"Oh, please, Father! Mustn't underrate your influence—I don't think that's so at all. And I can't let you go back without a drink—wine, tea—whatever you favor, and a little rest. You must be as tired as I am, sir. Please take my horse the rest of the way—I'd like to get the cramp out of my legs anyhow."

"Thank you, Baron, but I must go back at once. Is it to be a search, or must we let the boy go for lost?"

"My dear man, of course we don't let it go." The Baron had taken offense and made no effort to hide it. "We'll search. But this day will soon be spent. And this fellow and his hounds have walked fifteen miles."

"It is a human life," said Father Clark, and lowered his gaze, in fear of seeing some flicker of denial, some unspoken suggestion that Bruno was rather less than human. "There are nearly six hours of daylight left."

"Father, I beg of you! Exhausted men and dogs can't accomplish anything, not against brown tiger. If the tiger's taken him it's far too late for us to do Bruno any good. We can only hunt down the beast and this—this mythical person, whatever it is, that goes around with him. That I propose to do. With rested men and dogs, first thing in the morning and a whole day for the work."

"We don't know the tiger took him. We only know he's gone, and may be lost somewhere in the woods. These dogs can follow scent, can't they?"

"They can, Father. They follow it as hunters. They are not much used, I'm told, in work of mercy—too dangerous, hard to hold. And I understand that when they catch scent of tiger they can't be taken off the trail or they go berserk, nobody can handle them. Once we start after this beast we must stay with the hunt until the end—six hours might only be a small part of it if the quarry is traveling. Am I right, Horrow?"

"They folla, they do. Stay with. Folla till they can pull's guts out on t' grass."

"Hear that? He's made his kill, Poet—woods buffalo, I think. Now he'll feed and lie up a while, but we can go on if you like. He can always find us."

"I wish I could sing of our journey, of the journeys to come."

"No need. I always hear you and I'll sing for you. Look at the little orchids! Moccasin-flower—Lady's slipper, some call them. Often they grow where some tree has fallen and lies in decay."

> *Here in a lake of shadow*
> *It fashions the sunlight of itself.*

If love can wake and shine,
make and declare its own light,
there's no night too dense for journeying.

Hurley the Ironsmith followed a false trail that day,
after returning from the manor in anger and frustration. He had gone again to that rickety cabin by the
forge, stood in the bleak room wondering how a boy
could have lived there and collected almost no posses-
sions—a few spare clothes, another pair of sandals, all
neat as the cell of a monk, his bunk with the blanket
squared and trim, no clutter, no dust. As if Bruno had
never been here at all. No knife, but the boy did own
a good one, and so must have taken it with him—any
reassurance in that? Hurley had not been aware of his
wife coming in until she slipped an arm around him;
he saw she was weeping. "Will, why didn't we ever
know anything about him?"

"Ah, well, Ann. . . ."

"Why don't we ever *know* anything about others?
Why?"

"Baron's away to Nupal, Ann. Posse won't move
without he gives 'em word. So I have to go by myself."

"By yourself? Where the tiger is? I lose you too, and
then—".

"Have to go, Ann."

"I know you do." Small and gray, she rolled her
forehead against his chest and dug her fingertips into
his heavy rib cage. "So—so go *find* him, Will!"

Then Wilbur Hurley went out in the late morning
with his bow, and a long hunting knife and steel-
tipped arrows of his own making, searching for Bruno
whom (he now understood) he had loved more than a
little. He and Ann were childless, yet it was more than

160

that, as love is always more than the sum of its needless explanations.

Having no clue at all, he entered the forest by the same wood-road Bruno had traveled. He knew that knoll with the flat rock summit as well as Bruno—better, and knew an easier path to it than the deer-run; push through a thicket by this oak, a thicket no Maplestock forester would ever disturb, and you come out on a single-file but obvious path leading to the knoll and the flat rock, where even nowadays sacrifices are sometimes offered—libations of wine, fresh-killed chickens unplucked, a hunter's gift of rabbit or pheasant, maybe an egg with a phallic shape drawn on it in charcoal which means some woman desires to become pregnant of a male child. And it's true (even nowadays) the covens may be more active up there on May Night and Midsummer's Eve and Halloween than the Church cares to admit. Hurley knew the place from the years of his youth, which are the subject of another story.

He knew the knoll and would have gone there, but as he was moving down that obscure path, silent in his moccasins, eyes and ears intensely alert, he heard the music of a brown bird well known to him and loved, coming from his right and not very far away (he thought) but from a place where the hemlock grew so dense and dark that something of night was always present and something of the dreams of night. Hurley had more than once known the wood thrush to sing in this manner in the full daylight hours, though his time of glory is evening, when the robin's sundown music may join him, and perhaps the white-throated sparrow will be a third among them if human listeners are most fortunate and willing to stop their own noise long enough to accept it. But to hear the vesper song

161

of the brown bird in morning hours is not altogether a common thing, and Hurley felt in it the pull of strange. He parted hemlock branches, and moved off slowly following the sound, although he understood that it was remaining the same distance from him, and no haste of his would ever bring him up to it unless that should be the wish of whoever made the music. But a simple bird (Hurley knew) can do this quite well, merely keeping out of sight and perhaps wanting to lead the clumsy human thing away from a nest, no supernatural reason demanded. He followed— traveling, though he could not know it, in the direction opposite to that taken several hours earlier by Bruno and his friends: although in this forest directions cannot always be what they seem, and as some wise man commented maybe a thousand years ago, the longest way 'round is the shortest way home.

Hurley did not know this part of the woods, but felt (unaccountably) no terror of being lost, and it scarcely occurred to him to wonder how much time had passed while he followed the music—through green darkness of hemlock, and small glades where the sunlight was a green gold flowing down the tree trunks to slake the thirst of the wood spirits who often look like evanescent butterflies to you and me. He followed, recalling old things, as though the discovery that Bruno was a person, one who might well have been loved, had made it necessary for him to hunt back along some of the plains and hills of childhood, that era when you believed in wood spirits without any itch to offer a propitiatory smile. He recalled the grandeur of his patient father at the forge, and a dog called Bock always a snuffle of demanding love for him; and he recalled the country of somewhat later years, certain journeys in pursuit of the unattainable, the courting of Ann in her shining girlhood, her marriage dream that their son (never to be born) might win an education beyond their position in life, and so on to learning, glory, maybe even the priesthood—although Will Hurley himself would have been well content if a son of his simply grew into a good and patient ironsmith, for felt in his soul that there's a virtue in continuity. (Is it possible that some ages of man have forgotten this to their sorrow?)

He followed the music. Sometimes his mind would have it that the bird was singing: *"Will you follow? Love follows . . . Will you follow? Love follows."* He followed, delighting in the high clarity and tenderness of the song, yet doing so through the mist of his distress for Bruno, and against a growing distraction of pain, which centered in that massive rib cage and sent spurts and ripples of anguish down his left arm. *Why would no one come with me?*

"Will you follow? Love follows."

He followed the wood thrush, if such it was, until the forest ended where the trees had grown to the very edge of a drop, the end of it not seen. Grasping the last barrier branches, Will could look out and up with sunlight pouring over him, to watch at last the flight of the singing bird, a golden vanishing even now become a nothing in the wonderful wilderness of white vapor, and he called aloud: "I will go with you."

His wiser mind passed through its moment of trouble: *I must find Bruno. He may need me.* Then his heart burst; he was not breathing; even pain vanished; a wish to live commanded him to keep his grasp of the branches, but he could not. He fell, and the rocks far below took him with mercy.

Thus died, childless, Wilbur Hurley, our Ironsmith,

a good man and a generous one of the quiet spirits, on an errand of love; and who has ever supposed these errands can be run without peril?

In the first opening pallor of morning, Baron Ashoka rode up through the ground fog to join the men grouped leaderless on the steps of the Store. The Baron was followed by Horrow and his northern hounds, who slunk out of the mist so like a part of it that Tom Denario shivered and made across his chest the sign of the Wheel. "Good morning, Father," said the Baron; Father Clark bowed wanly. In the damp chill—fine drops glittered on the Baron's brown and orange hunting cap, and his square face was shining as if with sweat in the lamplight from the Store—the Baron studied the others, greeted them, and asked: "Where's Hurley Ironsmith? I was certain he'd be here."

"Wilbur Hurley," said Father Clark, "went to search the woods for Bruno yesterday morning and has not returned. His wife has still a lamp in the window. I prayed with her until an hour ago. I ought to have gone with him, Baron, but I did not know his intention, and besides, I am not brave."

"I am sorry to learn of his absence," said the Baron. He tapped his hat against his knee to knock off the wet, causing his mare to jump and fret a little; his white hair tumbled moist and lank about his ears. "Father Clark, I implore you, if there's any ill feeling between us let it be put aside while this work is to be done."

"There's no anger, Baron. Until we find Bruno and, please God, Will Hurley, I am only one of your hunters to do as you order. Bodwin has lent me a bow—I had some skill when I was younger." Elias Clark was trying to pierce the formidable shadows and heaving mist, to see beyond the gaunt malignity of Horrow and his hounds, to forget them, to smile. "I have no anger for anyone this morning, Baron, not even Father Death."

"Then let us go."

At Hurley's house, Ann Hurley had made up packages of food, and did not understand how they could not burden their hands with anything but weapons. She was a little silly with grief—fluttered and cried, too deferential to the Baron, rambling in her speech. Father Clark took her aside. She said: "You will find him, won't you?"

He was not quite certain which one she meant; perhaps she was not certain herself. "Of course, daughter. Wait and pray. If we are late beyond dark, put the lamp in the window again. Now rest in Abraham, and the peace of God be with you."

At the cabin by the forge, the hounds were given Bruno's spare blouse and loinrag to smell, and though the trail was two days old they made no great confusion of it but smelled on a course that took them to the wood road and then into the tunnel of the deer-run—moving indifferently it seemed, bored beasts performing a trick on demand, bored no doubt because the smell was only the familiar human scent that did not trigger their lust to kill. Nevertheless Horrow gripped the leashes firmly in one hand, the whip poised in the other, as the rawboned heads drove through the mist.

The Baron had left his mare in charge of Bodwin; a tiger hunt is no place for horses if you love them. But on feet, carrying like Denario and Short a long knife at the belt and a seven-foot spear, he was as much as ever Baron Ashoka of Maplestock, tribune of the Imperial Assembly, here in the gray dangerous morning by his own choice. He walked in the commander's natural place, well back of shambling Horrow and his hounds to leave them room. Behind him were the archers, Barton Linz and Father Clark and that lank man from the Baron's household whom Ashoka addressed as Kemp though no one else cared to use his name: we do sometimes try in this manner to shut them out from humanity, the bitter distorted ones, as though we had the authority. Then the other spear carriers Tom Denario and Dan Short. These seven, and the dogs; there were no others.

Climbing the ancient knoll, the dogs lost boredom, galvanized into frenzy. "Aahh!" said Horrow, and responded with a huge bulging of his left arm as the beasts plunged forward against the leashes, and a crack of his whip in the air, a kind of speaking. He addressed them in other ways too, as they circled the rock at the summit snuffing and yattering: "Eh, Jad? Eh, Jedda? What nah? Find? Find?"

The bitch of the pair lifted her long head and howled, her nose pointed toward those crowded hills in the west, remotely visible from the knoll across a sea of treetops, a darker part of the sky. Dawn had begun behind the hunters; the mist was retiring in rags, spent ghosts worn away with the perishing of the night. "Tiger," said Horrow. "It's tiger. Us knows, eh, Jedda? Eh, Jad? *Find!*" And he set the pace down the slope, westward and into the deep passages of the forest, a pace that went on through the morning and through a time when some of the day's moist heat filtered down below the canopy, a pace that would not slacken until the end was known. Mosquitos became a torment, butterflies passed on secret evergreen journeys; then the light above the trees no longer glittered, but turned gray, and a noise not unlike the

166

strange short roar of brown tiger was perhaps instead the first warning of the gray storm that was rolling toward them out of the west across the hills.

"That was a hound's cry, Poet, but I think it was very far behind. We were hunted by them once, in the north—Tiger killed three; he carries a scar on his flank where one closed with him. See!—he heard and he knows. I think there's a brook not far from here and we can walk down it a way, but Tiger won't understand—he'll jump the brook and follow us on the other bank. Are you afraid, Poet?"

Bruno shook his head.

They came to the brook and waded downstream where thickets grew on either bank; as Tiger Boy had known, their friend would not step through the water with them but jumped the brook. They knew his presence beyond the thicket, and when they came out in a clear space he rejoined them with cat displays of pleasure, fawning and arching his golden neck. "He may be the death of us," said Tiger Boy, "because he fears nothing and is not truly wise. And I see you are not afraid. But we should hurry on. We can tire them. They won't travel by night, but we can, Poet, as surely as dreams do."

They moved on quickly, ate quickly from a sack of dried meat and roots and mushrooms that Tiger Boy carried on his shoulder, and the morning spent itself with no further warning of pursuit. Tiger Boy was not reassured, for he could remember how the hounds kept silent on a trail unless obliged to check and separate in search. But later, when morning had passed, and noon, and they heard the thunder and saw the graying of the sky, Tiger Boy smiled and told Bruno: "That's good, that may help us. A rain would kill the

167

scent. But we must keep on. Are you tired, Friend?" Bruno nodded. "Maybe we can rest soon. Ah, look there!"

Ahead of them the trees thinned, revealing a long ragged slope of rock, too steep and firm for any vegetation but a little scrub, but not too steep to climb. And beyond the crest of it the sky was churning deep gray to black; already large single drops were falling and a snake of fire struck at distant earth. "We'll climb it, Poet, and let the rain wash our scent from the rock." He gripped Bruno's hand. The tiger flowed up the long slope in one airy run and waited for them, a golden silhouette gazing back along the country they had traveled. At the end of the climb Bruno was gasping, hardy though he was from youth and his good work at the forge. Tiger Boy supported him for the last steps, when the rain became a sudden torrent and the vast slanted rock face foamed and shouted like a waterfall. You're tired. Let's get over into the brush by that big rock, and rest. Oh!—have you hurt your foot?"

Bruno nodded. The pain was not too severe, only a wrench maybe, but Tiger Boy picked him up and carried him into the thicket, under the natural roof of a rock overhang that held off the flood and let it tumble as a curtain before their eyes. Within minutes the storm dwindled to a tranquil rain; the smell of wet earth and leaves came sweet, and through the curtain now thin and lazy they watched the air and the green life and a faint return of sunlight. The tiger lay beside them to lick his fur back into neatness; the thicket filled with his musky scent. Grown drowsy, Bruno whispered: "Is that lake far from here?"

"Maybe no more than eight days' journey now."

"And the big river?"

"Oh, much farther. But we'll come to it before the leaves turn, and where it flows in the south there's no winter ever."

> On that river mighty as a sea
> we shall build us a boat of firm timbers.
> One sail it shall carry of white linen
> from flax grown in a field of happiness.
> And we shall sail over the rim of the world
> to a country I made in childhood
> where no one weeps.

"Sleep a little, Poet. I will watch."

But as he spoke his words were smashed down by the roar of the tiger, who plunged out of the thicket and charged to the edge of the rock slope, and there received the arrow of Father Clark in his neck and the Baron's spear in the core of his heart, quickly dying. And Tiger Boy running forward would have cried out something to them all, perhaps a warning that he was human, but a cold thing in an orange and brown loin-rag delivered him an arrow below the heart, and shouted: "My shot, Baron! I got him! I got the bastard!"

Meanwhile Horrow, anxious to save a valuable hide that would be his perquisite, whipped the hounds away from the tiger's carcass. Still witless and berserk with the smell of him that was everywhere, in the thicket, the wet air, Bruno's clothes, they flung themselves on Bruno, who was stumbling to his friend, and brought him down. Moments passed before Father Clark, slashing with his knife and impeded by Horrow's prancing and gibbering, could destroy the hounds and take up his son's body in his arms, and learn there was no life in it.

Life lingered briefly in Tiger Boy, and the Baron knelt by him bewildered. "Why did you come upon us? *Why*? Why have you made us destroy you?"

"I was searching for a friend."

Later the Baron felt Father Clark's hand heavy on his shoulder. "They are both dead, Baron. We must take them back to the village where they shall have burial." The Baron nodded, stunned and vague. "We must look for Will Hurley. I suppose we have other labors, Baron, and certain years to be lived." They would return together, Father Clark knew, not in friendship but because this is the way the world goes, more or less, in daily necessities, compromises of good and evil, error and some vision and good intentions and growing old. They would consult with politeness as usual on parish affairs, would now and then dine together with the Abbot of St. Benjamin's, and would remember—imperfectly, more and more imperfectly. And the prior of St. Henry's at Nupal must of course be compensated for the loss of two valuable hounds.

Thus perished in the summer of the Year of Abraham 488 an unknown whom men called Tiger Boy. And in this manner died Bruno, like many of our other poets, his work unfinished.

THE WITCHES OF NUPAL

I will interrupt the secret work on my *History of Heresy* to write you a story of murder, love, and witchcraft.

When I read about the burning of witches in Old Time—reading snug down here in the cellars of the Ecclesia at Nuber among ancient books the Holy Murcan Church hasn't yet destroyed—I note that they were never called martyrs except by a few outraged historians of a later age which considered itself humanitarian. That was the same age that invented napalm, some kind of jellied fuel designed for the purpose of clinging to the skin and burning to the bone. And these historians, good gentlemen all, usually declined to believe that the victims were witches—an unkind cut. For martyrdom you must hold beliefs later guaranteed to be holy, as Joan of Arc did: had she been a true witch no one would have found her death noteworthy. Poor girl, I suppose she was one more homosexual who became important enough so that she had to be made first a devil and then a saint.

I am Fifth Assistant Librarian to the Ecclesia, and in this blessed century, third since the supposed birth and death of Abraham, witchcraft has been declared a delusion of barbaric and unmurcan minds. (I could still be burned for that "supposed," maybe, although

171

the bonfires are rapidly losing favor as public entertainments, but this code I write in is not likely to be broken by those muttonheads upstairs, and my explosive notebooks ought to be safe behind the massive *Complete Works of J. Fenimore Cooper*.) Fifth Assistant is a soft, hideaway job. Here in the Ecclesiastical State of Nuber we are within my native land of Katskil but not of it, as the antique papal state once sheltered within the body of Italy. I am a mean, cynical, respectable old man, almost invisible, less vulnerable than most citizens to arrest and torture in the cause of modern enlightenment. Down here in the cellars I read, scribble at my *History*, and am sometimes almost happy. I am the jolly worm in your apple, O Ecclesia—look to the bloom on your cheek! For I shall one day be transfigured by a printing press into a book, and chew my way out clear through you, and spread my wings, while you fall to the mud, and rot.

I am thinking back to the St. George's Hatchet Day of the year 266, thirty-five years ago. I will write this moral tale for your someday instruction, whoever you are—my fellow man, poor sod!—because I have found out where the powers of darkness reside.

We thirteen silly adolescents met that June day according to our bylaws in the clearing below Simon's Mound, and Rudi Zavier was talking to us, resting his hand on the Stone of Sacrifice. "You have been faithful, my twelve," he said. "You shall learn more about the Master of the Horns." If you listened to Rudi, already loving him, your common sense wouldn't be yours to use again until he said so. He was close to twenty, by several years the oldest of us, full of inner fires.

That day he wore a brass pin on his shirt, a cherry-and-hatchet symbol of St. George, the way any con-

172

ventional citizen might do. We knew Rudi scoffed at the Murcan Saints—it was part of our fun—but wearing such trash was what he called policy. He saw me look at the pin and took if off, grinning, making a half-motion as if wiping his arse with it, but his eyes were chilly, bits of blue sharp sky, probing us, searching and measuring. He was taller than any of us except me, but not weedy as I was—Rudi could bend the seven-foot bow. He stood by the Stone, easy and beautiful, and behind him rose the colossus, Mafairson's Oak.

I wonder if it still stands—but I'm not going back to Nupal. It was said to be the tree where they hanged Fiddler Mafairson for robbing the Kingstone mail coach in former days, and the brave fella broke his fiddle over a stone before they strung him up. Some claim it's only a story from an Old-Time song; and I don't know. That day a moody wind was intruding on our sheltered space. I thought of Mafairson's ghost, craving human sounds, interrupting them with a sigh.

The sun came out a moment on Rudi's bright hair. Almost white it was, silver spun to gossamer, an imitation of age above a face of youthful splendor, demonic, secret. Rudi (at the time I knew him, when his childhood was spent) was not one for explaining himself. Maybe he tried to when his mother was living. She was a big pale woman with suffering eyes, who died a year after his family moved to Nupal from Albani up in Moha.

That day maybe our youngest—fat Nell Kunak or Jo Makepeace or poor Jena Doren who never stopped loving Rudi—believed the sun came out because he summoned it. Not Piet Horver. I think that big unhappy boy, the only one of us who never laughed, was already feeling the Church drag him back from our

173

naughtiness. He had been the first member of the coven when Rudi started it, and worshiped Rudi fantastically for a while, but the bond was straining to the snapping point. Understand, my good readers of the future who may never exist, when I was a boy it was a common belief that witches could command the sun and moon, vagaries of storm and calm. And though today I see a few signs of reaction against such credulous nonsense, I promise you the multitudes will cherish it for a long time yet, for faith is easily generated, but the use of reason demands courage.

At seventeen I may not have believed that Rudi could dominate the sun and moon and rain. But there was a time when I think I would have jumped into the tarpits of Hell for him.

He had won me four years earlier, soon after he and his family came to Nupal. I was thirteen, all hands and feet and long bones—awkwardest damned boy in Nupal, my father said. Rudi won me by listening to my stumbling talk of becoming an explorer, when my sailor father couldn't hear it without a noisy snigger. And look you, for a few years I did that! In my early forties, as a Clerical in the company of only two scouts, I penetrated the southern jungle, marking out a new trail to the empire of Misipa. I know how its harbors gaze south over the sea, over the round turning world toward tropic-hearted Velen, cruel land of spices, coffee, mahogany, slaves for the brutal Misipan markets. But it's too late for me to go again, and I'll never sail to Velen. (Besides, those are other tales.) Four years after Rudi thus won me, I was still in subjection to his brilliance and power, my own will spellbound.

"You have been faithful," Rudi said to us. "When we formed this coven last year we swore loyalty. We haven't accomplished much yet—it had to be a time of testing. You've done nobly." We looked, we hoped, nobly modest. "I'm proud of you. No one has left our company nor betrayed our secrets—pity for him if he had!" According to our bylaws, the penalty for betrayal was death. I suppose none of us except Rudi (and maybe Piet Horver) had more than a dim idea of what we had agreed to there.

Our "secrets" included our naked romps and orgies in this clearing. At our feasts each of us was required to bring liberated goodies—liberated not just from family but from outside victims who might holler for the Nupal constables. And there were the sacrifices on the Stone under Mafairson's Oak. Stolen chickens mostly; but a month ago at the May meeting Elder Meehan's smelly old half-blind dog Prince had waddled along to the gathering at Jon Bright's heels and Jon had not been able to send him home. Poor fool, he shambled up to the slanted Sacrificial Stone, lifted his leg at it, and climbed on it gazing down at us, tongue dribbling. I remember milky spots where cataracts were forming on both his eyes; they were fuzzy at the iris and stupid with age. Before there was time for Jo Makepeace or any other softhearted one among us to protest, Rudi Zavier—no one else was allowed to touch the Sacrificial Knife—drove that knife into Prince's heart. Some of us trembled while his blood drenched the Stone.

(Elder Meehan, ancient and simple, searched all over town, speculating and grieving. We knew every pitiable move he made, and most of us were guilt-sick, but even little Jo Makepeace couldn't speak.)

I felt sometimes that Jo was with us as a sort of elfin observer. I don't mean a spy; I mean he inhabited the world itself like a stranger marveling at the darkness and occasional brightness of human ways. A fancy, of course—Jo was just a sweet kid with imagination, which is miracle enough, and maybe he let himself be drawn into Rudi's foolish coven because the poet in him wanted to discover what shadows are.

"Have I done wrong?" said Rudi, wiping the knife and smiling at us like bright death. "If so, let him who is without sin cast the first stone."

"How shall I become without sin?" That was Piet Horver, but what he said only began as a shout; it ended in a mumble, as Rudi walked to him and took hold of his fist, gently straightening the fingers.

"See, Piet," he said. "There's no stone."

If any townsman had found the Sacrificial Stone and the blood, other witches might have been blamed, though I doubt whether there were any in Nupal in our time; a hundred years earlier perhaps. Certainly in the remoter Katskil towns, deeper in the wilderness, witchcraft may well have been practiced. I wouldn't care to say it doesn't go on even nowadays, back in the hills. There's no mystery thicker than the things good people prefer not to mention.

Now at that June meeting in evening sunlight, Rudi said: "Because of your faithfulness I'll tell you one thing: what the Church says about the existence of only one god is the biggest of all the Church's lies. And soon I'll prove it to you."

We gaped—not at the notion of more than one god, which is probably natural to children, nor at the idea that the Church would tell fibs, but just at hearing Rudi put such things in words. We knew what would happen if any Church person heard him and passed on information to the College of Examiners at Nuber, that grim gang of inquisitors which was rapidly becoming the dread official conscience of all Katskil. Rudi's youth wouldn't save him from the bonfire. Public opinion might be saying no about witchcraft; not about heresy. We had also the thrilling second thought: *He is trusting us, saying to us what he would say to no others.*

And there was the mingy little chance that Jehovah *might* hear him, although thus far heaven had rudely ignored our toughest blasphemies. Believing in Lucifer does imply at least some belief in Jehovah. If you don't believe in a god, how can you defy him? The ones who truly don't believe, I 've noticed, are the only ones who don't get uptye about religion. (I'm giving this an entire chapter in my *History of Heresy.*) They leave the roaring and the acid forgiving to the true believers, and get on with their own affairs.

"There are many gods," Rudi said. "Little gods, great ones. Think of the thousands of happenings, all day long. How could one god deal with them?" To many of us ignoramuses this was a clincher. Jena Doren nodded her bright head; she had to believe that Rudi, who constantly hurt and humiliated her, couldn't be wrong. "But the one greatest of all gods is Lucifer, Master of the Horns—Lucifer, Son of the Morning. They say he fell from heaven, do they? Why, he rejected the god of heaven, found heaven to be a poor sorry place." Rudi spread his arms, holding us with his yearning, mocking eyes. A number of his tricks were borrowed from Father Rupet's pulpit mannerisms; more were his own. Rudi was original; the devil dwelling behind his eyes stayed consistent with itself, even to the end. (Remember, too, we were stuffed full of our juicy Third Century romances, those hell-love-and-disaster yarns that promise to bloom better than ever in the Fourth, with the growth

177

of printing houses and what passes for literacy.) "No, he didn't fall from heaven, my twelve. He flew down to us of his own free will, to be Lord of Hell and Lord of the Earth also—the Earth to which he brought the floods, the pestilence, the cleansing fire of Old Time—the Earth that he holds in the cup of his left hand."

I have heard more practiced soul-rousers since then, but none with Rudi's voice-music, his power to shove that voice under your skin till you felt on the edge of orgasm from sheer scare of goosepimples. "Serve him, serve the Master of the Horns! He is the lightning-fire of the dark!" He had us swaying and moaning, as the most devout Abramites do in church. The girls closed their eyes in ecstasy. I saw Anna Hiel's nipples stiffen under her thin smock, and she slid me a glance. "He is the spark in the tiger's eye." (Who cared about making sense out of Rudi's rhapsody?—the purpose was the music, not the meaning: it was our *Hear us, O Abraham* and our *Kyrie eleison*.) "He is the black wolf's cry, the blade of sacrifice, the blood that follows it. And you shall see him in the flesh."

He stopped, his silence shocking us out of our fuzzy trance. He was waiting and smiling. Rudi knew how to out-wait an audience. Then he leered and said in a luscious imitation of Father Rupet's cadence: "Ay-y-men." We laughed and pressed close with our questions.

Relaxed now and amiable, he said, oh, he just meant that at the next meeting we'd see him put on the attributes of Lucifer, that was all—yes, my good loves, including the horns—and when he did, the Master's spirit would enter him. He couldn't predict what he might then be obliged to do—we wouldn't mind kissing his arse, would we? He laughed, too, watching

178

us. In a true sense he would *be* Lucifer while the spirit made use of him.

The rest of that June meeting became an orgy as it grew dark. I chased Anna Hiels three times around the Oak and got her down squealing with her legs open. Jon Bright took her twice after I had spent. But we were uneasy, though we had sentinels posted. Maybe we felt ourselves under the regard of Lucifer and it chilled us, gave us the sense of something enormous, wanton, consuming, outside our trivial posturing and capering.

Adam Ganz, who loved boys, got into a fight with Piet Horver, who shouted that Adam's games with little Jo Makepeace were depraved—that from a witch! Sometimes we were more than comic. Rudi had to separate them when Piet earned himself a bloody nose and started to rave and cry. And Jena Doren fell to weeping, too, and couldn't stop, when we went through our Black Mass, the Maharba (Abraham said backwards), making her naked body the table for our mock communion.

Before the Fourth of July Night meeting, hell was loose in Nupal. Three young girls—Dora Mallon and Ethel Lyme, and Dasi Stiles, who was seventeen but queer in the head, or "tarded" to use a Katskil expression—were having fits and screaming of bewitchment. Dora and Ethel were cousins, and inseparable. Dora was a hunchback and for that reason suspected by some of being a mue, but the Church had let her live. Ethel's bland round face was purpled by a great birthmark on the left side. They had named no names, so far. When some fool asked whether one Mam Shiller might be responsible for their pitiable state, the wenches were supposed to have screamed louder.

179

At Sudler's Dairy, where Rudi and I were working that summer, Rudi told me our coven might be involved, if not up to the neck at least up to the balls. Dora Mallon, he told me, had suspected the existence of our group and approached him with hints, wanting to join. He had put her off with evasions. "She may have seen some of us, slipping away to Simon's Mounds," he said. "She's a bitch we don't need. Sharp, though. I don't think any of us would have betrayed the coven. Do you, Sam?" He was looking into me with ice-blue coldness. "Sam?"

"No, Rudi. No." His look changed then to one of dreaminess, and some kind of exhilaration. Rudi's job at Sudler's was a joke, possibly due to some democratic notion of his father's that it would be "good for the boy." The Zaviers lived in a great gloomy house with ten acres of fenced-in privacy and a mess of servants. But Rudi rather liked the work and it kept him in touch with me.

Here in my cozy cellars I have dug up and read some accounts of the Salem witchcraft episode of 1692, the addled trial, the hangings, the pressing to death of brave Giles Corey. In Nupal I suppose history was repeating itself with a big squeak, as it may easily do for any people who have discarded knowledge and kept no understanding of the past. In old Massachusetts, however, the madness was followed by a significant revulsion against that kind of emotional garbage: the outrages did clear the air. In Nupal we had no Robert Calef or Thomas Brattle to risk their necks by pillorying the holy ghouls with indignation and laughter.

Mam Shiller was a fierce old twice-widowed reprobate living in a shanty outside of town, off the old Kingstone Road (which hadn't gone through to the national capital since the earthquake of 260 and still doesn't). She kept chickens, a few goats, a garden cherished behind thick hedges. In her late forties, she was currently giving bed and board to a traveling tinker who had holed up with her, scandalizing the town. I never could see that she was depriving Nupal's good ladies of anything, except the tinker, who was perfectly useless.

Mam Shiller wouldn't have strangers near her garden; she believed their sole object was to trample her flower beds. She'd take out after them with a broom or anything else handy. She also believed the town was dead set against her, and in that of course she was right—they are always against the queer and the lonely.

Dasi Stiles may have started the outbreak. Dasi nourished an ungovernable passion for flowers. She didn't admire them—she ate them. They must have done her good, too, for she had the creamiest complexion of any chick in Nupal, along with the weakest mind. Mam Shiller had recently chased her a quarter mile with a pair of shears, Dasi chewing and strewing rose petals all the way. Slow to anger like any half-wit, Dasi did resent being chased, and I suppose Mam Shiller's roaring threats were impressive, though the old woman wouldn't have hurt a mouse. Dasi must have gabbled to the other girls.

All three were children of poor families in the shanty section, but when Dora toppled screaming and frothing on the church steps on Friday morning while the congregation was filing out, she got enough attention for minor nobility. Ask Baron Reilla—he was there, and gave a few orders.

They carried her across the street into the house of the Elder Meehan. His wife, Mam Clotilda, was as pious-vague and sweet and cloth-headed as he was, while his sister-in-law Miz Beulah saw to it that they remembered to eat and get up and go to bed. Left to himself, Elder Meehan would have sat reading the Book of Abraham until he dried up and blew away. The Meehans should have had children, everyone said. They made a huge tremulous fuss over afflicted Dora, and over Ethel who followed along shouting: "O my poor Dora, my darling, will they never cease a-persecuting you?"—at which words the people in their good church clothes did marvel. Baron Reilla remarked she could hardly have got them out of a romance book, since he didn't suppose she could read. And we all chewed on the fact that Ethel Lyme had said *they*. Ethel then flopped on the bed along with Dora, frothing and wailing like a skinned wildcat. Presently both were speaking with tongues—that's what the faithful call it when the gobbling sounds almost like words.

Dasi Stiles had squeezed in along with the rest of us. When the girls were well launched on that sad ecstasy, I'll be damned if Dasi wasn't down there prancing on all fours wagging her handsome big rump and barking like a dog.

Father Rupet tore over from the church, limping with his bad knee. At his arrival those three maidens really sucked up their lungs and tried for a record. I heard Ethel roaring, "Don't you dare touch me with that thing, you beast, you monster! I already said I wouldn't tell—*ooh, ooh, that hurts!*" I was crowded into a corner; being tall I didn't miss anything. Rudi was there, but didn't try to elbow forward; the girls may not have seen him. And then—I don't know quite how it started, or who asked the first question—

presently the name *Mam Shiller* was zizzing around the room like a captive hornet.

By evening Mam Shiller was secured in the town lockup. We heard she was to be tried when the Ecclesiastical Circuit Court arrived at Nupal in September. They said it required two men to get the chain fastened to her leg.

At the dairy, from the corner of his mouth as we were cleaning the milking stalls, Rudi said: "Those bitches are just warming up. They didn't name Mam Shiller first, they just picked it up. I don't know why Dora hasn't named us."

Men were nearby, pitching hay into the loft. I said in the same kind of voice: "Could she be trying to scare us, hoping to get admitted?"

"Jasus-Abraham!" He thought about it. "Just maybe. But I'm sorry for Mam Shiller. I'm sorry for her." I couldn't recall ever hearing him say that about anyone else; but the devil was shining out of him still, and that exhilaration.

"Could she be a witch, Rudi?"

"Mam Shiller?" Again I'd said something that made him think. "I don't think so, Sam. No, she's a victim. We ought to do something for her." He thought some more, and laughed under his breath. "Ayah, something to turn the bloody town upside down." He was standing on the milking platform; for a fact, that was the only thing that made him taller than me when he put his arm around my shoulder, but I felt him taller. I was remembering who and what would be occupying his body on Fourth of July Night and believing every bit of it. "My good love, are you with me? Sam?"

"What do you take me for? Of course I'm with you." Not smiling anymore, he asked: "To the death?"

"Of course, Rudi. . . . To the death."

"Sam, what happens if we're betrayed to the Gentiles?"

"Gentiles?"

He was impatient, shaking me; he'd taught us that word and I'd forgotten. "Gentiles means common folk, Sam. People like—oh, Elder Meehan, or even Baron Reilla, or my own crawling son of a bitch of a father." Rudi's father was a lawyer, bland and clammy, a busy deacon of the Church. I may have been the only person who knew how savagely Rudi hated him, for both masked their feelings in public very well—for that matter the deacon himself probably didn't know the whole of it, being so thickly concerned with his own righteousness that he may have seen those around him as not much more than animated dolls. Nobody could have liked rich and sanctimonious Deacon Zavier, nobody with any sense or warm blood, but Rudi's loathing went beyond anything I could imagine happening in my own insides. Rudi never spoke of his mother, that big sad-faced woman who was thought by some to possess the second sight. The deacon had remarried, a blowsy matron whom Rudi spoke of to me (and maybe not only to me) as The Sow. "So what happens if we're betrayed? Come on, Sam, think! We burn, don't we?"

Without thinking I made the sign of the Wheel, church-fashion. Rudi grabbed my wrist and forced me to make the circle out from the body and in, the witch way, instead of tracing it flat across the chest. You're supposed to make the witch motion with a closed fist too, middle finger stuck out to look like a cock. His eyes were probing at me unbearably, inches away. "But Rudi, there haven't been any burnings for—oh, for years. Since before we was born."

"Means nothing." He still had his arm around me.

184

"Hide your big dumb head if you got to." I could feel him using the contempt as a tool to push me around, and I couldn't be angry. "I was going to ask you to help me spring Mam Shiller, for that's what I'm going to do. But maybe you'd wish to be excused."

"I'm with you," I said, feeling all torn inside. "But Jasus-Abraham, Rudi, they got that lockup guarded day and night."

His eyes were spitting blue fire. "Buck Winters, night guard—if a flea goosed him he'd run a mile. My good Sam, I know one or two things about prison guards. You take my father for instance—he's sort of a prison guard, you might say, though too stupid to know it. I know one thing about prison guards, that's for *sure.*"

"All right—what?"

"They are mortal."

"Rudi! Rudi, you never would."

"Poor little Sam!" said that dear miserable devil, and he lifted up on his toes to kiss my cheek.

We got her free that same night, Rudi and I, with no word about it to the coven. Some of them, he remarked, were still mighty young, not to be counted on as much as he'd led them to believe when he was speechmaking. Me?—I was just about old enough to know I was being flattered by that confidence.

We stole down to the lockup wearing black cloth masks and tight caps to hide our hair, after midnight when the town was in bed. Rudi had been watching the lockup for two nights, and knew the guard Buck Winters' habits to the last yawn. The building was a small thing in a scrubby yard back of the town hall, approached by an alley; they'd had no one in it for years but an occasional tramp or drunk, and now no one but Mam Shiller. All we had to do was wait in the bushes near the back wall until Buck waddled out to take a leak. When he was squared away at the wall Rudi slid out shadow-soft and sapped him with a stone in a sock. You can kill a man easily with one of those, but we were lucky, or else somehow Rudi knew just how hard to hit without finishing him. Buck was tall as well as fat, but with not much muscle. I had the gag crammed in his mouth and tied back of his thick neck before he finished collapsing. He was already coming around by the time we had him blindfolded, legs and arms trussed. Rudi told him to stop moaning or he'd get gut-sliced; he stopped it. Then Rudi hissed in his ear: "We are of the Old Religion." A tremor shook his whole carcass; he couldn't answer but he went on breathing. Rudi snatched the key ring off his belt and we were inside.

There was a cubbyhole office for the guard, a storeroom, and a corridor with two cells, both empty. I carried the small lamp from the office for Rudi. Mam Shiller was crouched on a foul heap of straw, chained to the wall, and poor soul, she was naked. While Rudi was getting the cell door open she probably saw our masks. She said: "I can't tell you anything. Don't hurt me any more."

"Nay, we're friends." And to me Rudi said: "Go find her clothes. Take the lamp."

"O my lordagod!" she said. "O my good loves!"

"Nay, Mother, don't talk now. We'll get you out."

"O Jesus and Abraham! They've hurt me some, my good loves. Will I have to walk far?"

As I went to look for the clothes I heard him say: "Not far, Mother—nay, I don't know, it might be far." I had never heard him call any other old woman

Mother, though it's a common thing in Katskil. "You're not safe in Nupal," he said—"ever, I guess."

Her clothes weren't to be found, not in the office nor in a ghastly storeroom, where I blundered into a heap of rusty tools dating from the old days that the Church says need never come again—all we have to do is trust in the faith and pay the taxes and the tithes. When I returned to the cell Rudi had unlocked her leg iron. He still wore his cap and mask, so I kept mine. "No clothes. Nowhere."

Rudi was furious. but it was like him not to lash out at me or go looking where I'd looked. Mam Shiller was crying. "It's all right, boys—I won't try to find out who you are. I guess you're the good angels—you got fresh young voices like boys—never mind, I won't ask, I'll do anything you say. Is my man waiting for me? My Wat?"

That was the tinker. I never knew a last name for him. Nobody had glimpsed him since her arrest. "Gone," Rudi said. "He's no good."

"O my lordagod, don't say that!—no, never mind, I expect it's so, I never counted on him for nothing. A'n't anybody seeing to my goats, my little hens? They won't tell me."

"The town took them, Mam," I told her, talking soft like Rudi through the bottom of my mask. She looked at me keenly as if she might have recognized my voice, but I felt she'd never tell.

"The town," she said—"oh, the town, their balls can rot off and drop in the jakes, I won't cry. But boys, I can't travel without no clothes. I'm not decent."

"Wait," he said, "sit calm." He jerked his head at me. We slipped outside and skinned the clothes off Buck Winters and dressed him up again in the ropes. He

187

was wide awake now, eyes rolling, but he played it safe and chewed quiet on his gag.

"All right," she said, and chuckled. "They got a p'ison smell of polis about 'em, but we can't be choosers. It's my back hurts where they broke a stick onto me." She supported herself on Rudi's shoulder while she struggled into the trousers. They were tight for her in the leg but not in the rump, for old Buck had a spread bottom like a lump of warm butter.

"Have you friends outside of Nupal, Mam Shiller?" Rudi was treating her like a lady and she knew it. There was a big streak of gentleman in Rudi; I don't think he got it from his father.

"Ah, by the last hear-tell I heard, my old father's still alive in Maplestock. Used to say himself he was too mean to die. He'll be gone seventy, or past."

"Go home to him," says Rudi, gentle and mild. "He'll take you, won't he, Mam?"

Strength was rising in her just from the taste of freedom, though she'd been miserably beaten and likely half starved. "He'll take me," she said, "or I'll sit howling on his doorstep. Look you, there's milk-and-egg money under a stone in my garden if the town ha'n't smelled it out. Wat never knew about it. If it's there it's yours. Under the second flat stone behind the rodidenders."

"No, you'll need that, we won't take it. We'll see you safe up there, and then you better be off for Maplestock across country, and fast. But don't risk the roads after sunup, and wade upstream a piece through Myler's Brook, in case they go for dogs."

She was crying and blessing us. We got her moving, and out past the naked guard. She would have gone by him in the night dark, but Rudi stopped there. I could feel an ugliness rising, and when I put my hand on his arm he was tight as a drawn seven-foot bow, and breathing hard as if something hurt too much. "This bag of crap here," he said—"remind you of anybody?"

I remembered how he had talked wild about his father being like a prison guard, and I snatched hold of that frozen arm, my own strength surprising me. "*No!*" I said. "It's nothing but old Buck Winters, and you know it. Come on—we got to help Mam Shiller get clear." I think it was anyone's guess for a minute whether old Buck would live or die, but the moment crawled past and Rudi was coming along with us.

We saw Mam Shiller safe through the spooky sleeping town, as far as her shanty. It had already taken on that horrible haunted look that comes to any dwelling just because people have stopped caring; we stumbled over trash in the yard that looters had left there, and the shanty door was swinging wide and groaning under a little breeze. She found her money safe, though, and then we saw her a short way on the road to Maplestock, Rudi making her promise again to take to the woods before sunrise, and wade through Myler's Brook.

Maybe that moment with the bound guard was the first time I had thought of Rudi in words like "mad." And yet I loved him.

They made a wonder of it that grew every time Buck Winters told the story—that is, eight or ten times a day. Rudi had not only turned the town upside down, he'd shaken it, with just those few words whispered to Buck about the Old Religion. According to Buck, he *counted* five witches, and they made him climb the roof of the town hall, driving him with whips and pins. Given a week, good old Buck would

189

have worked in a trip around the moon. But another wonder crowded us, at about the time people were getting tired of listening to Buck.

Two mornings after we sprang Mam Shiller, Dora Mallon was found strangled in an alley near the shanty where she had lived with her parents; Ethel Lyme had disappeared. They had been last seen together, the evening before, walking toward Main Street on the way to the church, where Father Rupet was to hold a prayer meeting for guidance concerning their bewitchment and the prodigy of Mam Shiller's escape. They would have had to pass the opening of that alley.

Rumor and speculation fed the town's thunderstorm of terror. My own storm was worse. I lay awake all night after the discovery, maybe for fear that a nightmare would show me the truth, but I thought I knew it anyway. Rudi never came to work at the dairy that day, nor the next. Fourth of July Night was coming on, and to me that meant other nightmares.

The people did search for Ethel Lyme, but Nupal is a small town in a pocket of heavily wooded hills, several thousand acres of them. Search all the trails, gullies, thickets, bear dens? How?

The majority were convinced that Mam Shiller had murdered Dora, likely with supernatural help. Buck Winters, of course, was a wholehearted spokesman for that party. By then I'm sure he devoutly believed in his witches himself, all five of them. But some began remembering out loud that bland-looking Ethel Lyme possessed large hands and strong fingers, good at kneading bread dough. Those people also had it on firm authority that the Devil, given entrance to the body of a victim who (knowingly or not) invites him, can make that subject do just anything, even to murdering a close friend. Or it might be, they said (anxious to preserve good feeling), that Devil-occupied Ethel and Mam Shiller were out there working together. The upshot of all this earnest thinking was that nobody cared about scouring the woods even in a party of twenty with dogs.

After the third day of the so-called search for her, Dasi Stiles reported seeing Ethel Lyme chased by a big man with horns all the way to the beach of the Hudson Sea, where she grew fins on her arms and escaped him under water. Questioned eagerly by Father Rupet and other experts, Dasi smiled in her sweetest empty manner and said, why yes, sure, she dreamed it—thus making the public all the more certain of the vision's truth. There is no means, Confucius said, of persuading the human race not to believe whatever it chooses to.

Deacon Zavier announced to his respectable friends and clients: "You know, after all, there's got to be Something Out There." Or maybe he said "Something Up There." The views of a man with that kind of income are invariably sound.

And speaking of Deacon Zavier, I learned on that third day after the murder that the deacon had told Sudler's Dairy Rudi wouldn't be coming to work any more. He was going to stay home and read law with his loving father, and go to the University at Nuber in the autumn. This made no sense to me whatever, for Rudi hated the law as he did his father. Indeed I have never quite understood why Rudi, almost twenty, detesting his father and stepmother, hadn't struck out for himself long before. No opportunity to speak of in Nupal, but all Katskil was available. He could have found work anywhere and taken care of himself. What bound him? Not Jena Doren—I think girls to him were

191

little more than creatures to be used. Love along with the hate? He had it too soft there at the Zavier house, three carriages, a butler, and all that bit? Oh, I do myself no good with these questions now, when Rudi has been dead for going on thirty-five years.

After quitting work that third day I saw them walking together on Main Street, the deacon marching as usual like a well-fed secretary of the Lord, Rudi slouching half a pace behind. Rudi gave me a quick headshake, so I only waved to him from across the street; the deacon didn't even nod—he had to keep his recognition uncontaminated, for important people. I couldn't read Rudi, in that glimpse. Captive? Change of heart? Lying low? I couldn't read him at all.

In Rudi's place Sudler hired Jon Bright. Jon was rather big on muscle and short on brain, a nice kid. Like me he was a First Member of the coven and full of wonder at all Rudi's doings. Jon confirmed what I had already heard—none of our lot was getting through to Rudi. Jena Doren and Jo Makepeace went to the big house trying to see Rudi and were turned away by the acid old butler: Mister Rudi was busy with his law books and could not be disturbed, bang!

Jon and I met with a few of the others on the third of July, a fret session. Without Rudi our courage softened; we might be dangerous witches, but nobody was about to take on the Zavier establishment, certainly not when the town was in a lather about Mam Shiller's escape, Dora's murder, Ethel Lyme's disappearance. We agreed to keep the meeting date the following night, and couldn't think beyond that. What we would do if Rudi didn't show we hadn't a notion.

I think we were all feeling—Jon and Adam Ganz and Jo and Anna Hiels and I—that we had been following a dream, maybe a childish one, into a country of experience where dreams of that kind can't live. Or we had worn out our old fantasies and needed new.

Dora Mallon's body had been publicly viewed at the parlor of the Nupal Mourners' Guild. Father Rupet fancied himself a scholar of Old-Time lore—he called it Lost Knowledge and I think he sometimes tiptoed a little bit close to heresy—and somewhere he had happened on the legend that if a murderer approached the corpse of his victim the dead flesh would betray him—wounds would open and bleed, and so on. Nothing like that happened. But we all did file past the bier, practically everyone in Nupal who could walk, including Rudi in his father's company. We all saw the green-purple bruises on Dora's young throat, and the terrible mouth. And we of the coven wanted out.

The Fourth of July Night arrived in weeping darkness, with black overcast and flurries of rain. The time of our appointment was midnight, and we all came there, all twelve of us, sneaking out of our houses and groping through the wet woods. Adam Ganz told me nobody had seen Rudi all day. Adam had brought a pail of coals, so we started a fire under the tree cover in spite of the occasional drizzle. It reddened the clearing and showed us grimacing faces and lewd designs in the ancient bark of Mafairson's Oak, but we got little warmth from it because of a coldness inside us. We talked some, hush-voiced. Adam Ganz tended the fire, and Jo kept close to him for comfort. My mother, who was a cure-woman from Tappan, had taught me a little about telling time from the moon—any fool can read it from the sun—and I had passed on the tricks of it to Rudi. I knew it was drawing on close to midnight; if Rudi was anywhere about he would know it too. The actual moment would be told us by the beautiful voice of Nupal's town bell two miles away across the pastures and the woods.

"He won't come," said Anna Hiels. "His Da's got him hog-tied. It's all crap anyway." She wouldn't have said that, or thought it, two days earlier.

"Maharba!" said Jena Doren, who never forgot any of the words that Rudi had taught her. "You think Deacon Zavier's got any power to stop Lucifer if the god is a-mind to—"

"Hush!" said Jon Bright. He had the sharpest hearing of any of us, but soon we all heard it, a dreadful small whimpering sound from deeper in the woods, like a hurt cat, or a child trying not to snuffle. It came closer by slow intervals. We couldn't speak or think; we were just suffering ears, and once or twice we heard a rustling and shifting of underbrush. We had turned our eyes away from our fire. We tried to pierce the wet forest blackness, and we searched for I don't know what—gold-green eyes, red eyes maybe, set high above ground and approaching like certain damnation. But we found nothing except the dark and the timorous-fluttering shadows of our own small fire. The whimpering ceased, and the noises of motion too, for the longest silence I have ever endured.

Then the bell. Twelve clear strokes, human and brave, reaching us through the rainy night—but they were also the signal for Lucifer to come to us; and he was coming.

He parted the bushes and stepped forth monstrous toward our fire, his masked head lifting high the horns, black and inward-pointing, and he led a victim slowly to the Stone by a cowhide rope. His shoulders bulked huge and shaggy, and his hairy loins sprouted a prodigious phallus that glinted in the firelight now dead white, now scarlet.

Painted wood, of course. I knew that. I knew it was Rudi, just Rudi. I knew the horror on his head was nothing but a pair of woods-buffalo horns, likely some wall trophy of his father's strapped clumsily in place, and the shag at his shoulders and hips was simply hacked off from a buffalo rug, and the priapus probably carved and painted by himself—poor Rudi was never very good with his hands. I knew all that, and so did most of the others. Why, we knew it and we didn't know it. Proving that an image is a fraud will not necessarily convince the credulous that the original of the likeness does not exist, and in this they follow a fair logic.

Lucifer's victim was Ethel Lyme, what was left of her after three days of captivity and isolation without food or drink. We learned afterward that she had spent that time tied and gagged in Mam Shiller's shanty where no one dared go after Mam Shiller's supernatural liberation. There Ethel had stayed in misery, probably remembering the sight of her friend's murder, until Lucifer came horned and masked and shaggy to lead her to the Stone of Sacrifice. As for Lucifer, why, he had been detained at home or he might not have left her so, detained to read law books until he managed his escape on the Fourth of July Night. Did Lucifer's father suspect who he was?—it's possible. I never held any conversation with Deacon Zavier, never desired any.

Ethel's wits were totally confused, gone with shock. She was so dirty and tear-stained, the remnant of her dress so ruined, that without the birthmark we might not even have recognized her—pinched too, somehow fallen in on herself. She was reduced to the mindless

195

whimpering we had heard, and she lurched ahead obediently as Lucifer tugged the rope that was tied around her hands.

Jo Makepeace said: "*No!*" He ran to Ethel and struggled at the cowhide binding her hands. The god Lucifer roared at him in amazed fury and swung his black sharp horns, and I think little Jo, fighting the cowhide rope with no help from witless Ethel, was not even aware of it. He knew well enough who and what Lucifer was, by then.

I can't guess how much further we might have let it go, but for Jo Makepeace. As it was, his single-handed act of honest outrage got through to us, shamed us out of witchcraft for good. Whatever meanness or foolish wickedness we might stumble into in later times, it wouldn't be that. And then—no blame to Jo, who took no part in it—we went too far the other way in reaction: savages we were, and one brave kid couldn't change that.

The story's really over. I'll write the end as quickly as I can.

Adam Ganz snatched the other end of the rope out of Lucifer's grasp and shouted to us: "Hell, it's nothing but Rudi dressed up! Who's afraid of him?" I heard Jo say, clear and urgent: "Ethel, Ethel! Wake up! We're going to take you home." Then he and Adam were hurrying away with her—as they passed beyond the firelight I saw Adam scoop her up in his arms—and paying no heed to us, and certainly none to the mighty god Lucifer, who just stood there.

Anna Hiels cried: "*He* killed Dora Mallon! Look you, who else?"

And someone else yelled: "Stone him! *Stone him!*"

Someone else?—why it was Jena Doren who screamed that, over and over. And still I think that in

196

her own way she never did stop loving him: it was only the other side of the mirror. Maybe I still loved him too, even knowing what he had done to Dora Mallon, what he had done and would have done to Ethel Lyme. And I know (in my age, here in the cellars) that it is a great human folly to love the image, the aura of glamor that may hang about someone, instead of searching for the human self that may be someone altogether different from the dream.

Jena Doren yelled that; Piet Horver was the first to obey her, sweeping up a rock in his big fist and howling: "This in Christ's name! This for a murderer! This in Abraham's name!"

He hurled it true. It struck and knocked away the horns of Lucifer, who was Lucifer no more but only terrified Rudi, who couldn't understand what had happened, who called urgent things to us that our shouting drowned, and who then made the fearful mistake of running.

There were stones in all our hands. I saw Jena's arm swing. Hate and love were in us. Most of all there was fear, finding its voice in Jena's screaming. Rudi was lost, he was down.

I try to think there was love in me, or at least pity along with my panic terror, my resentment, my mindless need to make an end, when the stone left my own hand. For he saw me throw it, and after that blow he moved no longer.

Piet Horver became a priest, a good one I suppose, a missionary to the Salloren savages of the north country. Ethel won back her wits in a year or so, such as they were, and married a farmer. Jena married too—I think; it would have been after I left Nupal. Dear Jo Makepeace—ah, he grew up awhile, and went to the University, and became a poet, and died young.

197

MY BROTHER LEOPOLD

1
*Memorandum from Jermyn Graz, Frater Litera-
tus & Precentor, to his Beneficence Alesandar
Fitzeral, O.S.S., Abbot of St. Benjamin's at Mount
Orlook in the Province of Ulsta, November 21,
465.*

My dear Lord Abbot:

Your Beneficence has graciously requested information in writing concerning the life of my brother Leopold Graz, thirty-eight years deceased, for the attention of the Examiners from the Holy City when they
determine his spiritual status, whether the Church
shall declare him beatified. My days of delay have
been spent in prayer, wondering how best to comply.
In spite of time, my brother's death is new to me as
yesterday; I am troubled and uncertain.

For longer than I wish to recall, I have been more
an observer than a participant in the sorrowful com-
edy. I will try to write a narrative as simple as the
rings of a tree trunk. I have lived a long time, as my
brother Leopold did not, since we played together as
boys with Jon Rohan and Sidney Sturm, the four of us
a natural company, ever loyal (we thought)—one for
all and all (we thought) for one. I think I would have

198

died for any of them, certainly for Sidney, as we swore our readiness to do one day when Jon snagged his pinkie on a thorn and we hurried to make use of the fine fresh gore for writing purposes. Oh, how long ago!—I am bald and slow and wrinkled, and tonight my joints pain me.

I have made the common pilgrimages—to Filadelfia, Albani, the shrines of Conicut and Levannon. I never made the long pilgrimage in Abraham's footsteps to the Old City of Nuin on the Atlantic, but I saw that ocean once, when I traveled as a young man to the highland from which one sees the Black Rocks emerge at low tide like scarecrows in the mouth of the Hudson Sea, and beyond them the great waters. I have beheld other marvels, including adult loyalties that warmed me—but I don't find these more intense than those of boyhood, or less frail; seldom as joyous, since adult loyalties may be stained by cynicism, weariness, second thoughts.

I have been for fifteen years precentor here under your tranquil rule. You will remember I was a monk, inscribing after my name the good letters O.S.S.,* long before that. I am also proud of my secular name Jermyn Graz, for our artisan father came from an agrarian family descended from a commune of Old Time; yet I am content to be only your devoted Fr. Jermyn, precentor of this Abbey.

My brother Leopold was born December 13, 405. Thirty-eight years ago, in the reign of Emperor Mahonn and the patriarchate of Urbanus II, he was arrested under the name of Brother Francis, charged with treason, and transferred after ten months' imprisonment to the Ecclesiastical Court at Nuber on suspi-

* Ordo Sancti Silvani.

cion of heresy. And as you know, he was tried, condemned, and executed at Kingstone, October 28, 427.

I have never had the privilege of reading the trial transcript, but my memory lives. When they bound him to the stake the sky did darken and a torrent flooded the streets; the soldiers were obliged to pour oil on the faggots. Some murmured that this showed disregard for God's voice in the storm, but then the crowd fought in the usual way, trampling and shoving to snatch magic relics from the ashes.

None of our family survives him but myself. Our father died years before Leopold's execution, and our mother still longer ago, when Leo was seven. I think the Examiners may disregard the rambling of my mother's sister Lora Stone, who thinks my mother had had no carnal knowledge of our father Louis Graz in the nine months before Leopold's birth, but was impregnated by fire from heaven. My aunt is very old, fumbling at the past like a child with broken playthings. She did not come to live with us until a year after my mother died.

We are taught that none can be born without sin; that every birth delays the Liquidation, our destiny. But sometimes I sinfully wish I might have held in my arms a child of my brother Leopold.

And I am ravaged by doubts, my Lord Abbot, especially on summer nights after Matins when I should be attentive at prayer. I fall to imagining this earth not liquidated but inhabited by a people changed, no longer constantly at war nor obsessed by greed and fear, a people such as my brother spoke of as dwelling in a City of Light. They would deal charitably; they would enjoy their days. They might one day recapture the lost skill of Old Time and journey to the stars—but then I recall how little can be left of the resources of

200

earth that made this conceivable in Old Time, and I am back in the old cobwebbed halls of human folly without a candle. I have never mentioned these doubts in confession; I have hugged the small sin to myself for comfort, until now this question of my brother's sainthood has smoked me out. The study of history (under Church guidance) has been my life. I am forced to see Old Time as an age when men, by their own written admission, had so wasted and befouled the earth that it could no longer support their fearsome numbers, and nature cut them down with war, plague, famine, and that bearing of sterile monsters which nowadays follows intercourse like a tax paid to Hell. And still I persist in wondering whether folly must always be our nemesis. To me the beauty of earth, of its other dwellers less arrogant than man, often appears more sublime than our grandest achievements. Where nature spreads a floor of loveliness we scrape our feet and shit on it.

[*In the brittle faded original of this letter by Jermyn Graz the foregoing paragraph is marked by a marginal line and exclamation point, probably conveying indignation. This mark was undoubtedly made by Wilmot Breen, a justice of the Ecclesia and the ranking prelate of the Nuber Examiners in 465, for his initials in the same script and ink are attached to other marginal notes further on.*]

I know we are taught that in a few years the elect shall be taken into heaven and all others submerged as if they had never been, when the oceans rise entirely above the dry land, and the world as we have known it passes away, a drop of water in the firmament. Still, when the nights are in summer and I hear

201

the sad-merry clash of the crickets and katydids and trill of frogs in the moist woods beyond the monastery walls—my lord, I wonder and I wonder.

I alone live to remember Leopold as a child. Jon Rohan died in 435 from after-effects of a wound received in the War of 426–429. I lost Sidney before that: a devoted young doctor, he died in 430, the year of the red plague that followed the Moha War—a return, some say, of the epidemic that did so much to destroy the society of Old Time. I alone recall the voice of the boy Leopold in the choir of the Kingstone Cathedral, how it soared.

Here was a day of 413: Leopold seven, I fourteen, Jon Rohan twelve, Sidney fifteen. We met a black-browed Gypsy, old and horny-footed, in a meadow by Twenyet Road; we were wandering, not far from home.

We had been trained to fear and avoid Gypsies, as children are usually guarded against any strangeness that might illuminate the strangeness within themselves. We saw a sagging wagon in the meadow, a crowbait tethered on succulent grass, and would have slipped past. Something of mirage or phantasm was in the heaviness of the afternoon. It was that pregnant month, July. Before we saw the wagon, Leopold had been singing for us, casually; we had noticed a hawk high in the blue.

The Gypsy sat motionless on the gray stump of a tree beside the road, wearing a dull loinrag and colorless sandals. His knotty flesh was brown like the earth behind him, his gray hair speckled white like the quills of a porcupine. He had a shoulder satchel; a clay pipe dangled in his hand unlit. I smelled sweat and coarse Conicut tobacco.

I am not fey. I was born for the prosaic life, pas-

202

sions and marvels passing me as a parade might wind down the road past a child who cannot open the window and call. But I have a more than natural sense for stress and change in others. I knew Jon was startled by the Gypsy and hostile. Sidney was startled too, but pleasantly, the sweetness of his nature responding to anything that showed no enmity. I knew my brother Leopold felt a recognition outside my understanding, as if in some territory out of time where he and the grizzled Gypsy could meet as contemporaries with a shared language.

The Gypsy asked: "Would any of you gentlemen possess a tinderbox? Mine's in my wagon and I too lazy to go stumping after it."

I had a fine new one, a present from my father. Up I stepped, and when the old man had tamped in fresh tobacco I made a light for him, my sliver of flame stabbing down into the gurgling bowl. Sidney stood near, and I knew his thought was for my safety, but the Gypsy was smiling with all dusty wrinkles. "I thank you."

I said as I'd been taught: "It's nothing—you're welcome."

"Welcome—that's a variety of love, ain't it?"

His question seemed directed at Sidney, the oldest of us, the kind one, slim and golden in the sun. Sidney smiled. Jon was standing apart and frowning, working his toes in the dust.

"So everything comes from nothing," said the Gypsy, "and that's what makes the world go round? Am I right, Youngest?" This to Leopold, who had ducked in under my arm. Either Leopold nodded or the Gypsy pretended he had. "I'm right," he said, puffing, and it's not a bad arrangement, for if the world quit going round wouldn't we fly off like beads from the end of a busted string?" Then he lifted some articles from his satchel and displayed them in the palm of his left hand. "Anyhow, I suppose I'm among gentlemen who believe the world is round. True, Youngest?"

My little brother said: "My name's Leopold."

"Why, that's a sensible answer." Then the Gypsy's gaze was piercing me. "My Ma named me Aleites. You'll be Leopold's brother." Seldom did others notice a resemblance. In those days I was sandy blond; Leopold's hair was dark as walnut. Our other features differed: Leopold had a straight nose, a glorious high arch of brow; my nose was always puggy, my lips too full. But that Gypsy saw our brotherhood. "And the name people call you—?"

"Jermyn."

"Light and welcome—I must make you a return." He was moving his big right hand over his left, jumbling the oddments there like one preparing a throw of the dice. "Jermyn, I'd have you choose one from this lot—alas, worthless as men measure things in the marketplace. Choose something to please all your blithe company." I stared at his palm, incapable of decision; it looked big as a plowed field. "Here, for instance, my dear, is a bit of a garnet—I don't claim it gives the wearer invisibility; we're sensible people, aren't we? Here's the milk tooth of a chimera, which some say confers bravery if worn next the skin—I don't say it, of course. And this gold phallus no bigger'n a thumbnail—perky, ain't it? Made for a king's son likely, the way every wench he met in his travels was *supposed* to jump out of her skin to please him, since we all know that next to a big one they like a gold one; but I never tried it out, don't actually know a thing about it. I never guarantee a blessed thing;

204

that's why I'm a successful businessman." His old nag nickered at that, and he had the grace to look embarrassed.

I grew desperate. I thought Jon might like the chimera's milk tooth; he was always for games that tested our company's bravery, maybe from a need in himself to prove he was brave enough to meet the world head-on. Jon's father was a captain of engineers in the Second Ulsta Regiment, a loud, urgent man. I would have done anything to please Sidney, but couldn't imagine what he might like out of that jumble. Then I saw how my brother's eyes yearned at one thing there, a thing the Gypsy hadn't even mentioned.

This was a lump of clay no longer than my thumb, a trifle stouter, so worn by time you needed a second look to understand it was sculpture, the stylized figure of a little human male with arms folded against his chest, hands flat to the body. And on the other side of the lump—the Gypsy turned it over for me—was a woman's figure sharing the clay body, her face brooding like the man's and mild. I glanced again at Leopold, touched the image, said: "That."

The Gypsy gave me the dingy thing and dribbled the other objects back into his bag. Oh, the glitter of them, the gleam of what I might have had! "You've made the strange choice," he said. "Heaven knows what will come of it, or maybe Heaven doesn't know."

"That's heresy," said Jon Rohan.

"It's heresy," said the Gypsy, "or it's an outlander's way of talking, meaning no harm. Pipe's out—back to work. Bless you and good morning to you, gentlemen." He shambled off to his wagon, and we four straggled back home with our thoughts.

Leopold asked: "Maybe I can keep it for you?" So I

gave him the image, wishing it were any of a thousand better things.

Many times since then I have held the image before me, and it has taken me into contemplation; then I am like one caught up to the arch of heaven with no company but the falling stars. In his own fashion my brother must have responded for a while to this same power of the clay. I remember how lovingly he first dropped it into the pocket of his blouse and held a protective hand over it, as another child might cherish a pet. It was only a little later that I began hearing about Leopold's Companion, concerning whose existence the Church Examiners, I suppose, will wish more light.

My brother shared the bed with me in our attic room, a dear fidgeting nuisance. Our mother loved him best: this I had always known as children do know it. But the years that brought him out of babyhood carried her into exhaustion and invalidism, no strength left for contending with small boys. Losing her in these dim ways, we found each other. By the time Leopold was five I think my jealousy had dissolved in fondness, answering his natural warmth. Whether darker feelings still smoldered I cannot say—it was long ago.

The night after our meeting with the Gypsy, Leopold bounced under the covers holding the image, lost it during sleep, went frantic hunting for it in the morning. When we salvaged it from the bedclothes, he put it on a string to wear at his neck—not good, for the image was worn so smooth it had hardly a projection for the cord to hold. For Leopold's eighth birthday, Jon and Sidney and I collaborated on a solution. Sidney, brilliant with his hands, carved a box of applewood with a secret fastening; Jon bought a delicate silver chain in an antiquity shop—it cost him two months' allowance—and I joined the chain to the box in my father's workshop. Leopold was speechless with joy, opening and shutting the mysterious catch forty times a day. I have the box still, and the image secure in its nest that Sidney made, his magic as good as ever after half a century.

Our mother was going through a cruel pregnancy. Her time came on her not long after that day we met the Gypsy. For several weeks her illness had brought Leopold and me more than ever together; but there were times when he seemed utterly alone, in unchild-like contemplation of the image. Silent in a corner of the cobbler shop, he could have been on the other side of the stars.

Our house was one of the many shabby-genteel ones that cluster along the Twenyet Road in King-stone. The Old-Time city of the same name stood southeast of there, now mostly underwater of course. We lived about three miles from Rondo's Shrine, where the Old-Time course of the Twenyet Road takes it under Lake Ashoka. The modern detour curves over higher ground to meet the old road emerg-ing. In many places one still finds the gray rubbish, curious Old-Time road material, frost-heaved, pried loose, dumped out of the way. This work of clearance and improvement was done, I believe, more than a hundred years ago in the era of construction after Kat-skil became an Empire.* Farther out in the country, much of the gray junk has been hauled off by farmers to add to their stone fences. A great deal more of the

* Cf. *Harker Sidon, Old-Time Survivals in Imperial Katskil, Filadelfia College Press, 748. But Professor Sidon is mainly con-cerned with the physical survivals; one must look elsewhere for discussion of the mental inheritance.*

repulsive indestructible garbage of Old Time might be put to some use, if we would exercise more ingenuity.

Our section of the Twenyet Road was called The Crafts, because so many artisans lived there to catch the trade of travelers entering the city. Father was a shoemaker, dark-gloomy like the tanned hides he labored with, strict with Leopold and me in matters of decorum and truthtelling, but strict with justice and not unkind. He was one of those who fend off love with a grunt and then admit it anyway.

Our mother was soft, no disciplinarian. She enjoyed those romances the Church approves for the common people, for unlike our father she had learned to read, at a wise woman's school in her native village; sometimes housework waited while she dwelt in a storyteller's daydream—who could begrudge it to her? Between my birth and Leo's she had borne two mues. It was at her insistence that Father sent me to Mam Sola's day school in Kingstone, where I met Sidney and learned my letters and arithmetic. I have always been grateful for it: a little reading may prove a key to great reading. I cannot help thinking, my Lord Abbot, that a fairly widespread literacy might usefully supplement our Imperial Program of Universal Education.

I know nothing about those other two mues. This late pregnancy our mother was suffering was terminated by the birth of a monster, a twelve-pound hulk of flesh with four arms and, the priest told me later, no anus. He had quickly smothered the thing as the law requires, and it must have been buried quickly too, in the dark and without any ceremony, as is proper, in that sad tombless yard—Mues' Acre—that every church must maintain beyond the limits of its natural

208

cemetery. But while Fr. Colin disposed of it, the midwife could not prevent our mother from bleeding to death.

During this ordeal I was in the attic room charged with keeping Leopold out of the way. He was beside himself when the screaming began, though he heard my explanations. I held him fast and said over and over: "They're trying to help her." His heart hammered and his eyes were blind. We heard a last scream, beyond bearing, a flurry of voices, quick footsteps, orders. I must have relaxed my grip, for Leopold tore free and rushed downstairs. I caught up with him in the kitchen. Fr. Colin, that sardonic old man who always befriended me, was wrapping the thing in a cloth, but did not get it out of sight swiftly enough. Leopold saw it, and collapsed.

"Get him outside, Jermyn," said Fr. Colin. "Fresh air will bring him back to this delightful world." I carried him out into the moonlit splendor of a field behind our house. I kissed him and talked to him. He roused when I moved the locket with the clay image because it was making a hurting hardness between him and me. His eyes opened; he was back with me, gripping the amulet as if it were a bridge to life. "It's all right," I said. "It's all right, Leo." We both knew it was all wrong. Leo at eight understood how our human talk uses these flat reversals of reason. "Happens all the time—the priest says it's the will of God because men were so wicked in Old Time." I went on till I ran out of respectable words.

His night eyes watched me. He took the image from its box and studied it in the white light, turning it from male to female side and back. "Jermyn, why can't people make babies the way grapevines do?" Startled, I laughed. "You might've rested a part of you on the ground till I grew out of it and it was time to cut me free." He knew he was talking absurdly. He said: "I'll preach when I grow up."

"Well, sure. Mother's always wanted you to be a priest."

"No, I won't be a priest. But I'll preach. I'll say it about the grapevines. It's a—a—" Maybe he wanted to say "parable" and didn't have the word. "And I'll tell about the City of Light. The Companion will teach me how."

"The Companion?"

"He came yesterday when I looked at Two-Face. He stands where light and dark come together." He watched me as if he longed to explain further and could not. It was no play-acting. We were too close for that, in spite of the seven years; when any play-acting was to be done, we shared it.

I said: "Tell me about him. Please. What does he look like?"

"Not always the same. Only a voice sometimes."

I was frightened, and lacerated by jealousy. I saw this Companion taking Leopold away—as perhaps he did, even if we grant him existence only in my brother's mind. I asked: "What is the City of Light?"

"A place the Companion knows." He said no more, but he was not trying to mystify me.

In the house, Fr. Colin told us our mother was dead. "Try to be good boys to your father," he said, fumbling at the unsayable.

Leopold asked like a grown-up: "Is he with her now?"

"Yes," he said. "Take them in, Sister Alma." The midwife was fluttering, poor-boying us, another of the well-meaning ones. She took us where our father sat stricken beside that little dark lady once so well known, now gone secret, the blanket pulled to her chin and she with no more regard for anyone, not even Father. Fr. Colin said: "Leo, you'll understand better when you come to be a priest yourself. God has His reasons, child—it's only that we can't always know them."

But Leopold said: "I cannot be a priest."

Father lifted his head. "Leopold, what do you mean?"

"I can't be a priest." He said this, standing by our mother's body. I remember putting an arm around him because I feared the grown-up world was about to roar at him.

But no. Fr. Colin mumbled about our mother's wish that he might enter holy orders. I scarcely heard that, waiting for what Father would say. It was a gentle reply: "Of course, Leo, you can't be a priest unless you wish it yourself. We'll talk of it later."

But so far as I know it was never brought up again. From that time on, however—the Examiners may find this important—Leopold was intensely keen to share whatever knowledge I brought home from Mam Sola's school. He took to reading like a baby fish to swimming. He gulped down all I could transmit, with impatience for its simplicity, begging for more difficult tasks. "Where are the big books?" he'd demand of me. "*Where are the books?*"

I was not a bad student, indeed Mam Sola praised me, but beside Leo I was a stumbling mule. Two years after our mother's death I resolved to work full time in Father's shop, while Leo would attend the school in my place, but soon he reported that Mam Sola said he knew all she could teach him. She wanted him to go to the great Priests' School at Nuber, and this she and Father arranged for him, beginning in the winter of 415–416, when he was ten. He was the baby of his class among yeasty adolescents; luckily, some of them made a pet of him, sheltering him from the mindless cruelties the majority would have visited on him if they had dared. The priests loved him too after their fashion, seeing maybe a future Patriarch, who knows?

The years 412–418—being nearly my contemporary, my Lord Abbot, Your Beneficence will remember this fragment of time much as I do, and the gradual increase of hatred in our nation toward the Republic of Moha after the accession of the Emperor Mahonn. There was the Sortees Massacre, when Moha traders were set upon by a hysterical crowd—that might have brought war, but neither side was ready. There was the complaint that Moha was cutting us off from trade with Nuin—and nothing ever said about our monopoly of trade with the tropical wealth of Penn, the spices and tea and oranges. The Emperor Mahonn's accession brought a relief from uncertainty: now at least we all knew there would be war, and only the timing was unpredictable.

Those were also the six years when my brother grew from seven to thirteen, from jungle of childhood to river's edge.

Jon and Sidney and I found it natural that a small boy should believe in an invisible Companion: a common fantasy. I may have had such a dream myself before Leo was born. That it should continue beyond early childhood was not so natural—but we were credulous, ignorant boys, and in our different ways we too believed in the Companion's existence. We'd catch Leopold with the clay image in his hand, sunlight on his closed eyelids, listening, and we believed.

My lord, he spoke once of "my brother the sun." Now, it was not till many years later, in my historical studies, that I learned of a saint in ancient Christian times who used these words, and certainly before he went to the Nuber school my little brother had never heard of him; yet he did so speak.

We would keep watch for him, a sharp eye against intruders. Unless he himself was a-mind to discuss them, we never asked about those silent conversations. Had others learned of the mystery and bothered Leo, we would have gone after them like wildcats. Leopold had become to us an oracle, our mascot. After he began study at the Priests' School we had him only in the summers, but schoolboys live for that time anyhow. He was ours and he could do no wrong.

We fell into the habit of consulting him as if he possessed a magical insight; maybe he did. We would ask questions about whatever disturbed us—sex, making a living, religion, right and wrong conduct, superstitions—matters that lay far beyond the experience of his years (beyond ours too!). We would mull over his answers for nuggets of gold.

At that time I was not well instructed in the faith. Fr. Colin was swamped in the business of a parish priest's duties, his time for meditation and teaching chewed to bits by the million tiny mouths of everyday trivia. Our father was none too devout, and what early instruction we had from our mother had blended religion and romance in one blur of wishful dreaming. Father resented the tithes, the spending of time on devotion. During those six years, arthritis twisted his cobbler's hands; at times I heard him growl heretical complaints.

Jon Rohan, that chubby hero, was somewhat disciplined in religion. Sidney was agnostic, which frightened me, though he was always discreet—I would not say it now of my friend if he were not long dead, beyond reach of wounding. Later, deep in the humanitarian work of his choice, it seemed to me he was not concerning himself as much as he ought to have done with the safety of his soul; but good works, I am sure, have won him a place in Heaven, if Heaven exists.* It was not until after his death that I, adrift and wretched from the loss of him and of Leopold, took lay orders as a student of history, leading to my later work as a churchman. At the young time I am describing I had what I will call an undisciplined openness of mind. I found no heresy in believing my brother might converse with an angel.

I will write of an afternoon in early September in Leopold's thirteenth year when we had gone to a favorite clearing above the road to Maplestock. That forest belonged to the Ashoka family, long masters of the Maplestock region. Baron Ashoka's game wardens could legally have lobbed arrows into us on suspicion of poaching—shooting, of course, to cripple and not to kill.

I was twenty that September. Expert in my father's trade, I supposed I would remain a shoemaker. I already managed our shop: pain in the joints was making it nearly impossible for our stubborn old father to go on working. My aunt Mam Lora had kept house for us about five years now, her conversation all sniff and glare, making a cult of our mother as a martyred saint.

That afternoon was a Friday. In the morning we had gone to church, taking the rest of the day for a holiday as our customs then permitted. (My lord, I do dislike the modern trend toward a completely joyless

* In the margin, a note with the initials W.B.: "These are strange remarks for a precentor of your Abbey."

Sabbath.) Sidney was returning soon to the University at Nuber for his third year of medical study. On the journey he would be looking after Leopold, who was going back for his last year at the Priests' School—then the University for him too, we assumed, since he was certain to be granted a scholarship. And Jon too was leaving, for the Military Academy at Nupal. I would stay home and make shoes.

Jon had said goodbye to his sweetheart, Sara Jonas, in the grandeur of his Academy uniform; he told us about that parting, modestly. Sara owned a great share of him, a delicious girl pretty as a violet in the snow. We found that right for one of Jon's temperament, but his humor and good nature appeared to be jelling into a kind of sentimentality that made him no longer quite one of us. He in turn felt, I think, that he had outgrown us and was at eighteen the only adult in a gaggle of starry-eyed goslings. He took a deep melancholy joy in the war talk. He was like a prince condescending: Let us pursue our mundane plans; for him, the lonely glory of going forth to die in our defense, thinking of Sara in his last hour. Not that he ever spoke such corn as that, yet we felt something of the sort in him. My own discomfort at his swashbuckling may have been partly envy: what has a shoemaker to do with war? Well, he makes boots for soldiers to march in, for soldiers to die in.

This was 418, eight years before the war actually began. When it did come, Jon was a captain of infantry, blooded during the Slaves' Rebellion in the western provinces (fomented by Moha, some claimed) in 422. And when the last great struggle with Moha did begin, our Jon was in the thick of it. He was wounded in action, suffering the loss of his left leg from the infection of a spear wound, and the blinding of his right eye. He came back thus to goodwife Sara and his small children: halt, half-blind, the infection still burning in the stump of the thighbone and never quite healing, an old man in his middle twenties. This ruin came on him in our defeat at Brakabin Meadows, April 4, 427, which brought the Moha forces within a short march of Kingstone. No one then could have imagined our recovery, our victories of the following year; 427 was ebb tide, all Katskil breathing despair. For his bravery at Brakabin, Jon received a life's pension and the Iron Wheel of the Order of St. Franklin.

I have digressed again, my lord—forgive me.

A September afternoon of 418, and Leopold had not sung for us that day. At thirteen his voice had cracked; the Cathedral choirmaster warned him not to sing again for two years. We missed it. Entertainments were few. We had the huge sermons of Fridays and Lecture Days; the street-corner storytellers, the peep shows, visits from Rambler caravans that ignored national boundaries and carried amusement, news, messages everywhere; that was about all. We found it hard to lose the pleasure of Leopold's singing and know it would never happen again as it had been, since Leo singing with a man's voice would be another happening in another world.

We bathed in a pool and dried ourselves in the sun. Leopold was not used to the new curly hair on him or the breaking of his voice, but didn't mind our jokes and bawdy counsel. We found it strange to watch the Mascot enter adolescence as we were emerging from it. His body was becoming like ours; his mind occupied other dimensions.

Jon asked: "Leo, what does the Companion say about the war?"

Leopold had lately spoken of the Companion only enough to let us know the conversation had not ended. He said: "Not much, Jon. A war will come sometime, and make an end of—many things."

"Why," said Jon, "everybody knows that."

Sidney inquired: "Because there always has been war?"

"It's a reason," said Jon. "You can't change human nature."

"But it does change," I asserted. "The history books—"

Jon wanted to argue with Sidney, not to hear about history. "It's the cause, Sid. The future belongs to Katskil. How can we make progress with Moha like a log across the road?"

(And since then I have read much history of Old Time, and of ancient time, and how often have I stumbled over these same worn words! Including my own protests, and Sidney's.)

"The future doesn't exist," Sidney said.

I put in: "Only in the mind of God."

"Progress by smashing skulls," said Sidney. "Destiny. Shit."

And Leopold: "Mue-births are bad enough, without war." Perhaps the Examiners ought to know that from our mother's death to the time I lost him, Leopold was obsessed with the tragedy of mue-births. Moments came now and then when his fresh and healthy child's face incredibly foreshadowed maturity, even old age— I don't think I imagined this; and when I saw it I could be almost certain what trouble it was that darkened him.

"No use being a bleeding heart," Jon said. "Face facts!"

217

Sidney wouldn't get angry, even at that noise. "The facts stare me in the face, Jon, and I say there isn't one stupid thing between us and Moha that couldn't be settled at a conference table." ·

"But how can you trust 'em?"

Leopold said: "You're not hearing each other. . . ."

Later Jon asked about the Companion. "Do you still—*see* him?"

"As if my eyes were shut, and I knowing the shape in memory. He speaks, and it's like a memory of hearing."

"Then it's only thinking? Imagining?"

"Maybe. He startles me, and then later I understand." Leopold frowned. "He described the City of Light like—a real place."

Sidney asked: "Do you believe in his separate existence, Leo, the way you believe I'm sitting here bare-ass and beautiful?"

"Not that way. But I think there is a City of Light."

That day was forty-seven years ago. After he left with Sidney for Nuber, I did not see my brother Leopold again for eight years.

We had a letter from him in November. I recall our heady excitement when the Imperial Post rider banged on our door. Letters came rarely to poor districts like Twenyet Road; Leo was being extravagant, undertaking such an expense just to send us greetings. We shut out the urchins who had gathered to stare at the rider, and then my father was beside himself with impatience till I could read him the message. However, that letter was one any schoolboy might have written to content his family: he was well, studying hard, sorry he couldn't be home for Thanksgiving but looked forward to seeing us in the Week of Abraham,* love to everybody.

In early December came a letter from Sidney: Leopold was gone.

On the night of December 7, Leopold had gone to bed as usual in the Senior Dormitory—thirty-six boys in a long room where all-night candles burned and a priest sat wakeful to suppress giggling and other unseemliness. In the morning, Leopold was not there.

The monitor priest admitted he could have dozed off. The other boys under severest questioning confessed no knowledge, and I think they had none. Leopold must simply have dressed himself silently and walked out. The night watchman spent his hours mostly at the gatehouse; Leo must have climbed the Pine Street wall, hidden by evergreens.

Sidney had not seen Leopold for two weeks before the disappearance; nothing then had seemed to Sidney unusual.

When I read this letter to my father, he gasped and fell—his first stroke. I got word of this to Sidney and Jon. Jon was not given leave of absence; Sidney left Nuber at once and reached our house by evening on a fast horse. In his embrace I found the relief of tears, till then denied. And Sidney gave me the clay image with its applewood box and silver chain. "He *left it behind,* Jermyn. Under his pillow." This we never did

---

* *All nations of eastern Murca in the Fifth Century professed Brownism, celebrating the supposed birth of Abraham Brown on December 24 and making the whole week a festival: an obvious superimposition on the Old-Time Christmas. Brownism preferred mild methods of substitution and engulfment in its suppression of Christianity—one could almost speak of syncretism rather than suppression. The modern scholar is often puzzled to distinguish the newcomer from the ghost.*

understand; nor do I, altogether, in later years. But so the amulet did return to me, my lord, and it has not since left my possession.

Sidney helped me untiringly in caring for my father, who was always asking for news of Leopold, we understood, with his eyes and the one finger he could move. Then soon, mercifully, he had another stroke, and died. We watched the difficult life recede, leaving the shell of our good cobbler Louis Graz, my father, and Sidney closed his eyes for me with his steadfast kindness.

For eight years, no word. Soon after my father's death my Aunt Lora entered the nunnery of St. Ellen at Nupal, where she is now in her ninety-fifth year. Sidney returned to the University, was graduated with high honors, finished his licentiate in 422, and started practice in Kingstone. That was also the year of the Slaves' Rebellion in which Jon Rohan rose to the rank of captain. I sold our house and cobbler shop—another of the gray milestones that emerge in anyone's life story. The buyer was well known to me; he would have notified me if Leopold had ever returned to that house. With a donkey and my cobbler's equipment, I took to the roads.

I had not lost my passion for reading and history. But it was in some manner reinforcing my grief at the loss of Leopold. There can be a weariness, even acedia, in too much history. I wished to escape it for a while. History repeats much of its sorrow, error, lost opportunity. Though I had learned a great deal about the folly and corruption of Old Time, I found small consolation in comparing past with present—I can't see that we have learned much from that dark story. In my monastic years I have collected, edited, sometimes rewritten legends and true tales of our region, past and present. This labor also, though congenial, has done little to alter my view. Hope is a lost child stumbling across a battlefield.

I had stronger reasons for a wanderer's life. An artisan may follow the roads: people must have shoes in a country of thorns and serpents. A peddler-artisan may listen. (Our Gypsy by the roadside was listening.) If careful not to startle or offend, he may ask some questions. I would not believe my brother Leopold was dead.

Sidney never discouraged my search. Jon thought Leo must be dead or carried off by slavers, and scolded me for wasting myself. Sidney aided me, his fine house at Kingstone my home whenever I wished. We knew Leopold, thirteen, harmless, could have had no enemies, and he had no wealth to steal. Slavers would hardly have approached a well-guarded place like the Priests' School; besides, at that time the Nuber polis were said to be keeping those vermin clear out of the Holy City.

I searched—into Penn, Conicut, Levannon, down to the southern extremity of our Empire, that pine-barren country. The clay image went with me, on the silver chain, in the box Sidney had made.

Sometimes, my lord, I dreamed the image might bring the Companion to me, even with word of Leopold. This was superstition, I admit. I cannot guess who made the image or with what ancient purpose, but when I contemplate either of the faces of enduring clay, the present drops from me, time is a murmur behind a curtain, I see my own breed as a blurred commotion in a stream wider and deeper than we suppose. A face of the image may say to me: *Why trouble with those who must soon be gone from the earth altogether in total sterility, or another plague year, or another thousand years of good intentions?* To this I find doubtful answers, and I dare to ask in return: *Why then has God made them? Or is God the Creator only one more fancy of this apelike nobody?* Then the image returns me stare for stare.

I am admitting, my Lord Abbot, that the image carried so long in boyhood by Leopold Graz can indeed stimulate heresy. But remember, and I pray Your Beneficence will urge the Examiners to remember, Leopold was not carrying it when he went about as Brother Francis—I was. And though I have exposed my spirit to the clay, Your Beneficence knows I have lived in what we agreed to call virtue. I think no one would whisper that I am in the grip of the Devil.

In 426 came the first rumor of an itinerant preacher calling himself Brother Francis. I was in Penn and southern Katskil early that year. Everyone expected some clash that would at last fire up the war against Moha. Emperor Mahonn was occupying his pinnacle of majesty at the Summer Palace of Lakurs, far from the Mohan border, uttering ambiguities. Diplomats, those well-fed errand boys, bounced from insult to insult, but Mohan travelers came to our country no more. And under this tension began those religious revivals, opening with prayer and shifting into orgies of hate. There might be a choir; the people would sing the fine hymns from the Third Century religious renascence—*In pace gaudeo* or *Exultate gentes*. Then preaching and praying, and soon enough the frenzied roaring: *"Down Moha! Destroy! Destroy!"*

According to the story rumor brought me, a slim man, very young, in a robe that some thought marked him as a lay brother of the Silvan Order, appeared at a meeting in the Stadium at Monsella and asked permission to speak, saying he was one Brother Francis, a messenger. When the Bishop of Solvan asked his place of origin, he replied: "My lord, who among us knows that?" The Bishop, moved by the power of his presence, permitted him to address the gathering. The voice of Brother Francis, rumor said, was not loud but so pure and moving that the people stood rock-quiet to hear him. Yet he was only describing a thing they knew intimately: the countryside between Nupal and the Mohan border city of Skoar.

He spoke of farms and villages they knew, of the Maypole dances, the churches where on Friday mornings they heard the words of Abraham explained. He talked of gardens, orchards, common things—the town greens and their pavilions; pastures near woods where the deer showed their proud heads in morning mist. He did not deny what they all knew, that poverty, cruelty, greed, and ignorance devour us; that human beings die from incomprehensible sickness of Old-Time poison from the ground; that men are not altogether masters in the country of brown tiger and black wolf; that if our women escape sterility, at least one birth in every four is a mue. He denied no darkness, but he showed them their world as still a lovely thing. Then he told them in that same quiet voice: "If you follow the present direction of your lusts, the legions will walk here."

I suppose it was the voice and manner that moved them, for this argument has never yet deterred man from fouling his own nest. Some grumbled. One or two called, "God bless you!" Most were silent. When the Bishop sought their attention it was as though they could not quite catch the noise of him. They drifted away tranced abandoning the Stadium to the Bishop and a few twittering officials. And Brother Francis—at this point rumor whispered excitedly—

vanished. I suppose he stepped down to walk anonymously with the crowd.

Another tale reached me in May when I was returning to Kingstone. I discussed it with Sidney as we sat in his garden in the cloudy evening. "Miracles!" he said. "It was to be expected." Brother Francis had spoken at Grangorge, near the Moha border, and a man with a bent disordered spine, a cripple for years, tossed away his crutches and knelt to kiss the holy man's robe. Others were then and there healed of old afflictions. Sidney said: "The times are in a steamy state, Jermyn—it's this damned war, bound to come any minute. People have the need to believe. You notice the dear fella's preaching has no effect on the politicos. They hear only the noises of power."

"But here's power, if Brother Francis can sway a multitude."

"Yes, if." Sidney went on to speak of cures that baffled medical reason until one recognized the limited but amazing power of the mind over states of the flesh. "I'd want to know how well that man walked the following day," he said, "but that's the part of the story we never get to hear. . . . I see you still wear Leo's amulet." We talked on about my brother, remembering loved qualities at random—his occasional stammer, his yen for fresh bread, his shyness with girls.

Leaving Kingstone in June, I fell in with some Ramblers whose Boss I knew. He told me of a meeting at Brakabin, where Brother Francis had said: "I speak of the City of Light."

Thus I knew. My Rambler friend could tell me nothing more. I hurried to Nuber, inquiring at the Abbey of the Silvan Order. They had been pestered by similar questions and were short with me: the man's robe was *not* that of a Silvan lay brother—it lacked the symbols; they knew and wished to know nothing of any Brother Francis. I went on to never mind all that. Though frustrated for several more months, I did find him.

When the war began in September, 426, with the smashing of our garrison at the border town of Milburg, Katskil shivered at a prospect of Mohan columns driving south—down the Skoar River, through the hill passes, along the coast of the Hudson Sea. Had Moha tried this they might have won the war, but like our Empire, I daresay, they were ruled by the opaque stupidity of the military mind.

In those days of anxiety I caught word of a band of pilgrims who were marching up along the Delaware, intending to place themselves between the opposing armies in the no-man's-land that extended from Lake Skoar to the Hudson Sea, and these mad saints were led by Brother Francis. I hurried to Gilba, on the north shore of the lake, where they would pass if the story was true. I reached the town on a gleaming October afternoon, when the hills were purple under sunlight and rolling cloud shadows; but a section of the northern horizon was sullen with smoke—not forest fire, God knows, for the woods were soaked from recent rains. The pilgrims had arrived before me and were camped in a meadow at the edge of the town.

They were not saints but simple folk, some perhaps not even very religious, drawn by wonder at a truthspeaker. I have blamed Leopold for bringing them together in so vulnerable a crowd. Certainly his intention was to lead them between the opposing forces, armed only in their goodwill. And their innocent blood drenching the earth would have taught men what they have been taught through the millennia by

the blood of other martyrs: namely, nothing.* In this I
find the cruelty of the saint, who would have the devoted follow the dream—his dream, never understanding that it cannot be theirs for longer than the moment of enthusiasm. Since this particular massacre did
not occur in the manner he may have foreseen, I suppose the question of Leopold's blame will be tossed
about to the end of time, and no profit in it.

I asked a black-haired girl at the pilgrims' camp
whether I might speak with Brother Francis. She said
he was resting in his tent, but then she read my face,
and in her kindness took me to him. My brother was
asleep. Across eight years I knew him as though I had
just then waked beside him in our old house on the
Twenyet Road. At the girl's touch on his shoulder he
came awake quickly—he always had—and asked:
"Beata, my dear—is it time for prayers?"

"Not yet," she said, and I saw she loved him, not
only as a believer loves a saint, but as a woman loves
a man. "There's one here in need of you." Then she
stared amazed from his face to mine, and presently
left us.

I knelt by his cot, spoke his name, lost in the puzzled gaze of his so-familiar eyes. He said: "I'm sorry,
sir—are you in trouble? What can I do for you? Why
do you call me Leo?"

"Leopold, has your memory thrown me away?" For
an instant I thought he was shaken, that he really
knew me; then I could see in him only confusion. I
recalled how once he had gashed his left arm in falling from a tree. "Here," I said, and shoved back the
sleeve of his robe and found the scar, a jagged white-
ness. "The oak near Rondo's Shrine—a hot August

* W.B. writes: "Can he expect the Church to condone this utter-
ance?"

morning—I carried you to the shrine, where the priest bandaged and scolded you."

He searched my face, and told me he was sure I was not trying to deceive him; but was I not mistaken? "For my life began," he said, "in a night-time room where I woke and knew I must go out into the world and learn the ways of it and become a messenger. I knew this from the Companion who spoke to me there, and came with me on my journey out of Nuber." He was speaking slowly, reminiscently, as if partly to himself. "I worked on farms. Sometimes I lived in the woods among the wild things. You see, I have never lived before—everything was new. I was held in a Moha prison once, for vagrancy. But before all this, you understand, I can't have been anything more than a germ of thought at the heart of chaos."

"Did you not change to your young man's form from a bony thirteen-year-old boy just into puberty, with a certain scar on his arm?"

He answered reasonably: "I suppose I did. Maybe there was a life before the one I know; some tell me there must have been. Forgive me if it's unkind—I can't pretend to remember you."

"Sidney Sturm? Jon Rohan?" I watched the beautiful saint's face, my anger not quite dying; maybe it has not quite died. "Louis Graz? Louis Graz and his wife, who died giving birth to a mue?"

"I am sorry, sir. Who were they?"

"Your father and mother, and mine. I am Jermyn Graz. I cared for you and loved you. I do now." I pulled the amulet from under my jacket. "You left this behind, Leo, in the dormitory of the Priests' School at Nuber eight years ago."

He opened the applewood box. Now, Sidney had made the fastening with such uncanny skill that it was quite concealed; no one could open it without a fumbling search unless he already knew the trick. Brother Francis opened it without hesitation. He looked on the clay image and said: "Oh, no! I could never have seen this before." He let the box drop, as if it hurt his fingers.

Outside the tent began a screaming uproar, and two soldiers of the Katskil Imperial Guard burst in, seizing my brother by the arms. "Are you he they call Brother Francis?"

"I am Brother Francis."

"Then I have a warrant for your arrest on a charge of treason against the sovereign people and the Emperor."

"I have done no treason."

"Not for us to judge. You are to come with us."

He made no resistance. His eyes warned me that any effort of mine to help would only worsen this new trouble. I have tried to imagine that his loss of memory was assumed to prevent my involvement in the disaster that he knew was about to overtake him; but no—those eyes were surely not seeing me as Jermyn Graz. Following in my stricken obscurity as the soldier led him away, I saw how a platoon of the Guards was dispersing his followers with cudgels and whips, and gathering in some of them to be tied together like a string of slaves. The girl, that gentle Beata who had acted as my guide, flung herself at one of the men in a blind effort to reach Brother Francis, and was pushed to the ground. Her wrists were bound and she was carried off on a giant shoulder, unconscious, limp as a sack of meal.

As Your Beneficence knows, Brother Francis was taken to the military prison at Sofran and held there incommunicado for ten months. Through autumn and winter the war ground on. In April was fought the battle of Brakabin Meadows, and Jon Rohan, who had better have died there, wounded. Only after the war was over did I learn how another band of pilgrims had marched south from central Moha led by a disciple of Brother Francis, one Sister Adonaia. That group was intercepted in a mountain pass by Mohan soldiers, hunted down through the thickets, and butchered. As if, my lord, the two armies had agreed like feral lovers to sweep aside anything that threatened the consummation of their squalid embrace.

I will not try to tell of the trial. Let the Examiners study the transcript. Let them also consider the revulsion within the Church itself after the war. Let them consider how the new Patriarch Benedict denounced the verdict against Brother Francis on many counts, saying that it was tainted by political expediency as well as bigotry—the Church had been hired, he said in effect, to do the hatchet work of an insane Emperor. (There does seem no doubt that the Emperor Mahonn was witless in the last year of his life, and that he was dressed in a wolfskin and drinking fresh chicken's blood when the assassins found him.) Let the Examiners consider how Patriarch Benedict invoked the Third Century ecclesiastical law *Contra Superbiam*, placing the whole Empire under a year's penance. Without this extreme reversal of the Church's position I could not have entered the monastic life.*

Sidney and I were refused admission to the Patriarchal Palace during the Preparatory Interrogations. We searched out Jon Rohan. How embittered he was!—but he was drifting away from us even before the war. I

* W.B. writes: "He convicts himself under Contra Superbiam. Who is he to judge the Church and speak as though it were subject to change?"

told him of finding Leopold, of the refusal to admit us; we begged him to go in our place. A wounded veteran with the Iron Wheel of St. Franklin was less likely to be refused. But Jon would not believe Leopold could have become Brother Francis, whose very name Jon loathed. For some baffled words of mine defending the actions of Brother Francis, I thought poor distracted Jon would attack us with his crutch. His wife, disheartened, lovely Sara, begged us to go.

Then at Leopold's final trial and examination at the Lecture Hall of the Palace, I was admitted (but Sidney was not—perhaps they feared his wealth and distinction would weigh too heavily in the prisoner's favor) and the Archbishop of Orange permitted me to testify—what a mockery! Leopold, thin and haggard in his chains, denied me again; but not in quite the same way, my Lord Abbot. I felt he might be denying me for my own protection, lest I burn with him. Those judges were certainly determined to have his life. All but one perhaps: I read compassion in the face of one of them; but it was not a strong face, and he did not speak while I was there.

Quickly the Archbishop's questioning led to the clay image. I was prepared for that trap. Seeing more clearly than I, Sidney had persuaded me to leave the image hidden at his house in Kingstone. If those judges connected Leopold to it, they would make of it idolatry, witchcraft, who knows what? I did badly, my lord—stammered, wept, disgraced myself. I denied knowledge of the image, was called a perjurer (as of course I was), dragged from the Hall, and searched. Sidney and I were banished from the Holy City.

And Jon did testify, that day. They must have held him in another anteroom, for we never saw him. He—

I will not write of that. It must be in the transcript.

Condemned, Leopold was taken to Kingstone. Behind a chain of polis and soldiers he was drawn in a slow cart to the stake in the marketplace. I was not the only one who called to him in love—if he could have heard it. I struggled to the edge of the crowd. A guard recognized me, secured me with an arm bent up behind my back, and grumbled at my ear: "Quiet, fool! We don't want to arrest you."

They lit the faggots at my brother's feet. The wood was damp; the smoke flung itself upward in a dirty cloud. I heard my brother cry out: "My Companion, have you forsaken me?" Moments later, above the priests' chanting, the flames, the rumbling of the storm that was reaching over the city, he called me. Very clearly I heard him call: "Jermyn, I have remembered you."

Fr. Jermyn, O.S.S., Precentor

2

By Maeron of Nupal, Fr. Lit., Clericus Tribunalis Ecclesiae in the Patriarchate of Urbanus II: being a Digest of the Terminal Trial of the Heretic known as Brother Francis before the Court of Ecclesiastical Inquiry at Nuber, in the month of October in the Year of Abraham 427, His Grace the Archbishop of Orange Presiding Judge.

His Grace the Archbishop of Orange being present, the Court was opened on the ninth day of October, at or about the hour of Tierce, and before the judges were brought for final examination and judgment the prisoner calling himself Brother Francis and reputed by some to be one Leopold Graz son of the cobbler Louis Graz (deceased) of Twenyet Road in the City of Kingstone, this individual called Brother Francis being charged with heresy and certain related criminal actions as set forth in eight Articles.

Present on the dais were also the Most Reverend Jeffrey Sortees Lord Bishop of Nupal and, representing the Secular Estate, the Right Honorable Tomas Robson Earl of Cornal, Supervisor of the Ecclesiastical Prisons at Nuber.

The man called Brother Francis being present, the judge explained to the prisoner his rights at law, reminding him that during the Preparatory Interrogations he had refused the assistance of ecclesiastical counsel, and inquired whether he yet persisted in such refusal now that the matter had come to the point of final trial wherein he stood imperiled of his life.

The prisoner said he needed no defense but what he possessed.

His Grace said: Do you mean simply that you are in God's care?—but the Lord surely would have men aid one another in extremity.

The prisoner replied that he would not ask for counsel.

His Grace suggested that a defending counsel might aid that search for truth which was one of the major concerns of the trial. The prisoner replied that no other knew his heart, therefore no other should assume the burden of his defense.

Then, having been instructed concerning the sanctity of the oath, and that he ought to tell the truth as much for his soul's sake as out of respect for Church and Law, the prisoner said that he would tell the truth so far as he knew it, and so far as he was not forbidden to tell it by his conscience or by that Companion who to him was a second conscience and whose will he had accepted as a guide.

His Grace the Archbishop told him he could not

make any such reservations concerning the oath; and the Earl of Cornal also admonished him, saying that he was demanding a license to lie.

The prisoner said: Not so, my lord: I will not lie. But only God, if God lives, can command my mind; therefore I will not swear to tell everything, lest later I be forsworn.

His Grace asked: Do you doubt that God lives?

The man called Brother Francis said: Does any man live altogether without doubt, Your Grace? I have doubted it as one may doubt that the sun will rise.

His Grace said: It is perhaps a point of philosophy.

Bishop Sortees said: As for the reservation on the oath, Your Grace, is it not a reservation that any of us might make? If made out of true deference to the will of God I see no evil in it.

The Earl of Cornal said: But there is that matter of what he calls his Companion.

The prisoner then said that he would take the oath, but in no other way than he had stated, even if the torture were renewed and repeated until he died.

His Grace said: Well, let him be sworn to tell the truth as he understands it. I suppose no man can do more. We must not lose our way in irresponsible debate.

On these terms the prisoner willingly knelt, and having rested his forehead on the Book of Abraham, he made over his heart the sign of the Wheel and swore to tell the truth.

Then was read to the man called Brother Francis the First Article of the Charge.

ARTICLE I: *The man going by the name of Brother Francis is charged with making unproven claim to be a messenger of God.*

233

Questioned as to the truth of this, the prisoner said: I do not claim and have never claimed it.

His Grace said: But you have called yourself a messenger?

The prisoner said: I have, but cannot tell who sent me.

His Grace asked: Cannot, or will not, my son?

The prisoner said: I cannot, Your Grace. I do not know.

Earl Robson said: It might have been the Devil?

The prisoner said: I have never had reason to think so.

Reminded by His Grace that some of his followers had declared under the ordeal that they believed him to be sent by God, the prisoner said they must have spoken whatever their hearts believed, but not what they knew, since he did not know it himself.

Earl Robson of Cornal said: I can't understand this, a man who carries a message, or thinks he does, not knowing who sent him.

The prisoner said: But for the direction of my Companion, I would not call myself a messenger; and my Companion may well be of the chosen of God. I think he is; but he has not told me so.

The Earl of Cornal then remarked that, with deference to his colleagues of the Ecclesia, he considered the prisoner had already convicted himself under the First Article of the Charge. His Grace requested the view of the Lord Bishop of Nupal, who said that while he felt the prisoner had so far spoken with reason and humility, he would not further commit himself at this moment.

Then was read to the prisoner the Second Article of the Charge.

ARTICLE II: *The man going by the name of Brother Francis is charged with accepting guidance in all his actions from a being outside the common perceptions of men, whom he calls his Companion, in defiance of the First Law of Holy Church as laid down in the Book of Abraham, Chapter Five, Section Seven:* THOU SHALT SET NO AUTHORITY ABOVE THE AUTHORITY OF ALMIGHTY GOD AS DEFINED BY HIS ANOINTED.

Questioned as to the truth of the charge, the prisoner stated that he had accepted the guidance of his Companion in all actions, but only in the manner in which others might accept the guidance of priests, believing that their counsel would not be contrary to God's will so far as any human being can know it.

His Grace said: But you have no reason except your own opinion, the feeling of your own heart, to believe that this Companion can be regarded as one of God's anointed?

After reflection the prisoner said: No, Your Grace: it is true that I have formed this belief in the light of my own opinion and conscience.

His Grace said: You will admit, then, that unless it can be proved that your Companion is one of God's anointed, you stand convicted of heresy under the Second Article?

The Prisoner said: I can hardly deny it.

Bishop Sortees asked: But you have sincerely believed that your Companion would require nothing of you that violated God's laws?

The prisoner said: Yes, Father, I believe that.

The Earl of Cornal inquiring whether the prisoner had known his Companion by any other name, the prisoner denied it. Asked by the Earl to describe the Companion, the prisoner said he had seen him only with the eyes of his mind.

The Earl of Cornal said: You are unreasonable. You are attempting to confuse the Court with metaphysics.

The prisoner said: My lord, I use what words I find. I know my Companion; I do not see him as I see your lordship in the flesh.

His Grace the judge asked: Is he with you now, my son?

The prisoner said: No, Your Grace.

His Grace asked: Is it long since he has been with you?

The prisoner said: It has been long. He has not been with me since the day of my arrest.

His Grace asked: Never during the Preparatory Interrogations? He was not with you on the day when, because of contumacious refusals, it was necessary for you to undergo physical persuasion?

The prisoner said: Had he been with me then, Your Grace, I could have borne the torture with a better heart.

His Grace asked: Do you draw any conclusion from this absence of your Companion while you have been in the custody of the Church?

The prisoner said: I draw no conclusion, Your Grace. I remember too well that in the ten months of my imprisonment in the military prison at Sofran, when I was accused of treason but not of heresy, my Companion was not with me.

His Grace asked: Do you think it possible then that your Companion may have been only the substance of an illusion which has now passed from you? You must know, my son, that the Church has no wish to punish anyone for a malady of the mind.

236

The prisoner replied quickly and firmly that his Companion was no illusion.

Then the Earl of Cornal asked: Have you ever accompanied your Companion to certain meetings?

The man called Brother Francis said: He was often with me when I spoke to the people, to those who joined my company.

Earl Robson said: That is not the question. Have you ever gone, with this being you call a Companion, to meetings of any group called a coven, a meeting of those who deny the divinity of our Savior Abraham and of his prophet of Old Time Jesus Christ?

The prisoner said: No.

The Earl said: You will answer with respect.

The prisoner said: I know nothing of witchcraft, my lord, but I believe it to be a delusion.

The Earl said: Your Grace, is not that heresy in itself?

His Grace the Archbishop replied that the entire question of witchcraft was a matter of dispute, and that no doubt much light would be shed on it in the next Council on the Creed. He suggested also that with regard to this prisoner, this line of inquiry had apparently been exhausted, and with negative result, in the Preparatory Interrogations, and during the physical persuasion that the Earl himself had attended as Supervisor of the Prisons. His Grace then asked the prisoner: If your Companion should come to you while you are on trial here, will you know it?

The prisoner said: I will know it, Your Grace.

His Grace asked: And will you tell us of it?

The prisoner said: If my Companion permits it.

His Grace said: Have a care, my son, how you set the whim of this unknown Companion above the authority of the Ecclesia.

The prisoner said: I have already stated that I have obeyed all the directions of my Companion, even against my will.

The Lord Bishop of Nupal asked him: But if your Companion required you to perform some act forbidden by the laws of God, you would not perform it, would you?

The prisoner said: Father, I think this could not happen.

His Grace said: But you must answer the Lord Bishop's question, and do so remembering your oath.

The prisoner said: I think the will and the laws of God have always been explained by some human agency, and these are fallible.

His Grace said: My son, Bishop Sortees' most kindly worded question deserved no such response, which we find over the borderline of heresy. If you continue headstrong and impudent, you will compel us to find you guilty under the Second Article.

Then was read to the prisoner the Third Article of the Charge.

ARTICLE III: *The man going by the name Brother Francis is charged with claiming to have begun life miraculously, without father or mother, in the body of a boy about thirteen years of age.*

In response to the reading of this Charge, the prisoner declared that he had claimed no miracle but merely described what had happened to the best of his knowledge: that his conscious life had indeed commenced at that apparent age, with no memory of an earlier existence.

The Lord Bishop of Nupal said: But this would be

a miracle, astonishing as a virgin birth. No childhood?

His Grace reminded Bishop Sortees that cases of lost memory were not unknown, a malady of the mind that was very possibly a punishment for secret sins, and thus no miracle was necessarily involved.

The man called Brother Francis said: I think this may be, Your Grace. God may have taken my memory, but perhaps to strengthen me as a messenger, or for other reasons that I cannot know. I do know that I woke as if from a void: I was; and my Companion guided me.

Bishop Sortees said: I am amazed. I should have taken time to read the record of the Preparatory Interrogations. You woke, Brother Francis, knowing the speech of men?

The Earl of Cornal remarked it had been agreed that the prisoner was not to be addressed as "Brother" since he had demonstrated no right to the title, as would be stated in the Fourth Article. Bishop Sortees apologized for his error, reminding the Earl that he had come uninstructed to the Court in the place of the Bishop of Ulsta, who was ill. Then he repeated his question to the prisoner.

The prisoner said: I must have done so, Father, since my Companion spoke to me and I understood him.

The Lord Bishop asked: And no childhood, my son? No childhood?

The prisoner said: I cannot remember any, Father.

The Earl asked: Well, what kind of voice has your Companion?

The prisoner said he knew that voice with the hearing of his mind.

Earl Robson said: Oh, again, again! Metaphysics! His Grace the Archbishop then spoke of delusions wherein the deluded may be innocent of evil intent; and the Bishop of Nupal declared that he thought the prisoner spoke with no evil intent but rather like one impelled by a dream; and His Grace warned against premature judgments before completion of the reading of the Articles.

The Earl of Cornal said: But I ask myself, Your Grace, what motive the accused can have had for claiming this miraculous or seemingly miraculous thing, other than a wish to dazzle his befuddled followers.

His Grace said: Let us continue.

Then was read to the prisoner the Fourth Article of the Charge.

ARTICLE IV: *The man going by the name Brother Francis is charged with unlawfully assuming that title, being not a member of any religious body recognized by the Holy Murcan Church, and with wearing a robe simulating that of a lay brother of the Ordo Sancti Silvani.*

In response to this charge the prisoner stated that when he woke to life it was with the knowledge of the Companion calling him, and by the name Brother Francis; that the Companion had always called him by this name and no other, and that he could not remember responding to any other name. As for the robe, he declared it had been made for him by a woman of his company who knew nothing of religious orders. He also respectfully inquired whether there was an actual law of Church or State that forbade a man to call himself Brother or allow himself to be so addressed if he was not a member of a religious order.

The Earl of Cornal said: Verily the Devil is a lawyer. Everyone knows the title is proper only to a monk. Statute or no statute, can this fellow require us to overlook the tradition of the ages to suit his whim? And how should a woman make a monk's robe not knowing what she did?

His Grace said: My lord of Cornal, we must not assume too much. This may even be a case of true ignorance on both counts. The prisoner's robe, I remind you, did not carry the symbol of the Wheel, nor the symbol of crossed shovels that defines a lay brother's status. And to the prisoner His Grace said: We must warn you, however, that by accepting "Brother" as a title you have caused in some persons a mistaken notion that you spoke with the authority of the Church. This was at least a deception, whether or not by intent.

The prisoner said: Your Grace, I admit my error in this. I told those who joined me that I was no churchman; I ought to have told them not to address me in a way that could cause misunderstanding.

Earl Robson said: Your Grace, I think he buys a great sin with a small penance.

His Grace said: My son, you have spoken with humility, yet I feel a defiance in you still. Are you defiant, at heart?

After long silence, during which His Grace desired that the accused be not interrupted but given time to reflect and consult his conscience, the man calling himself Brother Francis replied: No, Your Grace, I do not think I am.

Bishop Sortees of Nupal asked: In accepting the title "Brother" were you perhaps intending to implement that ancient wish for the brotherhood of man which our Savior Abraham declared in the words: "Let us be born again together"—could this be?

The prisoner said: Those are words that I treasure, Father, but I can say no more than I have said. I woke, and my Companion called me by that name.

Then was read to the prisoner the Fifth Article of the Charge.

ARTICLE V: *The man going by the name Brother Francis is charged with speaking against the sacrament of marriage, has lived in open sin with a common harlot, and has inspired the women of his company with such a concupiscent hysteria that they believe him to be a god.*

Questioned as to this, the prisoner replied that he had once said, to those friends who marched with him to the meadow of Gilba, that he did not suppose marriage was the only good way men and women might live together. He said he did not think this amounted to speaking against a sacrament. As for the remainder of the charge, he said it was absurd.

The Earl of Cornal asked: Do you deny then that you lived in carnal intimacy, while going about under the name Brother Francis, with one Beata Firmin, a common prostitute?

The prisoner said: Beata Firmin was caught up in the life of a prostitute at an earlier time; she had abandoned it before joining our company. If it has a bearing on my trial for heresy, I do not deny that I loved her, but my Companion has commanded me to live chastely for the sake of my mission. Often Beata slept in my tent, but we had no carnal knowledge of each other.

Earl Robson said: More fool you, she's a handsome woman.

The man calling himself Brother Francis said: Well,

242

my lord, you cannot accuse me both of fornication and of the avoidance of it.

Earl Robson said: Nay then, nay, we must cease jesting. I remind you that you are on trial for criminal actions as well as for heresy.

The prisoner said: I cannot conceive how my friendship for Beata Firmin can be described as a criminal action.

Bishop Sortees said: My lord, surely any criminal actions, to be judged by this Court, must bear a relation to the charge of heresy.

The Earl said: Your Reverence, I think the relation can be shown. And to the prisoner he said: You are aware that the woman Beata Firmin believes you to be a god?

The prisoner said: I have been separated from her for ten months. Ten months ago I am certain she had no such delusion.

The Earl said: Why, man, she speaks of nothing but you and your divinity. She rants, she drivels, she bites her lips to make them red and pleasing against the dream of your return, she sits in her cell with a pillow under her smock and croons to it, saying she is with child by the Divine Brother and the child's dear name shall be Jesus. Is the Companion with you now?

The prisoner replied: My Lord Robson, if your prison has brought Beata Firmin to this state, I will pray God to forgive you in Hell, since it is beyond my human power to forgive.

His Grace said: Finish the reading of the Articles.

The Earl said: It seems I have been cursed by a witch.

His Grace said to him: My lord, my lord, no more jesting. Finish the reading, Clerk.

But Earl Robson of Cornal said: Your Grace, as

God is my witness I am not jesting. The moment after this prisoner cursed me I was taken with a violent pain in my right hand.

Bishop Sortees said: But he did not curse your lordship. He said he would pray for your forgiveness by the Almighty, and had I spoken as you did, I declare to you I would feel need of such forgiveness myself.

His Grace asked: Do you wish an adjournment, my lord of Cornal, or may we continue with the reading of the Articles?

The Earl of Cornal said: I ask no adjournment, Your Grace. I will bear it. But I wish this fellow to know, I say to him in open court, if he slips off our griddle here in the Court of the Ecclesia, I'll fetch him down with a charge of witchcraft under secular law, and it shall go hard with him.

Then was read to the prisoner the Sixth Article of the Charge.

> ARTICLE VI: *The man going by the name Brother Francis is charged with professing to heal the sick by miraculous means.*

In response to this the prisoner said that he professed nothing except his message; that some persons might have found healing in his presence, at times when the Companion was with him, and that if God had truly healed them it must have been done by his Companion rather than by himself.

The Earl of Cornal said: And your Companion, we understand, politely declines to be questioned by this Court?

The prisoner said: My Companion is not here.

The Earl said: A pity, a pity. I should admire to ask his opinion concerning the pain in my hand.

The man known as Brother Francis did not answer. Then was read to him the Seventh Article of the Charge.

> ARTICLE VII: *The man going by the name Brother Francis is charged with wantonly leading a band of his followers to a place of peril between the savage invading host of Moha and the defenders of the Empire.*

His Grace the Archbishop said: Since the fact itself is not in dispute, I will only ask how you explain this action.

The prisoner said: We hoped to illuminate the nature of war.

His Grace said: You must know the Church is deeply opposed to war. Why did you not work through the Church?

The prisoner said: That month, Your Grace, Masses were being said for the victory of the Imperial arms.

His Grace replied: Naturally. Since the Holy City is located within the Empire, an attack on Katskil is an attack on Holy Church; therefore the rights of the case are not in question. In any event, your followers were merely swept aside, as you must have known they would be. Why this empty gesture? You placed your people between fire and fire without a shield. Had the Guard not intervened and dispersed them, many lives might have been lost.

The prisoner said: I hear that many of my company were arrested, some questioned under torture, none released except by death.

His Grace explained that this was a political and military problem, not within the competence of the Ecclesiastical Court. The prisoner then stood silent a long time, and appeared like one listening, and there was whispering among the members of the Ecclesia privileged to attend as spectators, which His Grace the Judge was obliged to silence, the prisoner seeming unaware of this. At length the prisoner said: Your Grace, we sought to illuminate the nature of war. But I understand now that the greatest evil is not war itself but the love of war. However, Your Grace, is it not a fact that the armies did not meet that day?

His Grace said: What reasoning is this? They met later, and at that very place. Did you not hear in prison about the battle of Gilba?—I am told that Mohan forces still hold the highlands north of the lake. So what price your intervention? And the armies met at Brakabin Meadows in the following spring, another disaster. There is a witness to be called who was wounded at Brakabin. You shall see for yourself, sir, how effectively your dangerous dream has prevented war. Well?

The prisoner said: Your Grace, we never had great hope of preventing the continuation of this war; only, as I have said, to illuminate the nature of war. In any case, I did as my Companion directed me, and I would do the same again.

Earl Robson said: But maybe with fewer followers?

The man called Brother Francis replied: Maybe with a million followers. Or with two or three. I would do the same again.

His Grace then gently asked the prisoner whether he had been listening a moment past to his Companion, and the prisoner replied: I cannot answer that, Your Grace, because I am not certain.

The Bishop of Nupal said: Your Grace, I have read of some in Old Time who went up unarmed against the machineries of war. Certain priests and others burned their own bodies in protest at evils they found intolerable. It is folly perhaps; but so far I can find no sin in this man.

His Grace said: It is true this Article deals with a social and military issue. However, the wisdom of the Court has included it among the charges of heresy, and so we must consider it.

Earl Robson said: Does it not seem, Your Grace, that this prisoner has set himself up to judge between the nations as only God can judge? The issues of the battlefield, surely, are decided by God and God alone, not by fanatic preachers.

His Grace said: This will be weighed, my lord of Cornal. Does your hand still pain you?

The Earl replied: There is only one more Article to read. After that, if Your Grace thinks best, we might adjourn till tomorrow.

Then was read to the prisoner the Eighth Article of the Charge.

> ARTICLE VIII: *The man going by the name Brother Francis is charged with deluding his followers by talk of a coming heaven on earth described as a City of Light, in contravention of Holy Doctrine as set forth in the Book of Abraham, Chapter Five, Section Seven*: THOU SHALT CHERISH NO TREASURE ON EARTH OR IN THE THOUGHT OF EARTH, WHICH IS SOON TO PERISH AND PASS AWAY.

In reply to this, the prisoner said that he had never described the City of Light as a heaven on earth, or ever intentionally deluded anyone in any way.

His Grace asked him: What then is the City of Light?

The man called Brother Francis said: In the City of

Light no violence is done to the body of earth or to the human body or spirit. The light of the City is the light of understanding and love, the two inseparable.

His Grace asked: It is a dream of earth and not of heaven?

The man called Brother Francis said: It is not a dream of heaven on earth, for in the City of Light men may strive for perfection, I suppose, but they do not reject the good that is attainable.

His Grace said: And for this dream of earth you have endured imprisonment and physical persuasion, and may suffer worse: was this not for the sake of persuading others to share your dream, and leave their appropriate labors, and follow you?

The man called Brother Francis replied: I do not urge or persuade. I tell the vision as I see it, and I think those who followed me were sharing it for at least a part of my journey.

His Grace said: As far as the meadow at Gilba, where the armies might have rolled over them. My son, there have been visionaries before who perverted the just course of life. Do you not see the result when men turn aside from their necessary labors after a moonblink, an *ignis fatuus*? Who shall plow and sow, and tend the fields, and mind the harvest? You must have been taught, perhaps in the childhood you do not remember, how God has placed us on this miserable earth for a time of trial, so that souls deserving of Heaven may be winnowed out from the unworthy, and how then the earth shall pass away and be as a drop of water in the firmament. Do you not see, my son, that no other explanation of our presence here is possible, since we must believe that God is all-loving and all-powerful? Why do we concern ourselves with heresy at all, if not to protect our people from straying into disaster? To dazzle the credulous with your vision of a City of Light on earth is to betray them, to hide from them this truth that God's revelation through Abraham has made clear to us. And whether your heart's intent is evil or benevolent, the result is the same as though the Devil himself had stood at your shoulder and charmed the gullible with your voice.

The man called Brother Francis replied: Yet there is a City of Light. I said to those who followed and heard me: There is a battle of Armageddon, where good and evil confront each other for a decision, not for all time but for the time that you know; and there is a City of Light on earth, built by your labor not for all time but for the time that you know. Every day, every night the battle of Armageddon is to be fought, and won or lost: see that you find courage. Every night, every day something is given to the building of the City of Light or taken from it: see that your share is given, and with goodwill. The battle is within you; the city is for all your kind, not for all time but for the time that you know.

At this hour the session of examination and judgment was adjourned until morning of the following day.

His Grace the Archbishop of Orange being present, the Court was opened on the tenth day of October, at or about the hour of Tierce, for the second day of the final judgment and examination in the case of the prisoner charged with heresy who calls himself Brother Francis.

Present as before were the Most Reverend Jeffrey Sortees Lord Bishop of Nupal, and the Rt. Hon. Tomas Robson Earl of Cornal, who attended this session with his right hand covered by a bandage. His Grace the Archbishop graciously inquired whether his lordship was still in pain; the Earl replied he would willingly bear it rather than delay the trial, adding that all those present yesterday must bear in mind that they were witnesses to what had occurred.

The prisoner being then brought to the dock and chained, His Grace announced that one Jermyn Graz, itinerant Cobbler of no known address, had urged his right to testify before the Court, and that this request had been granted. Master Graz came forward and was sworn.

To him His Grace said: When you demanded admission to the Preparatory Interrogations it was denied, Master Graz, in view of the improbability of your story and the fact that the accused disavowed any knowledge of your name. Since then other information has come to us tending to support your claim to be heard. You are sworn; I must further caution you to limit yourself to the question put to you. I request you to look now on the accused and say whether you know him.

Master Graz looked on the prisoner and said: He is my brother, Your Grace. He is my beloved brother.

His Grace then directed the accused to look on the cobbler Jermyn Graz and say whether he knew him.

The prisoner said: I know him as the man who came to my tent at Gilba on the day I was arrested. If I ever saw him before then, the memory is gone with all my other memories of childhood.

Master Graz said: He is my brother. He disappeared from the Priests' School at Nuber in 418. It was the seventh of December.

His Grace said: Master Graz, when we learned something of this from another source, we spoke to the Headmaster of the Priests' School. The records do show that a boy Leopold Graz, thirteen (your brother we do not doubt), did vanish that day. But the Headmaster Father Ricordi was shown the man called Brother Francis at the prison, and would not say with any certainty that he was Leopold Graz, and you have now heard the prisoner testify that he does not know you. Then His Grace asked the accused: Have you any recollection of attending the Priests' School at Nuber, or any school?

The prisoner said: I have none, Your Grace.

His Grace said: But when Father Ricordi described to you the Senior Dormitory at the school as it would look by candlelight, you remembered this as the place where you had, as you say, waked to life?

The prisoner said: That is true, Your Grace.

Master Graz said: He is my brother.

An attending officer of the Court was then obliged to restrain the witness from climbing the barrier into the dock; the man was weeping and appeared beside himself. Being restrained, he apologized to the Court for his behavior.

His Grace said: Subject to your dissent, my lords, I think we may accept the probability that the man called Brother Francis is indeed Leopold Graz, once of Kingstone, who has suffered the loss of memory of his childhood, under what divine punishment we know not. There being no dissent, His Grace said further: We have then an identity for the prisoner, and will address him from now on as Leopold Graz. But I point out to you that this does not further our inquiry, unless the history of his childhood produces evidence bearing on the charge of heresy. I will ask you now, Master Graz, if you have recovered control of yourself, whether you are acquainted with a Captain Jon Rohan.

Master Graz said: I am, Your Grace, or I was. We were boys together, Jon and another friend and my brother Leopold and I.

His Grace asked: Have you seen Captain Rohan recently?

Master Graz said: Not for a month or more. I went to see him when I was refused admission to the Preparatory Interrogations, hoping he might be allowed to testify in my place. He told me he believed my brother was dead. As a soldier he hated and despised Brother Francis from what he had heard about him, and refused to consider that Brother Francis might be Leopold. Jon still suffers from an unhealed wound. He was not himself; I should have forgiven it. We parted in anger.

His Grace said: We have spoken with him, rather our representatives have, and with your other friend Dr. Sturm. You yourself are better known to us than you may suppose. What can you tell us concerning a clay image once in the possession of your brother Leopold?

Master Graz then appeared startled and confused, stammering and saying he knew of no image belonging to his brother.

The Earl of Cornal said: You are under oath, Master Graz.

Master Graz said: Ah, you mean *my* little amulet. I had one till lately, the sort I'm sure the Church hasn't disapproved. But my brother would never have cared for anything like that. He was always deeply religious, Your Grace. He would have found it sacrilegious.

His Grace asked: This idol is not now in your possession?

Master Graz replied: No, Your Grace. I lost it some time back.

The Bishop of Nupal would then have questioned him, but his Grace intervened, saying: My lord, whether or not he is lying about possession of the image, he has perjured himself on another count, as testimony that follows will show, and we cannot permit the Court of the Ecclesia to be contaminated by a perjurer. Attendant, take this man Jermyn Graz to the anteroom, strip him, and search him for the possession of any sort of charm or amulet. If any is found, he is to be committed to the prison for examination. If not, he is to be conducted to the border of the Holy City of Nuber and warned not to return within a year, and he is to consider himself fortunate in the leniency of this Court. Master Graz was removed, and His Grace addressed the prisoner: Leopold Graz, I note that you have become very white. Do you wish the help of a physician?

The prisoner said: No, Your Grace, a physician cannot help me.

His Grace asked: You do admit, then, that you may stand in need of help for your soul's sake? And when the prisoner appeared unable to answer, His Grace gently inquired: For your soul's sake, what can you tell us concerning a clay image, male and female, in a box of applewood fastened to a silver chain?

After much hesitation, the prisoner said: Your Grace, I have no knowledge of any such thing.

The Earl of Cornal said: Have you lost your memory for recent events also? Did not that man Jermyn Graz show you such an image in your tent at Gilba?

The prisoner said: No, my lord. No.

His Grace then called Captain Jon Rohan, who came from the west anteroom with the assistance of an attendant, and was sworn. His Grace asked: Captain Rohan, you are a veteran of the battle of Brakabin

253

Meadows, wounded in the service of His Majesty the Emperor?

The witness replied: I am, Your Grace.

His Grace asked: You testify here willingly, under no duress, Captain Rohan, and in accordance with our previous conversations at the time when you volunteered to appear before this Court?

The witness replied: I do, Your Grace.

His Grace said: I will ask whether in former years you were acquainted with a boy named Leopold Graz, son of the cobbler Louis Graz of Twenyet Road in Kingstone?

The witness said: I was, Your Grace. He was five years younger than I, and I was a playmate of his elder brother when he was born. I knew him until his thirteenth year, when he disappeared from the Priests' School at Kingstone.

His Grace said: Look on the accused, Captain Rohan, and say whether you know him.

Captain Rohan looked long on the man called Brother Francis and said: Yes, that is Leopold Graz, though greatly changed.

His Grace then directed the prisoner to look on Captain Rohan well and say whether he knew him. The prisoner said with apparent indifference: He is quite unknown to me.

Captain Rohan said: He knows me. He has betrayed his country and his people. He cannot hide behind mystery. He knows, Your Grace, he knows I understand him.

Bishop Sortees said: You are not here to judge, Captain Rohan. I pray Your Grace will instruct him to limit himself to the question.

His Grace said: You must do that, Captain Rohan. I

ask you now to tell what you know of the childhood of Leopold Graz.

Captain Rohan said: He possessed great charm, as a boy, but he was what people call fey. Strange, ungovernable, given to outrageous fancies. He became fascinated by an obscene clay image, an object indecently representing both sexes in one body, that his brother secured for him from a Gypsy when Leopold was about seven, and which I think was never out of Leopold's possession until he disappeared from the Priests' School.

His Grace asked: And this obsession with a clay image, was it associated with any other thing that you recall as unusual?

Captain Rohan testified: It was, Your Grace. Very soon after his brother gave him the image, Leopold was speaking of an invisible companion who gave him guidance.

The Lord Bishop of Nupal said: Captain Rohan, is this not quite a common thing in childhood? A child, especially a lonely one, is often given to such fancies, surely.

Captain Rohan said: But this did not pass away as we expect childhood fancies to do, Your Reverence. Yes, my own little daughter chattered of such a thing once, and I corrected her, and soon heard no more about it. But this boy Leopold continued to believe in his spectral companion—and does so still, I understand. We others, being ignorant boys, were much impressed by his talk, and I am sorry to say we encouraged it a while. I stopped doing so when I realized that it bordered on idolatry, or perhaps passed the border.

The Earl of Cornal asked: Do you say that he in fact worshiped this idol, this image?

Captain Rohan testified: My lord, he would hold it in his hands, and often close his eyes and appear to be listening; and then he might give us advice on matters of which he could have known nothing. It was, I remember, advice much more mature than belonged to his years.

His Grace asked: And what, if you know, became of this clay image?

Captain Rohan said: The boy Leopold left it behind when he disappeared from the Priests' School. I believe Sidney Sturm brought it back to Leopold's brother Jermyn, and it was still in Jermyn's possession a month ago when he and Dr. Sturm came to see me.

His Grace said: Leopold Graz, under oath before God to tell the truth, do you say you do not know this man Captain Rohan?

The prisoner said: I know his nature from the way he speaks.

His Grace said: You evade. Do you remember him from the past?

The prisoner said: I cannot answer that.

His Grace said: What? You cannot?

The prisoner said: I took the oath with reservations of which I made no secret. I cannot answer the question.

His Grace said: And you deny any knowledge of a clay image?

After hesitation, the prisoner replied: I do.

His Grace asked: This you say under oath? . . . Leopold Graz, you must speak so that we hear you, and stand upright if you are able. You declare under oath that you know nothing of any clay image?

The man Leopold Graz called Brother Francis said: The light of the City is the light of understanding and love, the two inseparable.

His Grace the Archbishop then said: There need be no more testimony, no more questioning. The rest, my lords, is for discussion among us three, *in camera*. We insist that there be no loose discussion of this troublesome case by those privileged to attend this hearing as spectators. The Court is now adjourned. Final judgment and sentence will be pronounced on the opening of this Court tomorrow.

3

Letter from Mgr. Wilmot Breen, Magister Theologiae, Director of Examiners under the Patriarchate of Pretorius IV, to His Beneficence Alesandar Fitzoral, O.S.S., Abbot of St. Benjamin's at Mount Orlook, November 29, 465.

To Your Beneficence, Greetings.

Speedily and with the help of God we have reached a decision in the question of the blessed Francis of Gilba, and have communicated our finding to His Holiness Pretorius IV by the Will of Heaven Patriarch of the World. It is now our great pleasure to convey to Your Beneficence also the substance of our findings, with gratitude for the assistance so graciously granted us by Your Beneficence in securing the document by Jermyn Graz, which in spite of its dubious nature sheds much light on the childhood of the blessed Francis.

We find that beyond doubt Francis of Gilba was divinely inspired in his teaching (so unfortunately never committed to writing) and that in particular his insistence on truthfulness, divine understanding, and divine love as the essence of the everlasting Brownist Faith is a great contribution toward the salvation of mankind. We feel confident that when sufficient time

has passed, this noble spirit will be declared sanctified. In the meantime Your Beneficence will be
pleased to learn that the arm bone of the blessed
Francis preserved at the Cathedral in Albani contin-
ues its work of healing to the manifest glory of God.

We have found that the Companion who appeared
to the blessed Francis in his visions was no other than
the blessed St. Lucy of Syracuse, martyred in ancient
time and venerated throughout the centuries. Understanding in this matter was granted to us in a dream,
wherein it was made plain that in speaking of the City
of Light, Francis of Gilba was approaching as nearly
as God permitted him to explaining the identity of his
sacred benefactress: LUCY from ancient Latin LUX,
meaning LIGHT. After this guidance it was a simple
matter to consult the records, wherein we found that
Francis of Gilba, vulgarly known as Leopold Graz,
was born on December 13, St. Lucy's Day since time
immemorial. Thus all doubt was dispelled: the dross
of argument and conjecture fell away and the intention of the Lord was made plain.

We find further, having questioned the benign and
ancient woman Mam Lora Stone at the nunnery of St.
Ellen at Nupal, that the birth of Francis of Gilba must
have been miraculous. St. Lucy, be it remembered, is
a patron of woman in childbirth. We need not pre-
sume any event so marvelous as a virgin birth, but
simply that the mother of Francis was gotten with
child by an angelic visitation. A clue to this is unwit-
tingly provided in the manuscript by the man Jermyn
Graz, in the passage recording the obscure saying of
the boy Francis that he was "born unto the Vine." The
Vine, as we know, is sacred to the Archangel Diony-
sus, the Male Principle, and now that the identity of
the Companion is known, the conclusion is obvious.

This brings us to a delicate matter wherein we must rely on the discretion of Your Beneficence. The manuscript of the man Jermyn Graz, which we had hoped to return for the archives of St. Benjamin's, has disappeared, owing, we believe, to the criminal dereliction of some minor member of our clerical staff; all of them are to be put to the question, and no doubt the truth will emerge. In the meantime, by the grace of God, a fair copy of the manuscript had been made, from which the gross errors and perversions of the man Jermyn Graz were eliminated; thus we now have a record that is reliable for all time, and if the original manuscript should be recovered, it will probably be the consensus of the Examiners that it ought to be destroyed, not preserved.

The miraculous generation of the blessed Francis of Gilba is rendered even more clear by the fact that Francis could not logically have been whole brother to this man who for many years has been precentor at St. Benjamin's, and who appears to have wormed his way into the affections of Your Beneficence, and whose opinions as they appear in the uncorrected manuscript are tainted with gross heresy and sinful pride and willful error. Your Beneficence will understand that this man Jermyn Graz must be instantly removed from any position at the Abbey, and held in close custody until the Examiners shall have had opportunity to study his literary output—collected stories, legends, commentaries on Old Time, we know not what—and determine whether to place them on the Index Expurgatorius and burn all copies.

Finally—and this is a matter of the utmost urgency—any amulet or image or the like found in the possession of the man Jermyn Graz is to be confiscated and turned over to us for exorcism and disposal. If no such object is found in his possession, he must be persuaded by any approved means to explain his disposition of it. The blessed Francis of Gilba himself repudiated this miserable idol with horror; other implications, we feel sure, will not escape the consideration of Your Beneficence.

Accept, we pray, the assurance of our continual esteem.

Wilmot Breen, M.T.

4

Note from unfrocked prisoner Jermyn Graz to His Beneficence Alesandar Fitzeral, O.S.S., Abbot of St. Benjamin's.

My dear Lord Abbot:

Pray accept my gratitude for the kindness of Your Beneficence in transferring me to this cell where an eastern window permits me a little morning light, and for allowing me these writing materials, and for permitting me to make this communication to Your Beneficence.

I will first take this opportunity to recant whatever confession of error I may have made under physical persuasion, and second, to repeat as clearly as I can that which I said to my examiners and which they would not accept, concerning my disposal of the two-faced clay.

After I had committed to the hands of Your Beneficence my Memorandum on the life of my brother Leopold, reflection made it clear to me that the discovery of the image on my person, considering the present temper of the times, might result in peril to the clay figure as well as to myself. I remind Your

Beneficence that I have been and still am a historian. To me, in this ugly little dab of clay, there is a beauty and a wonder that I cannot describe to you: these faces have seen eternity. Why it was rejected by my poor brother, if indeed it was, I shall never know; but I cannot repudiate it: these faces that have seen eternity are the faces of my own kind.

Therefore on leaving Your Beneficence I took myself for a long walk into the woods outside the monastery grounds, or perhaps beyond the woods, and I buried the image. It is in the applewood box that my beloved Sidney made for it, the silver chain is wrapped around it, and it lies in a place where it will not be found by any search—for even I, having smoothed the natural cover and moved away heeding no landmarks, could not find it again if I would. The Examiners and their servants cannot overturn all the trees and boulders or dig away all the earth in all the places where I might have buried it.

Let it lie there and be discovered again—maybe by a child, or a poet, or a wanderer, in a time when the passions of our day are no more remembered than those of Old Time.

Jermyn Graz

THE NIGHT WIND

I will do it somewhere down this road, not yet but after dark; it will be when the night wind is blowing.

Always I have welcomed the sound of the night wind moving, as the leaves are passing on their secrets and sometimes falling, but falling lightly, easily, because their time to fall is come. Dressed in high colors, they fall to the day winds too this time of year, this autumn season. The smell of earth mold is spice on the tongue. I catch scent of apples ripening, windfalls rich-rotten pleasuring the yellow hornets. Rams and he-goats are mounting and crazy for it—O this time of year! They fall to the day winds echoing the sunlight, the good bright leaves, and that's no bad way to fall.

I know the dark of autumn too. The night wind hurts. Even now writing of it, only to think of it. Ottoba was in me when I said to my heart: I will do it somewhere down this road, I will end it, my life, for they believe it should never have begun. (I think there may be good spirits down that road. Perhaps the people I met were spirits, or they were human beings and spirits too, or we all are.) And I remembered how Father Horan also believes I ought never to have been born. I saw that in him; he believes it as the town folk do, and what we believe is most of what we are.

For three days I felt their sidelong stares, their anger that I would dare to pass near their houses. They called in their children to safety from me, who never hurt anyone. Passing one of those gray-eyed houses, I heard a woman say, "He ought to be stoned, that Benvenuto." I will not write her name.

Another said, "Only a mue would do what he did."

They call me that; they place me among the sad distorted things—armless or mindless or eyeless, somehow inhuman and corrupted—that so many mothers bear, or have borne, folk say, since the end of Old Time. How could a mue be called beautiful?

When I confessed to Father Horan, he shoved his hands behind his back, afraid he might touch me. "Poor Benvenuto!" But he said it acidly, staring down as if he had tasted poison in his food.

So I will end it (I told the hidden self that is me)—I will end it now in my fifteenth year before the Eternal Corruption that Father Horan spoke of can altogether destroy my soul; and so the hidden self that is me, if that is my soul, may win God's forgiveness for being born a monster.

But why did Father Horan love me once, taking something like a father's place, or seem to love me? Why did he teach me the reading of words and writing too, first showing me how the great words flow in the Book of Abraham, and on to the spelling book and so to all the mystery? Why did he let me see the other books, some of them, the books of Old Time forbidden to common people, even the poets? He would run his finger through my hair, saying I must never cut it, or rest his arm on my shoulder; and I felt a need, I thought it was loneliness or love, in the curving of his fingers. Why did he say I might rise in the Holy Amran Church, becoming greater than himself, a bishop—Bishop Benvenuto!—an archbishop!

If I am a monster now, was I not a monster then?

I could ask him no such questions when he was angry. I ran out of the church though I heard him calling after me, commanding me to return in God's name. I will not return.

I ran through the graveyard, past the dead hollow oak where I saw and heard bees swarming in the hot autumn light, and I think he stood among the headstones lamenting for me, but I would not look back, no, I plowed through a thicket and ran down a long golden aisle of maple trees and into Wayland's field (where it happened)—Wayland's field all standing alive with the bound shocks of corn, and into the woods again on the far side, only to be away from him.

It was there in Wayland's field that I first thought, I will do this to myself, I will end it, maybe in that wood I know of; but I was afraid of my knife. How can I cut and tear the body someone called beautiful? And so I looked at the thought of hiding in a shock of corn, the same one where I found Eden idle that day, and staying in it till I starved. But they say starving is a terrible death, and I might not have the courage or the patience to wait for it. I thought too, They will look for me when they know I'm gone, because they want to punish me, stone me, even my mother will want to punish me, and they would think of the cornfield where it happened and come searching like the flail of God.

How bright they stand, the bound stalks in the sun, like little wigwams for the field spirits, like people too, like old women with rustling skirts of yellow-gray; their hair is blowing. Now I know I will remem-

ber this when I go on—for I am going on without
death, never doubt it, I promise you I shall not die by
my own hand.

I saw two hawks circling and circling in the upper
wind above Wayland's field. I thought up to them:
You are like me, but you have all the world's air to fly
away in.

The hawks are bound to the earth as I am, they
must hunt food in the grass and branches; men shoot
arrows from the earth to tear their hearts. Still they
enter regions unknown to us, and maybe they and the
wild geese have found an easy way to heaven.

Into the woods again on the far side of Wayland's
field I hurried, and down and up the ravine that borders it, shadowed ground with alder and gray birch
and a cool place of ferns I know of where sunlight
comes late in the morning and mild. The brook in the
ravine bottom was running scant from the dry
weather, leaves collecting on the bodies of smooth
shining stones. I did not go downstream to the pool
but climbed the other side of the ravine and took the
path—hardly that, merely a known place where my
feet have passed before—to the break in the trees that
lets you out on this road, and I thought: Here I will
do it, somewhere farther on in the shadows.

It is wider than a woodroad and better kept, for
wagons use it now and then, and it is supposed to
wind through back ways southeast as far as Nupal,
ten miles they say or even more—I never believed
much of what I hear about Nupal. The trading of our
village has always been with Maplestock, and surely
nobody goes to Nupal except those tinkers and gyppos
and ramblers with their freaky wagons, squirrel-eyed
children, scrawny dogs. A sad place it must be, Nupal,
more than seven hundred crammed into the one vil-

lage, as I hear it. I don't understand how human beings can live like that—the houses may not be standing as horridly close together as folk tell. Maybe I'll see the place in passing. I've noticed a dozen times, the same souls who sniggle about with ugly fact until it looks like fancy will turn right-about and ask you to believe that ugly fancy is fact.

I went down the road not running any more, nor thinking more about Father Horan. I thought of Eden.

Then I thought about my mother, who is going to marry Blind Hamlin the candlemaker, I'm told. She wouldn't tell me herself, the winds told me. (Toby Omstrong told me, because he doesn't like me.) Let's hope the jolly wedding isn't delayed by concern over my absence—I am not coming back, Mother. Think of me kindly while tumbling with your waxy man, or better, think of me not at all, the cord is cut, and anyhow didn't you pick me up somewhere as a changeling?

Hoy, there I was on your doorstep all red and nasty, wrapped in a cabbage leaf! Likely story. But we can't have it thought that *you* gave birth to a monster, even one begotten by a little shoemaker whose image you did your best to destroy for me. (But I saved some pieces, I try to put them together now and then. I wish I could remember him; the memories of others are not much more help than wind under the door, for people don't understand what I want to know—small blame to them, they can't hear the questions I don't know how to ask—and I think your memories of him are mostly lies, Mother, though you may not know it.) "He was a poor sad soul, Benvenuto." Was he, Mother? "He broke my heart with his unfaithfulness, Benvenuto." But Blind Hamlin is going to stick it back together with mutton-fat, remember? "He drank, you know, Benvenuto, that was why he could never make a decent living." Why, I will drink to you, Mother, I will drink to the wedding in Mam Miriam's best apple brandy before I leave this poor empty house where I am writing.

Don't destroy Blind Hamlin, Mother. I don't like him, he's a crosspatch bag of guts, but don't destroy him, don't whittle him down as you must have scraped my father down with the rasp of words—but I forget, I am a changeling. Poor Blind Hamlin!—there may be witchcraft in it, Mother. It troubles me that a man who can't see makes candles for those who will not. Don't destroy him. Make another monster with him. I'd like a monster for a half-brother—but there, never mind, I'm not coming back to Trempa, make all the monsters you wish. The world's already full of them.

I am not writing this for my mother. She will not be the one to find it here. Whoever does—I pray you, read this page if you like and the one before it that begins "She wouldn't tell me herself"—read and then throw away, in God's name. For I would like the truth to be somewhere in the world, maybe in your head, whoever you are, but I don't wish to slap my mother in the face with it, nor Blind Hamlin either. Blind Hamlin was never unkind to me. I am all soreness, the tenderest touch smarts on a burned skin. I will mend. I don't hate my mother—do I hate anyone?—or if I do, I will *mend*, I'll cease hating wherever I am going, and even forget. Especially forget. Read those pages and throw away and then, you too, forget. But save the rest, if you will. I don't want to die altogether in your mind, whoever you are.

Down that road I came. I think I left behind me

most of what had appeared certain in the world; the new uncertainties are still to find. Where did I encounter you? Who are you?—oh, merely the one supposed to find this letter. So then you are not the new person I need to find—someone not Eden, nor Andrea whom I loved, but some other. But with Andrea I understood that heaven would open whenever he looked on me.

In that road through the woods beyond Wayland's field the trees stand close on either side, oak and pine and enormous tulip trees where the white parrots like to gather and squabble with the bluejays, and thickets that swell with a passion of growth wherever an opening like that road lets through the sun. Oaks had shifted into the bronze along with the clear gold of maple trees when I passed by, yet I saw few leaves fallen. You remember some of the wise prophets in Trempa have been saying it'll be a hard winter, with snow in January for sure. The Lord must save a special kind of forgiveness for the weather prophets— other kinds of liars have some chance of learning better. As I looked along the slender channel of the road, I saw the stirring of distant treetops under the wind, but here that wind was hushed, cut to a modest breeze or to no motion at all. And suddenly the stillness was charged with the fishy loathsome reek of black wolf.

It is a poison in the air and we live with it. I remember how it has always happened in the village: days, weeks, with no hint of the evil, and when we have forgotten and grown careless, then without warning the sour stench of them comes on the air, and we hear their rasping howl in the nights—nothing like the musical uproar of the common wolves who seldom do worse than pick up a sheep now and then—and people will die, ambushed, throat-torn, stripped of flesh and bones cracked for the marrow. Some tell of seeing the Devil walk with them. He teaches them tricks that only human beings ought to know. He leads them to the trail of late travelers, to lonely houses where a door may be unlatched, or someone seized on the way to shed or outhouse. And yet they do say that black wolf will not attack by day; if a man comes at him then, even if he is at his carrion, he may slink off; now I know this is true. At night black wolf is invincible, I suppose. The smell hung dense on that woodland road, coming from all around me, so that I could not run away from it.

I had my thin strength, and a knife; my knife is from the hand of Wise Wayland the Smith, and there is a spell on it. For look you, no harm comes to me if I am wearing it. I was not wearing it when Andrea's family moved away and took him with them—all the way to Penn, God help me. I was not wearing it when they came on me with Eden in Wayland's field and called me monster.

In fear I went ahead, not trying for quiet because no one ever surprises black wolf. I came on the beast on the far side of a boulder that jutted into the road, but before that I heard the sounds of tearing. It had ripped the liver from the body. Blood still oozed from all the wounds. Enough remained of the face so that I knew the man was old Kobler. His backpack was not with him, nor any gear, so he had not been on his way to the village. Perhaps he had been taken with some sickness, and so the wolf dared to bring him down in broad day.

By this time Kobler will be expected in the village. They'll wonder why he doesn't come marching to the General Store with his stack of reed baskets and Mam

Miriam's beautiful embroideries and such-like, and slap down his one silver coin, and fill his backpack with the provisions for Mam Miriam and himself. True, he was never regular in the timing of his visits; another week or two might go by before anyone turns curious. People don't think much unless their convenience is joggled, and old Kobler was so silent a man, never granting anyone a word that could be held back—and Mam Miriam herself hardly more than a legend to the town folk—no, I suppose they won't stir themselves unduly. All the same I must leave, I must not be caught here by those who would stone me for their souls' benefit. Nothing keeps me in this house now except to wish to write these words for you, whoever you are. Then I will go when the night wind is blowing.

It was an old dog wolf, and foul, alone, his fangs yellowed. He held his ground hardly a moment when I walked down on him with the knife of Wayland flashing sunlight on his eyes. I did not understand immediately that Kobler was past help—then the wolf moved, I saw the liver, I knew the look on the old man's mask was no-way meant for me. Jon Kobler, a good fellow I think, Mam Miriam's servant, companion, and more. He shrank from the world as she did, nor do I see how you could hold it against either of them, for often the world stinks so that even a fool like me must hold his nose. It will not harm them now if I tell you they were lovers.

The wolf slunk off through the brush into a ravine. It must have been the power of Wayland's knife—or is it possible that black wolf is not so terrible as folk say? Well, mine is a knife that Wayland made long since, when he was young; he told me so.

He gave it to me on the morning of the best day of

my life. Andrea had come to me the day before, had chosen me out of all the others in the training yard—although I seldom shone there, my arm is not heavy enough for the axe or the spear-throwing, and in archery I am only fair, undistinguished. He challenged me to wrestle, I put forth my best, almost I had his shoulders down and he laughing up at me, and then presto! somehow I am flung over on my back and my heart close to cracking with happiness because he has won. And he invited me to go on the morrow with him and some of his older friends for a stag hunt through Bindian Wood, and I had to say, "I have no knife, no gear."

"Oh," says Andrea, and April is no kinder, "we'll find extra gear for you at my father's house, and as for a knife of your own, maybe Wayland the Smith has one for you."

I knew that Wayland Smith did sometimes make such gifts to boys just turning men, but had never imagined he would trouble with one so slight-built as I am and supposed to be simple-minded from the hours with the books. "You do hide your light," says Andrea, whom I had already loved for a year, scarcely daring to speak to him. He laughed and pressed my shoulder. "Go to him—and maybe he'll have a knife for you. I would give you mine, Benvenuto," he said, "only that's bad magic between friends, but come to me with a knife of your own and we'll make blood brotherhood."

So the next morning I went to Wayland the Smith with all my thoughts afire, and I found the old man about to draw a bucket of water from his well, but looking ill and drooping, and he said, "O Benvenuto, I have a crick in my arm—would you, in kindness?" So I drew the water for him, and we drank together. I saw the smithy was untidy with cobwebs, and swept it out for him, he watching me and rambling on with his tales and sayings and memories that some call wanton blasphemies—I paid little heed to them, thinking of Andrea, until he asked me, "Are you a good boy, Benvenuto?" His tone made me know he would like to hear me laugh, or anyway not mind it, indeed I could hardly help laughing at a thousand silly notions, and for the pleasure of it, and the joy of the day; and that was when he gave me this knife I always carry. I don't think I answered his question, or at least only to say, "I try to be," or some such nonsense. He gave me the knife, kissed me, told me not to be too unhappy in my life; but I don't know what one must do to follow that counsel, unless it is to live the way all others do, like baa-sheep who come and go at the will of the shepherd and his dog and must never stray from the tinkle of the wether's bell.

Oh, yes, that day I went on the hunt with Andrea, armed with the knife that was given me by Wayland Smith. We killed a stag together, he marked my forehead, with our own blood then we made brotherhood; but he is gone away.

There was nothing anyone could have done for old Kobler except pray for him. I did that—if there's anything to hear our prayers, if the prayers of a monster can be noticed. But who is God? Who is this cloudthing that has nothing better to do than stare on human pain and now and then poke it with his finger? Is he not bored? Will he not presently wipe it all away, or go away and forget? Or has he already gone away, forgotten?

You will not have me burnt for these words because you will not find me. Besides, I must remember you are simply the unknown who will happen on this letter in Mam Miriam's house, and you may even be a friend. I must remember there are friends.

When I rose from kneeling beside the poor mess that was what remained of Kobler, I heard rustling in the brush. That wolf had no companions or they would have been with him tearing at the meat, but perhaps he was rallying from his fright, hungry for something young and fresh. I understood too that the sun was lowering, night scarcely more than an hour away. Night's arrival would be sudden in the manner of autumn, which has a cruelty in it, as if we did not know that winter is near but must be reminded with a slap and a scolding. Only then did I think of Mam Miriam, who would expect Kobler's return.

When was the last time any of you in Trempa saw Mam Miriam Coletta? I had not even known she was daughter to Roy Coletta, who was governor of Ulsta in his time. Or was this only something she dreamed for me, something to tell me when perhaps her wits were wandering? It doesn't matter: I will think her a princess if I choose.

She was twenty-five and yet unmarried, hostess of the governor's mansion at Sortees after her mother's death, and she fell in love with a common archer, one of the Governor's Guard, and ran away with him, escaping from her locked bedroom on a rope made from a torn blanket. O the dear romantic tale! I've heard none better from the gyppos—their stories are too much alike, but this was like some of the poems of Old Time, especially as she told it me, and never mind if her wits wandered; I have ceased speculating whether it was true.

You think the archer was this same man who became Poor Old Kobler, marching into town fortnightly with his backpack and his baskets, and the embroideries by a crazy old bedridden dame who lived off in the Haunted Stone House and wouldn't give anyone the time of day?

He was not. That archer abandoned her in a brothel at Nuber. Kobler was an aging soldier, a deserter. He took her out of that place and brought her to Trempa. He knew of the old stone house in the woods so long abandoned—for he was a Trempa man in his beginnings, Jon Kobler, but you may not find any bones to bury—and he took her there. He repaired the solid old ruin; you would not believe what good work he did there, mostly with wood cut and shaped out of the forest with his own hands. He cared for her there, servant and lover; they seem not to have had much need of the world. They grew old there, like that.

Rather, he did, I suppose. When I saw her she did not seem very old. Why, I first heard talk and speculation about them (most of it malicious) when I was six years old; I think they must have been new-come then, and that's only nine years ago. Yesterday or perhaps the day before, nine years would have seemed like a long time to me. Now I wonder if a thousand years is a long time, and I can't answer my own question. I am not clever at guessing ages, but I would think Mam Miriam was hardly past forty; and certainly she spoke like a lady, and told me of the past glories as surely no one could have done who had not known them—the governor's mansion, the dances all night long and great people coming on horseback or in fine carriages from all over the county; she made me see the sweaty faces of the musicians in the balcony, and didn't she herself go up one night (the dance at her tenth birthday party) to share a box of candy with them? She spoke of the gardens, the lilac and wisteria and many-colored roses, the like you

274

never saw in Trempa, and there were odd musky red grapes from some incredible land far south of Penn, and from there also, limes, and oranges, and spices she could not describe for me. Telling me all this simply and truly, she did seem like a young woman, even a girl—oh, see for yourself, how should I know? There she lies, poor sweet thing, in the bed Jon Kobler must have made. I have done what I could for her, and it is not much.

I am wandering. I must tell of all this as I should, and then go. Perhaps you will never come; it may be best if you do not.

I prayed for Kobler, and then I went on down the road—despising the wolf but not forgetting him, for I wish to live—as far as its joining with the small path that I knew would take me to Mam Miriam's. There I hesitated a long while, though I think I knew from the start that I would go to her. I don't know what it is in us that (sometimes) will make us do a thing against our wishes because we know it to be good. "Conscience" is too thin a word, and "God" too misty, too spoiled by the many who mouth it constantly without any care for what they say, or as if they alone were able to inform you of God's will—and please, how came they to be so favored? But something drives, I think from within, and I must even obey it without knowing a name for it.

You see, I had never followed that path. No one does. The road like the old stone house itself is haunted. Anyone who ventures there goes in peril of destruction or bewitchment. So far, I am not destroyed.

Once on the path—why, I began to run. Maybe I ran so as to yield no room in my thought to the fear that is always, like black wolf, waiting. I ran down the path through a wilderness of peace. There were the beeches, gray and kind—I like to imagine something of peace in their nearness. I know that violence might be done in the presence, in the very shadow of the beech trees, as in any other place where the human creature goes; a little corner of my mind is a garden where I lie in the sun not believing it. In their presence on that path I ran without shortness of breath, without remembering fear, and I came to the green clearing, and the house of red-gray stone. It was growing late, the sun too low to penetrate this hidden place. In shadow therefore I came to Mam Miriam's door and pounded on the oak panel. But gossip had always said that the old woman (if she existed at all outside of Jon Kobler's head, if he didn't create those dazzling embroideries himself out of his own craziness and witchcraft) was bedridden and helpless. So my knocking was foolish. I turned the latch and pushed the heavy sluggish thing inward, closing it behind me, staring about half-blind in the gray light.

The house is trifling-small, as you will see if you dare come here. Only that big lower room with the fireplace where Jon cooked, the bench where he worked at his baskets, clogs, wooden beads, and this other room up here with the smaller hearth. There's this one chair up here where I sit now (Kobler used to sit beside his love's bed, you know) and the little table I write on, which I am sure they used drawn up beside the bed for their meals together, for the night pitcher of water she no longer needs. You will be aware now that she did exist. There's the roll of linen cloth—Kobler must have gone all the way to Maplestock to buy that—and some half-finished table mats, pillow slips, dresser covers. There's her embroidery hoop, the needles, the rolls of bright yarns, and thread—I never knew there were so many sizes and colors. And there she too is lying. She was; she lived; I closed her eyes.

I looked about me in that failing evening, and she called from upstairs. "Jon, what's wrong? Why did you make such a noise at the door? You've been long, Jon. I'm thirsty."

The tone of her voice was delicate, a music. I cannot tell you how it frightened me, that the voice of a crazy old woman should sound so mild and sweet. Desperately I wanted to run away, much more than I had wanted it when I stood out there at the beginning of the path. But the thing that I will not call Conscience or God (somewhere in the Old-Time books I think it was called Virtue, but doubtless few read them)—the thing that would never let me strike a child, or stone a criminal or a mue on the green as we are expected to do in Trempa—this mad cruel-sweet thing that may be a part of love commanded me to answer her, and I called up the stairway, "Don't be afraid. It's not Jon, but I came to help you." I followed my words, climbing the stairs slowly so that she could forbid me if she chose. She said no more until I had come to her.

The house was turning chill. I had hardly noticed it downstairs; up here the air was already cold, and I saw—preferring not to stare at her directly till she spoke to me—that she was holding the bedcovers high to her throat, and shivering. "I must build you a fire," I said, and went to the hearth. Fresh wood and kindling were laid ready, a tinderbox stood on the mantel. She watched me struggle with the clumsy tool until I won my flame and set it to the twigs and scraps of waste cloth. That ancient chimney is clean—the fire caught well without smoking into the room. I warmed my hands.

"What has happened? Where is Jon?"

"He can't come. I'm sorry." I asked her if she was hungry, and she shook her head. "I'm Benvenuto of Trempa," I told her. "I'm running away. I must get you some fresh water." I hurried out with the pitcher, obliged to retreat for that moment for my own sake, because meeting her gaze, as I had briefly done, had been a glancing through midnight windows into a country where I could never go and yet might have loved to go.

Why, even with gray-eyed Andrea this had been true, and did he not once say to me, "O Benvenuto, how I would admire to walk in the country behind your eyes!"

I know: it was always true.

(But Andrea brought me amazing gifts from his secret country, and nothing in mine was withheld from him through any wish of mine. I suppose all the folk have a word for it: we knew each other's hearts.)

I filled the pitcher at the well-pump downstairs and carried it up to her with a fresh clean cup. She drank gratefully, watching me, I think with some kind of wonder, over the rim of the cup, and she said, "You are a good boy, Benvenuto. Sit down by me now, Benvenuto." She set the cup away on the table and patted the edge of the bed, and I sat there maybe no longer afraid of her, for her plump sad little face was kind. Her soft too-white hands, the fingers short and tapered, showed me none of that threat of grasping, clinging, snatching I have many times seen in the hands of my own breed. "So tell me, where is Jon?" When I could not get words out, I felt her trembling. "Something has happened."

"He is dead, Mam Miriam." She only stared. "I found him on the road, Mam Miriam, too late for me to do anything. It was a wolf." Her hands flew up over her face. "I'm sorry—I couldn't think of any easier way to tell it." She was not weeping as I have heard a woman needs to do after such a blow.

At last her hands came down. One dropped on mine kindly, like the hand of an old friend. "Thus God intended it, perhaps," she said. "I was already thinking, I may die tonight."

"No," I said. "No."

"Why should I not, my dear?"

"Can't you walk at all?"

She looked startled, even shocked, as if that question had been laid away at the back of her mind a long time since, not to be brought forth again. "One night after we came here, Jon and I, I went downstairs—Jon had gone to Trempa and was late returning—I had a candle, but a draft caught it at the head of the stairs—oh, it was a sad night, Benvenuto, and the night wind blowing. I stumbled, fell all the way. There was a miscarriage, but I could not move my legs. An hour later Jon got back and found me like that, all blood and misery. Since then I have not been able to walk. Nor to die, Benvenuto."

"Have you prayed?" I asked her. "Have you besought God to let you walk again? Father Horan would say that you should. Father Horan says God's grace is infinite, through the intercession of Abraham. But then—other times—he appears to deny it. Have you prayed, Mam Miriam?"

"Father Horan—that will be your village priest." She was considering what I said, not laughing at me. "I believe he came here once some years ago, and Jon told him to go away, and he did—but no charge of witchcraft was ever brought against us." She smiled at me, a smile of strangeness, but it warmed me. "Yes, I have prayed, Benvenuto. . . .You said you were running away. Why that, my dear? And from what?"

"They would stone me. I've heard it muttered behind windows when I passed. The only reason they haven't yet is that Father Horan was my friend—I thought he was, I'm sure he wanted to be, once. But I have learned he is not, he also believes me sinful."

"Sinful?" She stroked the back of my hand, and her look was wondering. "Perhaps any sin you might have done has been atoned for by coming out of your way to help an old witch."

"You're not a witch!" I said. "Don't tell yourself that!"

"Why, Benvenuto! Then you do believe in witches!"

"Oh, I don't know." For the first time in my life I was wondering whether I did, if she in all her trouble could be so amused at the thought of them. "I don't know," I said, "but you're not one. You're good, Mam Miriam. You're beautiful."

"Well, Benvenuto, when I am busy with my embroideries, I sometimes feel like a good person. And in Jon's embraces I've thought so, after the pleasure, in the time when there can be quiet and a bit of thinking. Other times I've just lain here wondering what goodness is, and whether anyone really knows. Bless you, am I beautiful? I'm too fat, from lying here doing nothing. The wrinkles spread over my puffy flesh just the same, like frost lines coming on a windowpane, only dark, dark." She closed her eyes and asked me, "What sin could you have done to make them after stoning you?"

"The one I most loved went away last spring—all the way to Penn, God help me, and I don't even know what town. I was lonely, and full of desire, too, for we had been lovers, and I've learned I have a great need of that, a fire in me that flares up at a breath. In Wayland's field a few days ago, where the corn shocks are standing like golden women, I came on someone else, Eden—we had been loving friends, though not in that way. We were both lonely and hungry for loving, and so we comforted each other—and still, in spite of Father Horan, I can see no harm in it—but Eden's people found us. Eden is younger than me—was only driven home and whipped, and will suffer no worse, I hope. Me they call monster. I ran away from Eden's father and brother, but now all the village is muttering."

"But surely, surely, boy and girl playing the old sweet game in an autumn cornfield—"

"Eden is a boy, Mam Miriam. The one I love, who went away is Andrea Benedict, the eldest son of a patrician."

She put her hand behind my neck. "Come here awhile," she said, and drew me down to her.

"Father Horan says such passion is the Eternal Corruption. He says the people of Old Time sinned in this way, so God struck them with fire and plague until their numbers were as nothing. Then he sent Abraham to redeem us, taking away the sin of the world, so—"

"Hush," she said, "hush. Nay—go on if you will, but I care nothing for your Father Horan."

"And so God placed upon us, he says, the command to be fruitful and multiply until our numbers are again the millions they were in Old Time, destroying only the mues. And those who sin as I did, he says, are no better than mues, are a *kind* of mue, and are to be stoned in a public place and their bodies burned. After telling me that, he spoke of God's infinite mercy, but I did not want to hear about it. I ran from him. But I know that in the earlier days of Old Time people like me were tied up in the marketplaces and burned alive, I know this from the books—it was Father Horan taught me the books, the reading—isn't that strange?"

"Yes," she said. She was stroking my hair, and I loved her. "Lying here useless, I've thought about a thousand things, Benvenuto. Most of them idle. But I do tell you that any manner of love is good if there's kindness in it. Does anyone know you came here, Benvenuto?" She made my name so loving a sound!

"No, Mam Miriam."

"Then you can safely stay the night. I'm frightened when the night wind blows around the eaves, if I'm alone. You can keep the fright away. It sounds like children crying, some terror pursues them or some grief is on them and there's nothing I can do."

"Why, to me the night wind sounds like children laughing, or the wood gods running and shouting across the top of the world."

"Are there wood gods?"

"I don't know. The forest's a living place. I never feel alone there, even if I lose my way awhile."

"Benvenuto, I think I'm hungry now. See what you can find downstairs—there's cheese, maybe sausage, some of the little red Snow Apples, and Jon made bread—" Her face crumpled and she caught at my hand. "Was it very bad—about Jon?"

"I think he was dead before the wolf came," I told her. "Maybe his heart failed, or—a stroke? I've heard black wolf won't attack in broad day. He must have died first in some quick way, without pain."

"Oh, if we all could!" That cry was forced from her

282

because her courage had gone, and I think it was only then that she really knew Jon Kobler was dead. "How could he go before me? I have been dying for ten years."

"I won't leave you, Mam Miriam."

"Why, you must. I won't allow you to stay. I saw a stoning once in Sortees when I was a girl—or maybe that was when my girlhood ended. You must be gone by first light. Now, find us some little supper, Benvenuto. Before you go downstairs—that ugly thing over there, the bedpan—if you would reach it to me. God, I hate it so!—the body of this death."

There's nothing offensive in such services, certainly not if you love the one who needs them: we're all bound to the flesh—even Father Horan said it. I wished to tell her so, and found no words; likely she read my thought.

Downstairs everything had been left in order. Jon Kobler must have been a careful, sober man. While I was busy building a fire to cook the sausage, arranging this and that on the tray Jon must have used, I felt him all around us in the work of his hands—the baskets, the beads, the furniture, the very shutters at the windows. Those were all part of a man.

In some way my own works shall live after me. This letter I am finishing is part of a man. Read it so.

When I took up the tray, Mam Miriam smiled at it, and at me. She would not talk during our meal about our troubles. She spoke of her young years at Sortees, and that is when I came to learn those things I wrote down for you about the governor's mansion, the strange people she used to see who came from far off, even two or three hundred miles away; about the archer, the elopement, all that. And I learned much else that I have not written down, about the world that I shall presently go and look upon in my own time.

We had two candles at our supper table. Afterward, and the night wind was rising, she asked me to blow out one and set the other behind the screen; so all night long we had the dark, but it was not so dark we could not see each other's faces. We talked on awhile; I told her more about Andrea. She slept some hours. The night wind calling and crying through the trees and over the rooftop did not waken her, but she woke when for a moment I took my hand away from hers. I returned it, and she slept again.

And once I think she felt some pain, or maybe it was grief that made her stir and moan. The wind had hushed, speaking only of trifling illusions; no other sound except some dog barking in Trempa village, and an owl. I said, "I'll stay with you, Mam Miriam."

"You cannot."

"Then I'll take you with me."

"How could that be?"

"I'll carry you. I'll steal a horse and carriage."

"Dear fool!"

"No, I mean it. There must be a way."

"Yes," she said, "and I'll dream of it awhile." And I think she did sleep again. I did, I know; then morning was touching the silence of our windows.

The daylight was on her face, and I blew out the candle, and I told her, "Mam Miriam, I'll make you walk. I believe you can, and you know it too." She stared up at me, not answering, not angry. "You are good. I think you've made me believe in God again, and so I've been praying that God should help you walk."

"Have I not prayed?"

"Come!" I said, and took her hands and lifted her in the bed. "Come now, and I'll make you walk."

"I will do what I can," she said. "Set my feet on the floor, Benvenuto, and I will try to lift myself."

This I did. She was breathing hard. She said I was not to lift her, she must do it herself. "There's money in the drawer of that table," she said, and I was puzzled that she should speak of it now when she ought to be summoning all her forces to rise and walk. "And a few jewels brought from Sortees, we never sold them. Put them in your pocket, Benvenuto. I want to see you do that, to be sure you have them." I did as she said—never mind what I found in the drawer, since you have only my word for it that I did not rob her.

When I turned back to her, she was truly struggling to rise. I could see her legs tensing with life, and I believed we had won, even that God had answered a prayer, a thing I had never known to happen. A blood vessel was throbbing fiercely at her temple, her face had gone red, her eyes were wild with anger at her weakness.

"Now let me help," I said, and put my hands under her armpits, and with that small aid she did rise, she did stand on her own legs and smile at me with the sweat on her face.

"I thank you, Benvenuto," she said, and her face was not red any more but white, her lips bluish. She was collapsing. I got her back on the bed Jon Kobler made, and that was the end of it.

I will go into the world and find my way, I will not die by my own hand, I will regret no act of love. If it may be, I will find Andrea, and if he wishes, we may travel into new places, the greater oceans, the wilderness where the sun goes down. Wherever I go I shall be free and shameless; take heed of me. I care nothing for your envy, your anger, your fear that simulates contempt. The God you invented has nothing to say to me; but I hear my friend say that any manner of love is good if there's kindness in it. Take heed of me. I am the night wind and the quiet morning light: take heed of me.

BIBLIOGRAPHY

NOVELS

West of the Sun, Doubleday & Co., Inc., 1953
A Mirror for Observers, Doubleday & Co., Inc., 1954
A Wilderness of Spring, Rinehart & Co., Inc., 1958
The Trial of Callista Blake, St. Martin's Press, 1961
Davy, Ballantine Books, Inc., 1965
The Judgment of Eve, Simon & Schuster, 1966
The Company of Glory, serialized in *Galaxy,* 1974

SHORT STORY COLLECTION

Good Neighbors and Other Strangers, Macmillan, 1972

SHORT STORIES AND NOVELETTES

"Angel's Egg," *Galaxy* magazine, June 1951
"The Singing Stick," *Ellery Queen's Mystery Magazine,* 1952
"Mrrrar!" *Ellery Queen's Mystery Magazine,* 1953
"Music-Master of Babylon," *Galaxy* magazine, November 1954
"Bottle Babe," *The Magazine of Science Fiction and Fantasy,* June 1956
"The Red Hills of Summer," *The Magazine of Science Fiction and Fantasy,* September 1959

"The Wrens in Grampa's Whiskers," *The Magazine of Science Fiction and Fantasy*, April 1960

"The Good Neighbors," *Galaxy* magazine, June 1960

"The Golden Horn," *The Magazine of Science Fiction and Fantasy*, February 1962

"A War of No Consequence," *The Magazine of Science Fiction and Fantasy*, March 1962

"Maxwell's Monkey," *Galaxy* magazine, October 1964

"A Better Mousetrap," *Galaxy* magazine, October 1965

"Wooglebeast," *The Magazine of Science Fiction and Fantasy*, January 1965

"Longtooth," *The Magazine of Science Fiction and Fantasy*, January 1970

"The Children's Crusade," *Continuum*, Berkley Publishing Corporation, 1974

"The Legend of Hombas," *Continuum*, Berkley Publishing Corporation, 1974

"The Witches of Nupal," *Continuum*, Berkley Publishing Corporation, 1974

"Harper Conan and Singer David," *Tomorrow Today*, Unity Press, 1975

"Tiger Boy," *Universe 2*, Ace Publications, 1972

"My Brother Leopold," *An Exaltation of Stars*, Simon & Schuster, 1973

"The Night Wind," *Universe 5*, Random House, 1974